Blood Descent

H. Leigh Cornwell

H. Leigh Cornwell, Publisher, USA

Printed in the United States of America.

ISBN: 978-0-9837490-0-4

www.blooddescent.com

Cover Design by Berni Stevens
Cover Photo by Caleb Cornwell
Edited by Kristin Burns

For those that share my love for the immortals.

Prologue

The Times Square clock clicked over to twelve midnight. A slight weasel of a man leaned against the cold brick wall in the shadows of a dark New York City alley. He watched the night foot traffic of the sidewalk, searching. Perched like a predator in the cover of darkness, he scanned the oncoming crowd, seeking his prey. There she was, oblivious to her surroundings, chatting on her cell phone. She wore designer labels from head to toe. Her purse alone would be a decent payday. But that only meant there was more treasure to be found within. His pulse quickened as the streetlights glinted off her jewelry. This would be a good score.

He reached into the frayed pocket of his worn jeans, pulling out his knife, ready for action. Sometimes these things got messy. It wasn't always easy to get these stupid bitches to give up their shit. A few more steps and he would make his grab. Once he got her in the alley...

A bottle skid across the cold damp pavement behind him, shattering against the wall. He spun around, his heart thumped loudly in his chest. His eyes made out the silhouette of a man standing only a few yards from him. The motionless figure watched him in silence.

"What the fuck are you lookin' at?" the slight man snarled.

No movement and no sound came. Anger fueled him to take a few steps toward the intruder. His knife opened with a click. Again came no response.

"Are you stupid?"

The words were a growl through his gritted teeth. He closed the distance between them, knife poised to strike. There was no time to react. The cold hand of the intruder shot to his throat and slammed his body against the wall, forcing the breath from his lungs with a choking gasp. His knife clattered to the street somewhere beneath his dangling feet.

Any attempt to free himself was futile but he still clawed in desperation at the hand clamped to his throat. He was losing consciousness. His hands fell limp to his sides. All he could do was stare back into the cold, black eyes that peered into his.

A glimmer of hope came to him when, once again, he felt the alley beneath his feet and the grip on his neck ease. His rubbery legs were having trouble holding him up.

The tormentor smiled, his eyes still void of emotion as he spoke, "I did not appreciate the way you were looking at my sister."

As if on cue, the weasel's mark stepped into the alley. She crossed her arms in front of her, wearing a smug look on her face. His attempt at an apology came out a strained gargle, forcing him to wince in pain. The last noise he heard was his own choked scream as teeth ripped into his flesh before everything faded to black.

1

The morning sun sliced through the drapes like a luminous razor. Its warm glow overtook the gloom, forcing the darkness to merely exist as shadows. I glanced at the clock and realized the peace and quiet of the new day was about to be terribly disrupted. Reaching toward the would-be culprit, I managed to silence the alarm before it had a chance to spoil my blissful moment of silence.

Today would be a good day, for a Monday. It would mark the beginning of the end of working for Edwards & Novak, the firm I had been pimping myself out for the past seven years. Now, I should say that it wasn't always so bad and I obviously loved the people I worked for or I wouldn't have lasted so long. Dealing in high end real estate made me quite a comfortable living. However, the clients start to kill your will to live after a while. I definitely had enough of the dead-behind-the-eyes trophy wives and their arrogant, self important husbands. It was time to move on, reclaim a life lost to long hours and impromptu travel.

The last appointment of my career was kind enough to be in the early evening. Not being much of a morning person, I was pleasantly surprised by the client's request. But I was still not spared an early rise. There were files to gather and paperwork to sort. I figured since I would have a freshly signed land deal to drop by the office tomorrow, it would be to my advantage to hand over the remaining client files in my possession as well. Better to attempt to get it done today than have to rush to get it done tomorrow.

As I descended the staircase, the glorious aroma of coffee met me half way. Whatever did people do before coffee makers had timers? The passing thought abandoned me as I entered the kitchen, filling my favorite mug to the brim and gingerly continued to my office.

Motivation greeted me when I stepped through the door into the tidy, organized area. The space had an uncanny ability to awaken me even more than the steaming contents of my mug. I always made a conscious effort to keep this area business only. Having the luxury of working from home, one cannot allow distractions. Every detail from the furniture, to the objects of décor, to the color of the walls was specifically chosen for a place of work.

I did, however, allow myself a few personal pictures to keep it from feeling too cold and sterile. To the right of my computer monitor was a picture of my parents taken the last time they came to visit me. I personally captured this moment eight months ago while they sat on my front porch swing. My father's arm casually draped over my mother's shoulders as they seemed to be sharing a private joke. To me, they had always been the poster children of true love. The ease with which they related to one another was a trait that they didn't pass on to me. My track record in relationships seemed laughable at best.

To the left of my monitor was a picture of my best friend Claire and me standing in front of the Bellagio Hotel and Casino in Vegas two years ago. Memories of that trip always brought a smile to my face. Then again, it would be quite a challenge not to have a good time with Claire. She could make laundry day seem like a fun and exciting adventure.

I carefully placed the hot mug on the desk next to my keyboard and roused my computer from its slumber. Coffee and email were the daily staples of my morning routine. I don't know that I could really have one without the other.

The contents of my inbox filled my screen. All the usual suspects were there calling for my attention. First and foremost was an email from Glenn Edwards, president of the previously mentioned firm. He was an old college friend of my father and like an uncle to me.

Yeah, so I got a job courtesy of daddy. But it was, in fact, my father's stellar career as an architect that began my interest in real estate. So it wasn't like I took the job for lack of something more interesting, it was exactly what I wanted to do. I started working for them while in high school. General office help at first, then I ambitiously worked my way through the ranks and got my realtor's license. The rest, as they say, is history.

Glenn's email was quick and to the point, much like the man himself.

Jack,

Good morning. I trust you took the time to look over the papers for Mr. Talbott, as I have not received any questions about the file I gave you. I'm sure you also noticed I took the liberty of printing out directions.
Karl called me this morning and told me he could be out of the hospital as soon as Wednesday morning. You know he is going nuts, such a work-a-holic.
Let me know how the meeting goes. Thanks again for covering for Karl.

Glenn

Glenn calling his business partner Karl a work-a-holic almost made me choke on my coffee. They could both use a serious vacation according to anyone who knew them.

My final client was actually not even *my* client. Trinnian Talbott and his family had been with the firm longer than any other client I could think of. Karl Novak usually handled all their affairs, but last Tuesday he suffered a heart attack while taking a stress test for a routine physical. Normally his son Julian would stand in for him but he was with clients in Los Angeles for the next two weeks. He left yesterday morning after being assured his dad would be fine without him.

Glenn met up with me at the hospital Saturday to visit Karl and discuss my meeting with Mr. Talbott. Of course Karl, being the consummate professional, pushed aside any concerns for his health to discuss the matters at hand.

My response to Glenn's email was just as quick and to the point, "Yes, I reviewed the documents, thanks for the directions (although I was sure I'd be placing my fate in the hands of my navigation system) and great news on Karl's release date."

The next email was from Claire. She'd just gotten back in town from the Capriccio Festival of Kites.

Jax,

I know I always say this, but I had a blast! The festival was incredible, the art was amazing and the food was worth not fitting into any pair of jeans I own!
BTW, you still haven't gotten back to me on Oktoberfest.
Call me when you get a chance,

Claire

Now there was a girl with a job to envy. Claire worked for a travel publication called *Go See! Magazine*. She had her own column that focused on festivals, anywhere and everywhere. So, basically, she went on vacations for a living. Maybe that was why she was determined never to leave Manhattan, because she was never actually there. We didn't see each other as much since I left the chaos of the city for the much quieter and slower pace of Upstate New York. But we still managed to maintain our friendship via modern technology.

Ugh, again with the Oktoberfest! The part of me that would love to see Germany was at war with the part of me that yearned for vacation. And, by vacation, I was referring to wearing pajamas for three months while freaking out about being unemployed. Glenn was convinced that he would have me back in no time and all I really needed was a break. He was probably right. He usually was.

CHAPTER ONE

After allowing myself a small amount of internet time, I got down to work. I discovered more files and paperwork in my possession than I originally estimated. By the time I managed to neatly pack everything in a collapsible file box to return to the office, it was almost three. I planned to be on the road by five to be on the safe side. Thanks to Glenn's map I had an idea of where I was going, never actually having been there. So I figured two hours to make an hour and a half trip was safe.

With an early dinner and a quick shower I felt like a new woman. After a fresh application of makeup, I actually even looked ready to face the world. My eyes seemed more green than blue today, like my father's. I could thank my mother for my peaches-n-cream skin tone, high cheek bones and rich auburn hair. I appeared to be well rested—something I hadn't felt in a long time. Maybe seeing Karl getting back to his old self on Saturday gave me a new outlook on life. We never know when our time will be up, so it isn't worth wasting what time we do have letting stress and the pressures of life hasten us to our demise. Of course, it only takes me seconds to contradict my latest train of thought by deciding I should wear my hair up in effort to look more professional.

The wardrobe selection went much quicker than usual. I suppose the inspiration came from the corporate upswept hair do. The only debate was between the gray suit with slacks or with a skirt. The decision was made by the fact that Mr. Talbott was accustomed to dealing with Karl, so slacks it would be.

My professional clothing collection, embarrassingly enough, was all courtesy of my mother. She was a buyer for Nordstrom's for twenty-one years before she retired last October. I personally couldn't tell one designer from another, whereas she could practically do it blindfolded. So whenever I felt the need to add some fresh corporate to my closet, I had to wait for mom to come into town.

Slipping into my favorite black pumps, I surveyed myself in the mirror. The suit fit perfectly. I guess that was one advantage to being average height and build. The jade silk blouse was the perfect pop of color to liven up the gray and black ensemble. Even after all these years of playing dress up for clients, I still never felt comfortable in this façade. I could pull it off flawlessly but I was truly a t-shirt and jeans kind of girl.

I made my way back downstairs to the office to gather up everything I would need to take with me. Earlier I prepared my briefcase for the trip, making sure to put the Talbott paperwork neatly inside and placing the map on top in plain sight. I took a mental inventory of everything I needed as I headed for the door: briefcase, map, purse, keys and cell phone. Satisfied that I wasn't forgetting anything, I flicked on the porch light and locked the door behind me.

The one part of my corporate façade that I did enjoy was my vehicle. Looking the part of a grown up business woman meant I had to drive like one. My birthday present to me this year was a black Volvo SUV. I always thought people that claimed to be in love with their automobiles maintained a bizarre set of personal values. Once I drove off the lot, I understood completely. I guess it was like finding the perfect mate. You don't believe it's possible until it happens to you.

With my portable office stashed neatly on the passenger seat, and my destination plugged into the navigation system, I started my journey.

Since I had about an hour and a half travel time to kill, I figured what better way to pass the time then to catch up on phone calls? My first call would be to my mother. She called me yesterday evening, and for whatever reason, I never heard my phone. By the time I saw the missed call she would've been fast asleep. She usually allowed twenty-four hours to respond before she started leaving the guilt messages.

My efforts to keep the conversation short failed miserably as they always did. The more I spoke to her, the more I believed that she retired too early. She became obsessive about finding ways to fill her time. The amount of clubs, charities, projects and classes she crammed her schedule with simply boggled the mind. Needless to say, she never ran short of things to chat about.

When the conversation turned to Karl, I knew I was about to get my much needed escape from yet another marathon call. Dad spoke to Glenn before I called and was told that Karl was doing so well his doctor was definitely going to discharge him Wednesday morning. I thanked her for the update and told her I was on my way to take care of some business for him.

The phone call ended with the usual endearments and promises to talk soon. I shook my head in amazement when I noticed I left the house thirty five minutes prior. The thought of making another phone call was quickly banished from my mind. Instead, I decided to turn on some music and enjoy the drive.

Traffic was sparse, making it easier to fully appreciate the scenic trip. Trees with leaves of orange, magenta, and golden yellow made a beautiful canopy of warm fall colors overhead, softly diffusing the fleeting late afternoon sunlight onto the road. It was only the middle of September and already the trees were displaying their enchanting fall shades. Deeper and deeper into the mountainous woods I traveled. All that was visible, as far as the eye could see, were trees and outcroppings of rock, characteristic of the area. Dusk settled in making the details more difficult to distinguish.

The calm female voice of my navigator brought me back to reality, informing me that I should prepare to take the first available right hand turn. Sure enough, there was a break in the forest where an unmarked road twisted and turned even deeper into the ever thickening woods. When it seemed I would sooner hit the Amazon River than any hint of civilization, the trees gave way to unveil their hidden treasure to me.

Searching the depths of my mind, I felt a sense of awe as I grasped desperately for the words to describe the beauty before my eyes. Nestled amongst the trees, a stunning eighteenth-century limestone mansion in absolute pristine condition came into view. The arrangement of artificial lighting added to its dramatic appearance.

Rounding the circular driveway with care, I parked and tried my best to exit the vehicle gracefully. I took a few steps back so I could fully appreciate the splendor of the hulking gray beauty. To witness it lit up in contrast to its dark surroundings only added to its mystique. If I hadn't been able to see my vehicle with my peripheral vision, it would be difficult for me to believe I was still in the twenty-first century.

I counted five stories, assuming there would be a basement. The expansive building's roof was a mixture of slate gray peaks and cones. The stone work was artistic perfection. The middle section of the house sat squarely forward, as if to present the hand carved double doors to would be visitors. Where it met the main house, tall rounded towers joined it to the structure. The landscape was limited to a few simple, yet well placed shrubs. From my vantage point, I could see there was ivy growing up the left side of the mansion and hear the soft bubbling of a creek.

Quite frankly, I could've gazed at the miniature castle all day. However, I was there for another reason. Hoping nobody witnessed me gawking at their home like a crazy person, I returned to my SUV to grab my briefcase and purse. I slung them over my shoulder and walked toward the beautifully crafted doors.

Three wide stone steps led up to the porch. On either side of the entrance sat a planter containing a ten foot tall topiary tree. Each door displayed an elaborate brass lion's head in the center with a large ring hanging from its gaping mouth. Reaching forward, I grabbed the ring in front of me and knocked it three times against the backing plate. Its summoning thuds were much louder and deeper than expected. Then again, so was the prompt response to the summons itself.

2

The huge door drifted open effortlessly, without a single groaning protest from its hinges as one might expect. I found myself staring into the darkest brown eyes I had ever seen, complemented by the angular perfection of the face that laid claim to them. If this was Trinnian, my cakewalk assignment just got difficult. Ever since I could remember, I always tended to get a bit tongue tied and scatterbrained around good looking men. Apparently it was something I never grew out of. Somehow, I managed to pull my wits together and speak.

"Good evening, my name is Jacquelyn Livingston." Astonished and comforted by my professional tone, I continued. "I have a seven o'clock appointment with Trinnian Talbott."

A kind, welcoming smile that threatened to sabotage my valiant attempt at composure adorned his face.

"I am Trinnian." He paused, then added hesitantly, "Forgive me, but when Glenn called Friday and said Jack would be filling in for Karl, I just assumed..." His apology trailed off. There was a warm, soothing tone to his voice.

"As do most people...you're forgiven," I said. The words managed to come out with less difficulty. Oddly enough, the result of Glenn's uncharacteristic slip in professionalism seemed to help me relax a bit.

"Where are my manners? Please, come in." He stepped back and gestured with his free hand toward the foyer.

I walked past him into the large open space, my eyes devouring the lavish antique pieces that inhabited the area. To my left, a large tapestry that depicted a great battle scene nearly covered the entire stone wall. Beneath it sat a long sofa with navy blue velvet seat cushions, its back a rich mahogany ornately carved with leaf and vine details. To my right was a wide staircase that narrowed slightly as the first six steps led to a small landing that turned sharply at a ninety degree angle from their origin. The steps ascended, hugging the wall to the second story. The rich, dark wood banister continued on past the stairs to serve as a railing for the second floor hallway, which overlooked the entire span of the foyer until it abruptly ended at the wall holding the tapestry. In front of me was an archway leading into the residence. On the left of the archway stood an ancient grandfather clock and on the right was a seven-foot tall bronze statue of a rearing stallion.

The door closed behind me. I turned back to face my host. He leaned casually against the door. His arms were crossed as he watched me, allowing me to fully absorb my surroundings. The word handsome didn't do him justice. Even in a pair of old blue jeans and a long sleeved green t-shirt, his short, dark brown hair tussled, he was quite stunning. His skin tone was fair like mine, which made the contrasting darkness of his hair and eyes all the more intriguing. He had the kind of lean muscular physique that made him seem taller than what he actually was, which if I had to guess, I would say six feet. If he was older than me, it wasn't by much.

"Your home is amazing," I managed to say, trying to bring my focus back to the fact that I was there on business.

"Thank you, but I cannot take all the credit. It has been an ongoing labor of love for my family and me. An eternal project it seems."

While he spoke, I noticed suitcases that were concealed by the door where I walked in.

"Oh, I'm sorry." I motioned toward the suitcases. "If today isn't good for you…"

"No, no. An old friend was in town, we spent the week at his place in Manhattan," he offered.

10

CHAPTER TWO

I hoped I was successful in not cringing at the word 'we'. If I wasn't, his expression didn't show it. Of course there was a 'we'! Could I realistically have thought this devastatingly handsome man was single?

His eyes did, however, notice something else entirely different above me.

"Speak of the devil." He nodded in the direction behind me. I slowly turned as he continued. "Jacquelyn, this is Olivia…Olivia, Jacquelyn. She is with Edwards and Novak, filling in for Karl."

Olivia walked along the second floor hallway toward the stairs as if she was on the catwalk of a Parisian fashion show. Peering down at us, she smiled at me and descended the stairs as she spoke.

Gorgeous, go figure.

"Hello, Jacquelyn, it is good to meet you," she said in a sincere tenor.

Ok, gorgeous and nice. Can I go now?

"Good to meet you too, Olivia," I replied, reflecting her tone of sincerity.

She could've sauntered straight out of the pages of Italian Vogue, wearing a pair of snug fitting, dark denim jeans and spiked, knee-high black boots. Her blood red, v-neck cashmere sweater clung to her perfect figure sinfully.

Crossing to the suitcases, she pushed her long, silky light brown hair over her shoulder and bent over to pick them up.

"Olivia, I can get those!" Trinnian protested as she straightened with the suitcases in hand.

"I thought you were supposed to be doing some sort of paperwork?" Olivia teased, her smile touching her pale green eyes as she made her way back up the stairs. "I will handle this. You handle…whatever it is you are doing." She smiled and winked at me.

I returned her smile.

Gorgeous. Nice. Fit. Personality. Ok, she wins.

11

"She is so stubborn. I do not know how Collin puts up with her," Trinnian joked, staring down the hall in the direction Olivia disappeared.

Collin? Did I miss something?

"I heard that!" Olivia exclaimed, laughing from somewhere down the hall.

"Collin is my brother. He and Olivia live here with me," he explained, as if answering my unspoken question.

"Got it," I said, feeling an absurd sense of relief. "I guess it would be difficult to live alone in a house this big."

"Yes, it is," he agreed. "Look at me being rude again, I bet that briefcase is getting heavy. Let us go into the dining room so you can put your things down and have plenty of space to work."

We headed through the archway, which was actually more like a short, arched hallway. Halfway down its length, we came to an intersection. Here we went left, entering a huge dining hall. A massive chestnut table surrounded by twenty chairs served as the center piece of the room. The furnishings weren't as intricately carved as in the entry but were as elegant in their simplicity.

The windows to my left faced the front of the property. In fact, I could see my Volvo parked outside, under the glow of the outdoor lighting. The wall on the other side of the table held paintings that were beautiful landscape interpretations of meadows and wooded areas. Beneath the paintings sat a long chestnut sideboard and buffet.

Trinnian continued to the table and pulled out the first chair on the right side. Politely, he gestured for me to take a seat.

"I believe you will have plenty of room for your things if you sit here," he suggested.

"Thank you."

Placing my purse and briefcase on the table, I realized how heavy they had become. I opened my briefcase, pulling out his file and began sorting through the papers.

"Can I get you anything? Are you thirsty, hungry?"

"No thanks, I'm fine. I had an early dinner," I answered. Then added thoughtfully, "But, please, feel free to grab a little something for yourself."

"Is it going to be that bad?" He chuckled as he turned to take the chair at the head of the table.

"I've seen worse. It's more time consuming than anything," I replied, continuing to sort through the stack of papers.

"I have got nothing but time." He smiled easily and leaned back in his chair like he had not a care in the world. Realistically, he probably didn't.

The hour that followed involved the usual read this, sign that. Karl told me the Talbott's owned numerous properties worldwide. What I wasn't told about Trinnian was the fact that he dealt with his family's property holdings and acquisitions for a long time. Unfortunately for him, we were well over half way through the stack when I realized, much to my embarrassment, he could've done it all without my presence.

Finally, the last papers were signed and placed neatly on the corresponding stacks. One contained copies for him, and the other, copies to be returned to the office. I turned and tried to glare at him. My feeble attempt to restrain a smile was just that, an attempt.

"Congratulations, Mr. Talbott, you're now the proud owner of the thousand acre tract of land to the north of your existing property," I stated flatly.

He looked back at me, trying to feign innocence. However, he too lost his battle as a devilish smirk overtook him.

"What?" He snickered. "I always just let Karl do his thing and then do what is requested of me. Why am I getting the evil eye for allowing you to do your job?" His amused expression was purely honest.

"My job is to translate the legal jargon and make sure you sign where appropriate, not to hold you hostage while I drone on dissecting contracts that you could probably recite from memory," I explained. "I'm pretty sure there are more interesting things you could be doing this evening."

"No, not really." He stood up, looking down at me. "You see, I spend the majority of my time lately with Olivia and Collin. It is nice to have a new face in the house." Rounding the edge of the table, he extended his hand to me. "I apologize sincerely for not confessing my proficiency in this matter and would be honored if you would stay for a glass of wine."

The look in his eyes reflected truth in his words and his pleading grin was too damn irresistible. Besides, I really didn't want to leave.

"I suppose it would be rude of me to turn down such an eloquent invitation," I teased mockingly, as I slid my chair back and took his hand. "I would love to stay for a glass of wine."

When I grasped his hand, I noticed his skin was soft. Not much of a surprise there, since I was sure he didn't spend his days doing backbreaking labor. But his hand was slightly cooler than mine, which to me was a bit surprising because mine always seemed to be cold.

After he gently, and needlessly, assisted me from my seat, I released his hand with remorse to push in my chair and pack up my things.

"Shall we?" he asked when I finished.

He walked toward a door past the side board, opposite of the one we entered. Beyond the door was another arched hallway much shorter than the last. Ahead of us was a pair of doors, each with a round window, like restaurant kitchen doors. To our right was a rustic plank wood door that Trinnian opened and flicked on the light switch inside.

"Watch your footing," he said over his shoulder as he descended the stone steps. "The stairs are fairly steep."

Thankful for the railings on both sides of me, I carefully made my way down the stairs. The passage opened into a spacious, very well stocked wine cellar. In the center of the room stood a sturdy wooden table, the only furnishing to be found. All four walls were lined with racks containing wine bottles from floor to ceiling. Judging from the amount of dust and cobwebs, I could've easily guessed which ones were the oldest.

"Pick a bottle, any bottle." He requested with arms wide, presenting the challenge.

"Um, we may be here for a few days if you're seriously asking me to choose!" I answered his invitation incredulously.

"Well, we do have plenty of room…" He shrugged in a matter-of-fact way, "But I am pretty sure you have more interesting things you could be doing this evening." He smiled openly, using my earlier words against me.

"Touché…well done, sir!" I laughed, shaking my head. "Well, could I at least get a little assistance?"

"Ok, how about this, what is your favorite type of wine?" He leaned against the table. His expression was curious, anticipating my reply.

"Merlot," I answered.

My response seemed to put him in deep thought for a second, and then his face lit up with a satisfied smile.

"Purely for selections sake, what year were you born?" he asked, innocently enough.

"Didn't anybody ever tell you it's rude to ask a woman her age?" My attempt to look insulted failed miserably as he laughed freely at my response.

"I did not ask you how old you are," he managed between chuckles, "and if I had perceived you as being uptight, I would have never asked the question in the first place. So just work with me here and answer the question, or at this pace you *will* be stuck here for a few days!"

I could no longer hold back my own amusement as laughter spilled easily from me and I answered his question. It was nice to feel at ease so quickly with him, simply being able to be myself. This was fast becoming the most enjoyable work assignment I ever had.

With my information at hand, he turned from me and scanned the room, lost in his mission. It took less than five minutes to acquire a selection of seven bottles, placing each carefully on the table with the labels facing me. The vintage year was all they had in common. Each bottle of merlot had its own unique label. I figured it would be safe to assume there was some sort of order to the way the bottles were stocked, although I didn't see any pattern revealed in the method of retrieval.

Maybe I should've specified that I *like* wine, the selection of it I always left to more capable hands. The extent of my wine knowledge is as follows: Wine is made from grapes and grapes grow on vines in vineyards.

Trinnian waited patiently, standing behind his selection for my final decision when his expression became one of curiosity.

"How many months were you at the Volvo dealership?" Sarcasm coated his question and I became instantly aware of the warmth spreading across my cheeks.

"Open the middle one," I quickly muttered, hoping he didn't notice my blush. However, I doubt the smirk he wore was due to my choice of wine.

He walked to the end of the table, opened a drawer and pulled out a corkscrew, opening the bottle with ease.

We made our way up the stairs and back through the dining hall. Trinnian explained to me that almost half of the wine selection came about courtesy of his good friend Owen, the friend that they spent the week with in Manhattan. Owen was a born adventurer, constantly traveling with no particular focus, whatever came to mind at any moment. His idea of picking up souvenirs for his friends was to hunt down the best bottle of local wine wherever he happened to stop. In fact, the bottle Trinnian held was compliments of Owen. It was the first run of merlot for a well established California family vineyard that decided to introduce something new to their collection.

Once again, we entered the main hallway. This time, we turned left with the foyer to our backs. We emerged from the hall into an oversized living room—so large it contained two different sitting areas. The front seating area offered a plump, taupe damask sofa with coordinating club chairs, surrounded by expertly hand crafted birds eye maple end tables and a matching oval coffee table. In contrast, the area in the back had an English Country estate feel with the way its worn brown leather couch and over sized chairs surrounded a wide stone fireplace. The furnishings and accessories were a clever mix of antique and modern that worked together brilliantly.

"Please, make yourself comfortable," Trinnian said.

CHAPTER TWO

He strolled over to a large maple cabinet, opening the doors to reveal a bar area. Plucking two wine glasses from the hanging rack, he neatly poured the wine.

Joining me in the front seating area, he placed the glasses on the table between us and settled into the sofa next to the chair I had chosen. Following his lead I took a sip of wine, savoring its exotic aroma and rich, fruity flavor. I set my glass back on the table when I realized he was staring at me thoughtfully.

"Well? What do you think?" His eyes searched mine while he awaited my verdict.

"It's absolutely delicious, thank you," I answered sincerely, ignoring the feeling of self-consciousness that tried to overwhelm me under his gaze.

He seemed slightly relieved with my answer. More than likely because the thought of having to choose another made him cringe on the inside.

The conversation that followed remained casual. He inquired about Karl and I told him the good news I received earlier, which in turn led to the topic of my career with the firm and my decision to leave. I made sure to let him know he wasn't like any of the clients that were prompting me to end my time with Edwards & Novak. They were polar opposites of him. Quite frankly, if I met him randomly, perhaps at a bookstore, I would have a hard time believing he came from money at all. His wealth didn't seem to define him, it was something he had. He didn't feel the need to hide behind it or depend on it to make him someone.

Strange as I found it, I didn't mind that he kept the focus of the conversation on me. He listened intently—almost like a child at afternoon story time in the library—as I entertained his questions about my family, friends and life in general. His curiosity was genuine. At no time did I feel he was prying, rude or judgmental, he was polite and down to earth. Throughout our meandering conversation, his keen wit and observations fascinated me. Trinnian was not only beautiful on the outside. It also came from a place deep within his being.

"Would you care for another glass?" asked my gracious host.

Looking at my watch, I realized it was almost midnight!

"Wow, where'd the time go?" I asked in disbelief. "No, thank you, I should get going." I stood up reaching for my glass.

"No, please, I will take care of that. Let me help you collect your things," he said, escorting me from the room.

I picked up my purse from the dining room table, explaining that the folder I left behind contained his copies of the paperwork. He said he would deal with it later. Carefully picking up my briefcase, he led me back to the foyer.

When we reached the door, he turned to me, "Thank you for filling in for Karl today."

"If there is anything else we can do for you, please don't hesitate to call," I said, then added with a smile, "It was truly a pleasure meeting you."

"I enjoyed meeting you as well," he said, emulating my sincerity. "I am glad you stayed for a glass of wine."

"Me too," I replied.

He handed me my briefcase and opened the door. I turned to leave but was suddenly frozen in my tracks by a tall attractive man standing in front of me on the porch.

"Oh!" I gasped in surprise.

Maybe it was his build, posture or choice of hair style, but he reminded me of a Marine—minus the uniform. He had the same dark eyes and hair as Trinnian. Stature was where the similarities ended, his shoulders were broader and he was taller. His demeanor softened quickly, becoming apologetic upon realizing he caught me off guard.

"I am sorry to have startled you," he said politely, his gentle tone betraying his intimidating frame.

"Jacquelyn, this is Collin," Trinnian explained, walking through the door to stand beside me. "She is Karl Novak's stand in for the day."

While he spoke, his expression changed slightly, as if taking a cue from Collin's disposition.

"Good to meet you, Jacquelyn," Collin said to me, then turned gravely to Trinnian and said, "Silas is back."

3

I found myself back in the wine cellar standing at the foot of the stairs. The light was soft and golden, illuminating from no particular source, offering no mercy from the musty chill in the air that coated me like a second skin. Walking toward the table, I could hear faint breathing behind me. Hesitant to turn around, I continued to the edge of the table until it halted my progress. I felt the solid cold wood beneath my palms, the pressure of the edge against my hips.

Glancing down, I noticed I wore the same short silk nightgown I put on before bed. This was a dream. Confident with my new realization, I chanced a glimpse over my shoulder. There was Trinnian, shirtless and barefoot, wearing only his old, worn jeans. His face expressionless but his eyes filled with smoldering hunger as he watched me from across the room. He stalked toward me like a predator approaching its prey.

Turning to face him, I felt the cold, hard edge of the table against my lower back. Within seconds he stood in front of me, his body inches from mine.

My breath came slower and deeper. I tried to force myself to relax, but the reality of my surroundings dared to push me to the limits of reason. The sensation of the cold wood on my back, the rough stone floor under my bare feet and the damp cool air that enveloped me tried to contradict my decision that I was dreaming. I was no longer certain I was safe in my bed.

Trinnian was so close I felt a whisper of his breath caress my face. I looked into his eyes, which glistened in a way I could only describe as urgency battling restraint. With a tormented tenderness, he grabbed my wrists and brought my arms up around his neck. His gentle hands slid down my arms, sides and hips. When they reached my thighs, his hands slid behind them pulling me roughly against him and heaving me up onto the table in one smooth motion.

There was no way I could've imagined the firm surface I sat on, or the feel of him standing between my thighs. Any attempt to make sense of what was happening to me blurred away to nothing as his hands moved back up my thighs, over my hips, crossing my lower back to pull me closer to him. My arms locked around his neck, pulling him to me in return. I could feel the crush of his smooth, cool chest against mine, the hard line of his jaw on my shoulder and the soft rhythm of his breath against my neck. His hand slid up my back and I felt his fingers tangle themselves in my hair, forcibly pulling my head back. A shudder passed through me as his lips brushed against my skin, delicately tracing from below my ear to the front of my neck, my head tilting back to allow him access. His fingers relaxed their grip in my hair, allowing me barely enough movement to look into his eyes. His acute stare bored into mine. Fear sent a fresh shiver down my spine. His eyes narrowed and his grip tightened once again, forcing my head back awkwardly. A deep guttural growl escaped from him as his face plummeted back to my throat.

I bolted upright in bed. My hands automatically flew to my throat. The alarm blared. My nightgown clung to me, damp with sweat. Quick, ragged breaths racked my body. I turned off my alarm, reassuring myself it was only a dream. After all, I was home in the safety of my own bed, wasn't I? The acknowledgement of my surroundings did seem to help a bit, at least my breathing returned to normal—or shall I say I was no longer on the verge of hyperventilation?

Where does the subconscious mind come up with the things dreams are made of? In reality, I couldn't imagine being in fear for my life in Trinnian's presence. How could any part of me turn such a gentle, polite, considerate, intelligent, chivalrous and kind man into a ravenous beast? Any therapist would have a hay day with that one, all too eagerly attributing a deep seeded mistrust of men to any failed relationship I've had.

A long hot shower turned out to be the cure for the wretched start to my day. By the time I shut off the tap, a feeling of normalcy had returned. I busied myself getting ready for a trip to the city. Claire and I had a late lunch date, which in turn would somehow involve shopping. She had a knack for always slipping a store or two into any plans we made. I called her on my way home from Trinnian's to tell her I had to drop off his paperwork at the office. She insisted on having lunch to hear all about my new friend. It really doesn't take much to get her fired up about any guy I meet. I think she was more determined to break my bad relationship streak than I was.

I had to admit, there was a bit of giddiness in the air on my drive home from Trinnian's place, combined with a bit of intrigue surrounding the mystery of the one named Silas. The change in Trinnian was obvious as soon as Collin uttered the name. His effortlessly gracious manner became strained by the serious shift in mood as he bid me goodnight and they vanished into the mansion.

The dreaded drive into Manhattan was relatively painless. In fact, I arrived at the café early, unfortunate for me since I was having lunch with the notoriously late Claire. I sipped an espresso and watched the city hustle along in its predictable break neck pace. Honestly, I didn't miss it. Well, maybe the food and entertainment, not the everyday mayhem. I'd grown accustomed to leaving my windows open at night and being lulled to sleep by the rhythmic chirp of the crickets. It was quite a refreshing change from trying to shut out the howling sirens and confrontational horns of the grumpy late night cab drivers, in my opinion.

It was a beautiful day for lunch outdoors. The sun was shining and the temperature was in the mid seventies. According to my watch, Claire was twenty minutes late, so that meant she would arrive at any minute. Twenty minutes tended to be her standard.

Lo and behold, are those blonde curls I see bouncing through the crowd?

Sure enough, it was Claire, her waif-like frame strutting towards me as if she owned the city. She had a poise about her that would make a queen jealous, but it was her girl next door manner that won the hearts of those that met her. I honestly couldn't think of one person that didn't like Claire. As soon as she sat down, the excuses would erupt as sure as Old Faithful. So I figured I might as well get her started.

"You're late," I stated flatly over my cup as she plopped herself down in the chair next to me.

Claire looked effortlessly cute, as usual, in her favorite black leather jacket paired with a pink shirt and skinny jeans. Sliding her oversized, hip sunglasses down her nose, she made a pouting face over the top of the frames at me. Sun light sparkled off her golden ringlets giving her an angelic appearance, as if divine intervention assisted in her defense. She tossed her glasses on the table with a big sigh and the flood gates opened.

"You could at least pretend you notice my hair." Her long lashes fluttered, attempting to look innocent while searching for sympathy. Both of which she quickly abandoned once she realized I was having none of it.

I crossed my arms and stared at her with one eyebrow arched.

Ah, so it would be the hair stylist excuse this time.

"Ok, I'm sorry, but you know how Rafael is? It's like you become his prisoner when you sit in his chair. People only put up with him because he owns the damn salon and he's like the hair whisperer or something. Trust me, I've tried to leave him before. You remember my green hair fiasco?" She paused for a shiver. "Anyway, I finally had to tell him to shut up and finish, he was making me late for an appointment." Excuse given, she broke into her best apologetic smile, her big blue eyes pleading for clemency.

"I would actually love to see the look on your face if one day I didn't wait the mandatory twenty minutes to be blessed with your company," I mused, tapping my finger on my lips and staring off into the crisp Manhattan sky.

"You wouldn't dare!" she exclaimed. Her eyes wide with fake indignation that melted into her contagious laugh. "Enough of your empty threats for one day, bitch, tell me all about this Trenton guy from yesterday."

"Trinnian," I corrected as our waitress showed up. She took our orders and disappeared into the bustling café. "What can I say about the most gorgeous, smart, funny and sincere man I've ever met?" Pausing in retrospect, I could see his flawless face in my mind. "Except that I'll probably never see him again, so what does it matter?"

"Don't say that! You never know..." Instantly her face brightened. "Hell, just call him!"

"No!" I gasped, barely succeeding in not choking on my water.

"Why not?" she asked, like it was the only logical thing to do and couldn't believe I didn't agree.

"Because he's a client, Claire!" The words came out a bit harsher than I would've liked so I took a breath and continued in a calmer tone. "How much more unprofessional could I possibly be? I spent half the night at his house drinking wine with him!"

"Whoa, whoa, wait a minute," she said, raising a hand as if to physically stop me. "Back up. You what?!"

I hung my head for a second, silently collecting my thoughts. Lifting my gaze, I met her impatient stare. My story took the whole lunch to recount. Claire didn't utter a single word as I spoke. She sat there mechanically eating her salad, staring at me the entire time. Then I relayed my dream from this morning, the details of which left her inadvertently dazed.

"And there you have it, my five hour business meeting with Trinnian Talbott." I finished my tale, slumping back in my chair, pushing away my picked over food.

"Wow," Claire whispered faintly, shaking her head, her eyes still fixed on mine. "Jax, I want to help you with this, I really do. But first, you're going to have to repeat the whole part about the dream again."

"Claire!" Aggravation flared in my voice.

"Take it easy, I was just joking!" she smirked. "Although I have to admit, the dream was my favorite part. Ok, ok, stop rolling your eyes and listen. The dream is the manifestation of your uncanny ability to deny yourself pleasure. In this situation, there's one part of you that would love to have this smoldering hot stud molest you in his basement—ok, ok, wine cellar. The other part of you believes these feelings aren't ethical due to the *work* relationship." She stopped and stared at me as if this was the part where I was to come to the same conclusion she had so obviously come to. Frustrated by my inability to play her game of fill in the blank, she shook her head and continued. "Not only is he not *your* client, *you* no longer work for Edwards and Novak."

"Tell Glenn that. He's convinced that all I need is a vacation and I'll be back to work in no time." Even as I repeated his words I still wasn't convinced he was entirely wrong, which only succeeded in frustrating me more. "Besides, if Trinnian wanted to see me again, he would've said so. Lord knows he had plenty of time to do that much."

Claire studied my face for a moment. Exhaling in defeat, she finally spoke, "Alright then, I'll let it go for now but I won't be surprised when you hear from him by the end of the week." She used that infamous tone of hers that was usually followed by an 'I told you so' at some point. The only option that remained was to cross my fingers in hopes of hearing those four little words that weekend.

We sat for a while longer talking, and of course, Oktoberfest came up again. I told her I was still undecided and she informed me the only way I was getting out of it was if I spoke to Trinnian by the end of the week.

Didn't she say she was going to let it go?

As if she read my mind, the topic quickly turned to shopping. She mentioned offhandedly that she passed a few good sales on the way to the café. Happy for subject change I made no protests in joining her. I did inform her that I had to head to the office before six to drop off the paperwork, to give myself a decent time frame to work with. Delighted in the mere fact I put up no argument, she assured me we'd be done with time to spare.

The shops were busy. It seemed as though half the women in Manhattan had been lured in by the same sales that caught

Claire's eye. I actually found quite a few things I liked, not usually one to have much luck or patience with shopping.

We finished in time for me to get to the office before everyone left for the day. Claire invited me to come back by her apartment after I finished at the office. That way I could wait out the worst of the grid lock. She claimed she had no plans for the evening. I tried not to look puzzled by her lack of something to do and told her I'd call her when I was done.

The office still hummed with activity when I arrived just after five thirty. The receptionist, Gloria, was on the phone so I decided to pass off Trinnian's paperwork to Glenn. He was with a client when I got to his office, so I simply waved from outside his window and gestured that I was giving the papers to Gloria. Eyeing my ensemble from head to toe, he shook his head in disapproval. It drove him nuts when I showed up at the office in casual attire. I was sure if the client asked, he'd say I was a courier or delivery person of some sort. It wouldn't be the first time.

I was pleased to find that Gloria finished her phone call by the time I returned. Handing her the neat folder of papers, I explained whose they were and that I'd gone in Karl's place. She happily informed me that Karl was definitely being released the following morning. I told her I heard and was relieved he was doing so well.

There had been rumors for years about her involvement with Karl. I think that was the first time I ever thought they might be true. She was absolutely glowing as she spoke about his recovery. Gloria was lovely. She had been a model well into her late thirties, which was unheard of even in her time. At fifty-six, she could still turn heads. I could definitely see the attraction, on Karl's end anyway.

Making my way to the door, she stopped me mid stride.

"Jackie, wait!" she called after me. I turned in time to see her reaching for something on the floor next to her desk, obscured by the small fortress of her reception area. When she stood up, she held a rectangular box wrapped in brown paper tied with twine. "I almost forgot this came for you by courier about a half hour ago."

"Hmmm, do you know who it's from?" I asked, eyeing the package curiously as I accepted it from her. Only a few of my clients knew I was leaving.

"No, when it arrived I was too busy to even ask. I signed for it and went back to the call I was on."

"Thanks, Gloria," I said, taking the package to the empty waiting area.

The outside of the package bore no writing or any other identifying marks. The only thing left to do was to open it.

With the string untied, the paper came away easily to expose an unmarked wooden box. The front panel slid open length wise, revealing a small envelope on top of packing material that resembled a fine bed of hay. 'Jacquelyn' was the only thing written on the envelope, sending my mind racing to think of anyone that even called me by my full first name. Family, co-workers and clients called me 'Jack' or 'Jackie' and my friends called me 'Jax'.

I opened the envelope, pulled out the card and quietly read it to myself.

Jacquelyn,

This is the one I was hoping you would choose.

Trinnian

My face felt flushed as I read the card over again, admiring the perfect artistry of the calligraphy lettering. I hadn't even noticed that the same skilled hand penned the envelope. At the time I was too concerned about who sent the package. What I did recognize was the signature, the same one I saw yesterday a dozen times over. Knowing Trinnian actually took the time to write this himself gave way to butterflies in my stomach. In my mind I heard Claire's voice, 'Just call him.' The very idea practically knocked the wind out of me, encouraging the butterflies to dance wilder.

Eager for a distraction, I slid the card back into the envelope and tucked it into the wooden box. Pushing aside the hay I examined the contents. It was a bottle of Italian merlot. My fingers traced the label and a smile crept across my face, thinking about the prior day's wine selection.

This was my chance to call him, if only to say thanks. After all, he did make the first attempt at contact. I stared at my cell phone for a good ten minutes before I could bring myself to press send. Fighting the urge to end the call on the third ring, the decision was made by the sound of his voice.

"Hello?" His timbre made it more of a question than a greeting, but hanging up was no longer an option.

"Trinnian, this is Jacquelyn Livingston." It took more effort to sound casual than I hoped. "I'm not interrupting anything am I?"

"No, not at all. I take it you got my retirement gift?" I could hear a smile in his voice.

"I did. Thank you very much but you really didn't have to do that."

"It is nothing really, even though our supplies are limited around here," he teased.

"Now I feel terrible!" I said, playing along. "I'm done here at the office. I could swing right by and drop it off if you like, wouldn't want to deplete your limited supply."

"As appealing as that sounds, I actually will not even be home. Olivia reminded me about a gallery opening this evening that I wanted to attend…" He paused briefly, "Would you like to join me?" I was fairly sure I quit breathing, not positive I heard him correctly. Obviously taking my lack of response as me thinking of a way to let him down nicely, he quickly added, "I know it is terribly short notice and I am sure you already have plans…"

"No, actually, I don't," I informed him, taking advantage of his pause. "What time does it start?"

Somehow I managed to pull off the cool and collected imitation of an adult that I was aiming for, all the while resisting the urge to jump up and down screaming.

"Eight O'clock. However, we will have to show up fashionably late. Owen has decided to stick around for a while and I promised to join him for dinner. I hope that does not influence your decision in a negative way."

Was he kidding? I would've waited five hours through a blizzard sitting on a curb if I had to. There was no way I was going to pass up a chance to spend time with him!

"Actually, that would be perfect. Claire wanted me to come by her place after I finished up here at the office."

"Excellent, then I will call you after dinner."

"Sounds good to me," I said. No longer able to contain my smile, I remembered my excuse for calling in the first place. "Thanks again for the wine."

"You are welcome, Jacquelyn," he said, ending the call.

Vaguely remembering my trip to Claire's apartment, I was still on cloud nine when I arrived. Naturally she assumed I lied about calling him, knowing what a chicken I was. She actually insisted on looking at my phone, convinced this was all just my lame attempt to get out of Oktoberfest. The real proof for her was the gift he gave me.

Stabbing her finger in my direction, victory gleamed in her eyes as she got to blurt out her favorite phrase, "I told you so!!!"

Her celebration cut short as she eyed me from head to toe, just like Glenn had, but she actually gasped in horror. Herding me into her bathroom, she informed me that I had to shower and start from scratch. She stalked off toward her closet, I barely made out her muttering to herself that no self respecting woman would go to a gallery opening in a ponytail and jeans.

Time flew by while Claire magically transformed me into what she promised would be drop dead gorgeous. I hadn't been allowed access to any reflective surfaces to check my progress and had never before given her to the green light to use me as her own personal mannequin, so I wasn't sure what to expect.

After we finished our Chinese takeout, she handed me a black dress, convinced it was safe to put on now that food was out of my reach. The finishing touch to my makeup was the lipstick she skillfully applied and then she carefully removed the hot rollers from my hair, raking through it with her fingers.

She stood back, gave me the once over with her eyes, clapped her hands together, and excitedly told me to go look in the mirror. I took a deep breath, closed my eyes and stepped in front of the full length mirror. Thinking it was already past eight, and I wouldn't have much time to tone down the ridiculous amount of makeup I'd seen Claire go through, I tentatively opened my eyes.

My hair fell slightly past my shoulders in supple wavy curls that framed my face perfectly. The makeup was skillfully applied in evening shades that were smoky yet subtle, accented by the translucent burgundy tint on my lips. Courtesy of Claire's sister was the classic little black dress. I lucked out on this one, there was no way I could fit into Claire's size zero wardrobe. The dress was perfect. It had three quarter length sleeves and a deep-v neckline that stopped tastefully before revealing too much. The top portion clung all the way to the hips and the skirt had a slight flair stopping above the knee. Adding a good four inches to my five foot five frame, the black stiletto heels were the last faultless touch.

"Drop dead gorgeous," I whispered Claire's words to my astonished reflection in the mirror.

Overcome with joy, I spun around and threw my arms around her neck, thanking her ecstatically. That was until my cell phone rang. The celebration broke off abruptly, leaving us to stare wide-eyed at each other.

Allowing myself a calming breath, I managed to answer the phone on the third ring. Hearing Trinnian's voice, the butterflies that had gone into hibernation were back with a vengeance. I gave him directions to Claire's apartment, as requested. He insisted it would be rude to make a lady show up for a date unescorted. I laughed in agreement, unable to tell if he was joking but too flattered to care. He hung up after stating he would pick me up shortly.

It didn't take Claire long to request that I sit down to avoid pacing clean through the floor. Her relief was obvious when we heard a light rapping on the door, I was confident my look was the exact opposite as the butterflies whirled into a frenzy.

4

Claire sat on the sofa pretending to read a magazine while I attempted to answer the door in a nonchalant manner. Not quite sure what to expect, I braced myself as best I could, which in this situation wasn't good enough. Trinnian stood in front of me wearing a pair of black slacks, a charcoal wool jacket and a black silk turtleneck. His hair was smoothed just enough to pass for sophisticated. A grin tugged at the corners of his mouth when he spoke.

"You look exceptionally stunning this evening," he said with an earnest smile.

"Thanks, you too," I said, barely managing to avoid giggling like a school girl. "Please, come in. I'd like you to meet Claire."

He passed into the room. I closed the door, turning in time to see Claire stand. She leaned forward to shake his hand as he extended his to her.

"It is a pleasure to meet you, Claire, Jacquelyn speaks very highly of you." Charm infused every word as he took her hand in his.

"And you as well," she offered back cordially.

I was happy she didn't feel the need to clarify the statement, judging from the odd look she chanced my way.

We only stayed long enough for the required pleasantries. When Trinnian opened the door for me I glanced back at Claire. Her eyes were practically bugging out of her head mouthing, 'Oh my God!' to me behind his back. My 'thank you' to her was equally silent, trying to convey that I definitely owed her one before I turned to leave.

The gallery opening was quite the event. It was in fact invitation only, which to me translated into a who's who of New York's invitation only elite. Everyone in the room seemed to know each other. Not surprisingly, I recognized a few clients from the firm. I decided I'd pretend not to notice them unless they directly spoke to me. Did I honestly think that quitting my job would spare me from the arrogant sector of society?

A gentle hand on my lower back broke me out of my disappointed evaluation of the assembly. I turned to my charming escort, leaning in to speak to me.

"I am sorry about the crowd. I usually turn down invitations to these types of events but an artist friend of mine has a couple of pieces on display tonight that I wanted to see."

"I'm fine," I reassured him. "It's just like being at the office."

He chuckled at my sarcastic attempt to sound comfortable and evidently took it as a signal to hunt down the bar. His hand sought out mine, leading me through the growing crowd. He smoothly towed me along, oblivious to the double takes and the whispers of the ladies left in our wake. A few of them offered me faux smiles upon discovering my notice of their behavior.

At the bar, his hand returned to my lower back, situating me beside him. He discreetly hailed the bartender. The man took our order, offered us a pleasant smile and was quickly off to fill our request. Trinnian whispered in my ear that he may have to fight the bartender for the pleasure of my company this evening. The thought appeared to amuse him, as I rolled my eyes, shaking my head.

The bartender returned with two glasses of Bordeaux. He placed them in front of us, inclining his head in response to my thank you. His eyes lingered on mine for a split second before he was off to attend to another customer. I picked up my glass and heard Trinnian clear his throat unnecessarily. He appeared to be trying to compose his face, hiding a smug look of satisfaction accredited to the prolonged glance from my alleged admirer. My elbow caught him just below the ribs. His new indignant expression allowed me my own smug look of satisfaction.

We wandered through the gallery admiring the unique assortment of art that didn't seem to have a common theme, much less medium. Timeless oil paintings held their own next to harsh metallic sculptures that embodied modern abstract forms. Fragile glass pieces delicately redirected the light diffusing through their very composition, sat content alongside a rich earthy clay formation that was intricate yet primitive in the same breath.

Each new artist we came across brought with it conversation about their work. Trinnian seemed to appreciate the pieces influenced by the more classic styles of art than the severe interpretations of the modern genre.

It was at that moment while I studied an impossibly delicate relief carved in pure white marble that I realized how quiet Trinnian had become. When I looked over at him, his face was blank as he stared out a window near the front of the gallery. His eyes locked onto something I couldn't see. Whatever it was commanded his full concentration. I opened my mouth to say something when I heard my name on the opposite side of me. Trinnian also heard it and met my perplexed stare before I turned to acknowledge the person vying for my attention.

Robert Westbrook was one of Karl Novak's long time clients, a retired investment banker who was borderline obsessive about buying land. The joke around the office was that he was aiming for world domination. When we hadn't seen him for almost a year, we figured he gave up.

I shook his hand, commenting that it had been a while, before introducing him to Trinnian. I told Robert offhandedly that he too was a long time client of Karl's.

As they talked, Trinnian appeared to be back to his normal self. For some reason, his obvious distraction from mere moments ago was still on my mind. It wasn't like he zoned out for a second, it was more like he was watching something. Then it dawned on me. I'd seen that same expression on his face when Collin mentioned that name Silas the prior evening. Trinnian's eyes flickered to mine for a brief second as if I said the name out loud. But I was obviously letting my imagination get the better of me once I realized Robert was addressing me, asking how Karl was doing. He didn't seem to notice my delay in answering him as I explained the situation. Robert then told me he called the office Friday to set up an appointment, which was how he heard Karl had been admitted to NYU Medical Center. He went on to reveal he wasn't surprised to hear he was doing so well there and that he himself had been admitted there after his third heart attack.

On that note, he excused himself, stating he saw somebody he needed to speak to, and as quickly as he appeared, he was gone. Trinnian's expression became mischievous, declaring it was probably Robert's cardiologist. I tried in vain to subdue a laugh but practically choked myself, which in turn made Trinnian laugh.

Even his laugh was beautiful. Everything about him seemed to be effortless and beautiful, which was a little intimidating. By the time we collected ourselves enough to behave like adults, I'd forgotten about his odd mood shift.

Our wandering resumed until we finally came across the two paintings he came to see. His friend Augustine turned out to be a master of impressionistic painting. I immediately recognized the style from the paintings in Trinnian's dining hall, my suspicion of which he confirmed, though the subject matter here was darker. One was of an angry sea, its waves smashing with immense explosive force against black jagged rocks at the foot of a sheer menacing cliff. Moonlight glinted off the wet surfaces and frantically clung to the waves, yet there was no moon to be seen. Lush dark shades of plum and cobalt blue represented the hauntingly mesmerizing sky. The second painting had an even more sinister feel. It was a tangle of thorny leafless trees in silhouette against the same moonless sky of plum and cobalt blue. The pale light of the absent moon accented the foreboding points of the ominous thorns. Both paintings were extraordinary, unsettling and seductive.

"Most people cannot seem to gaze upon them so long."

The voice came from behind me. It was low and carried a noticeable Italian accent. I looked at Trinnian, he gestured behind us. I turned a little farther to discover a man stood there. He wore a rich, burgundy velvet smoking jacket and black leather pants. His short sandy brown hair was naturally curly and long black lashes emphasized his hazel eyes as if he wore mascara. There was a boyish cuteness about him that was contradicted by a sensuality that smoldered in his eyes. Apparently his comment was directed toward me.

"Actually, I'm having a hard time looking away. They're almost hypnotic," I replied honestly.

"I could not ask for a more sincere compliment," he responded gratefully, with a hint of a theatric bow.

"Jacquelyn, may I introduce you to my outrageously talented friend, Augustine."

"I'm fast becoming a fan of your work. I absolutely love the paintings in Trinnian's home," I confessed.

"Would you like them? Trinnian, do not be so greedy with my things and give them to this captivating young lady!" Augustine chided.

Trinnian laughed, shaking his head.

"Augustine, she starts trouble like this all the time, do not fall for it for one second. I may even have to challenge the bartender to a duel later." He said, giving me a wink.

My mortified glare, accompanied by the planting of my fist on my hip, compelled him to change the subject. They talked about Augustine's new paintings and other projects he was working on. Evidently Owen was supposed to come tonight. I wasn't sure I was meant to hear that so I pretended to be engrossed with a hulking metal sculpture beside his paintings.

Part of me felt bad that I may have stolen Owen's spot. But the majority of me was thankful to be there. I wandered a little bit away to give them some space to talk.

To my surprise, I heard Augustine mention Silas. He asked Trinnian if he knew Silas was back, to which he replied he did. Augustine then asked what it was that Silas wanted. Trinnian's response was glacial, "Chaos, is that not what he always wants?"

CHAPTER FOUR

We didn't stay much longer after we found Augustine. I, for one, was ready to go. Not that I necessarily wanted to end my time with Trinnian but, more or less, be away from the crowd.

I was thankful I didn't have to make the drive all the way home. Claire invited me to spend the night at her place. She may have had her own selfish reasons for the invitation and her motivation didn't entirely have to do with her concern for my safety on the long drive home. I knew I'd return to her place to discover she'd waited up for me, salivating like one of Pavlov's dogs, eager for details of my evening.

Trinnian and I talked the whole way to Claire's place, as we had on the way to the gallery. Conversation was easy with him. Subjects flowed together seamlessly, never feeling forced or awkward.

When we got to Claire's building, he opened my car door for me and walked me to the stairs of her brownstone, offering to escort me up.

"I think I can manage, besides, you have a long drive home."

He smiled and proudly displayed a bronze key, "On the contrary, I will be invading Owen's place tonight."

"Ahh, your resourcefulness is but a drop in the bucket of your endless supply of talents."

"If that impresses you, now I regret not challenging that bartender to a duel," he smirked.

"No need for all of that, he was no competition and you know it!" Immediately, I wanted to clamp my hand over my mouth as I felt my face flush bright red.

He stared at me in silence for a moment, a touch of his smirk lingered on his flawless lips. Stepping closer, he reached up hesitantly. His fingers traced my cheekbone and pushed back a lock of hair. They barely felt like a whisper as they rounded my ear, coming to a halt on the side of my neck, his eyes never abandoned mine for a second. My heart sounded like it drummed inside my head it beat so hard. It was almost as if he waited for some sort of protest from me—that wasn't coming—while his thumb tenderly caressed my cheek. Until something flashed in his eyes...reluctance maybe, I couldn't be sure, but his hand left my skin and returned to his side.

"Please forgive me for being so forward," his gaze broke from mine. He looked down, studying the space between us, as if gathering his thoughts. When his eyes met mine again, there was a hint of sadness in them that was inconsistent with his content manner. "Thank you for joining me this evening. I truly enjoyed your company."

Oh. Ok.

I fought with everything I had in me not to let the profound feeling of confusion become the last emotion I registered visibly tonight. My mind ran through the last few minutes, trying desperately to figure out what just happened. What did he see in me that altered the situation so drastically? I wanted to ignore his change of heart, throw my arms around his neck and kiss him. But if he felt his actions were too forward, what would he then think of mine?

Taking a breath, I swallowed my disappointment. I composed my appearance into what I thought would pass for appreciation and spoke, "No really...thank you for inviting me."

And just like that, he was gone.

It took me a few minutes to open the door to Claire's since I knew what awaited me on the other side. Bracing myself for the inquisition, I slid my key into the deadbolt and turned the knob. Claire burst out of the bathroom in her pajamas, with her toothbrush sticking out of her mouth, eyes as wide as last I saw her. Upon seeing my face, hers collapsed into the mirror image of mine. With shoulders slumped she retreated to the bathroom to finish her task.

I sank into her sofa and stared blankly at the ceiling, waiting for the dreaded twenty questions to begin. But to my surprise, when she reemerged, she was dressed as if ready to leave.

"Go change, we're going to the pub." Her tone informed me 'no' wasn't an option, so I grudgingly did what I was told.

The 'pub', as we called it, was an old Irish dive a block away from her apartment. I always had my suspicions it was one of her deciding factors when she first found her place. Between the staff and the regulars, it had a homey kind of feel. When I lived in the city it was our Friday night hangout. For a Tuesday night, it was pretty busy but we still managed to find two stools available at the bar.

"Well look what the cat drug in," Shane, the owner, grumbled in his thick Irish accent. No questions asked, he poured us two Black Velvets, each pint sporting a shamrock in the foam of the Guinness. "For fuck's sake, Jax, where've you been? Claire and I were just talkin' the other day about puttin' your picture on a milk carton."

Had it been that long? Shane was cute but a bit ruff around the edges. Claire has been harboring a crush on him for a few years now. She didn't want to ruin her favorite hangout should things go down badly. Which I always thought sounded a little lame but I wasn't going to stoop to her level of harassment.

"Good to see you too, Shane, glad to see you haven't changed," I replied in a mockingly sweet tone.

"I only say it because your girl here gets a couple pints in her and starts brooding about the good old days," he gestured to Claire with an exaggerated consoling gaze.

Her only response, a carefully selected finger displayed in his direction.

"You see that, you've gone and pushed away the only girl in this town that would willingly sleep with you," I jabbed, bracing for the impact I knew was coming. This time it was a kick to my shin under the bar. "Ow!" I winced, rubbing my shin as Claire and I exchanged a vexing glare.

Shane chortled, moving on to serve another customer.

"Just because you apparently didn't have a good night, why must I suffer?" Claire asked.

Her attention shifted to something over my shoulder as she finished her sentence. I followed her stare to the seat next to me. A man settled into the recently vacated stool. He reminded me of the guy on the Captain Morgan bottle. His black hair flowed to the middle of his back in loose curls and, judging from the perfection, he probably spent hours maintaining his goatee.

I looked back at Claire. She shifted her position, putting her elbow on the bar to prop her chin up. If I didn't know better, I would think she was prepared to listen intently to how my night went. However, this was Claire and there was a good looking man in the vicinity. Which didn't necessarily make her a bad friend, even Superman had kryptonite.

"Should I warn Shane he has some competition?" I asked. The sour expression I wore snapped her back.

"No, Jax, I'm sorry. We came out to talk about your night. What the hell happened?"

Once you got it, Claire would give you her undivided attention. If anything, she was a good listener. I presented her with a brief overview of the evening, sticking to the facts. Even as I recounted the part where he dropped me off, I could still not make sense of how it all ended. Neither could Claire, since all she could manage to say from her place somewhere lost in contemplation was, "Huh." She looked away from me and stared at her pint glass as if she tried to mentally solve a riddle.

"There was no future commitment offered, like 'let's do this again soon' or 'call you later'?" she asked, while she eyed me deep in thought.

I shook my head and waited patiently, giving her time to think in peace. She was always good at this sort of thing. Finally, she looked back at me confounded.

"I got nothin'," she said.

"Well if you can't figure it out, I guess I'm screwed."

I summoned Shane with a subtle wiggle of my empty pint glass. It was going to be a long night.

"Oh shit!" Claire's face turned pale as she tried to duck out of sight. "Did he see me?"

I looked up to see her on again, off again boyfriend, Scott Vincent.

"I'm pretty sure...he keeps looking over here. It looks like he's with his buddies but you better go over there and say something so he doesn't feel the need to come join us."

Unwillingly, she meandered over his way. A preemptive strike if you will. I couldn't stand him but, for Claire's sake, I tried to be civil. So whenever they were in an 'on again' stage, I had to play nice. Thankfully, they were in the 'off again' phase, so I didn't feel I should have to talk to him. She claimed she was finally through with him this time. I could only hope that was true. She could do so much better than him. My train of thought was derailed by a simple phrase.

"Excuse me."

I turned to discover the smooth voice belonged to the Captain Morgan look-a-like. His ice blue eyes unassumingly searched mine to make sure I wasn't bothered by his interruption.

"I do not mean to be rude but I could not help overhearing a name you mentioned," he paused as if still testing the waters. I was more curious than bothered, which must have spurred him on. "I have an old acquaintance named Trinnian. It is not the most common name, so I thought maybe you were referring to him. Trinnian Talbott?" He must have noticed the blood drain from my face as he quickly added, "I should clarify I have not spoken to him in years…in fact, I am fairly certain I never will again."

Shane returned with my fresh pint and placed it in front of me. He suspiciously eyed the man speaking to me before he turned his questioning stare my way. My subtle nod was taken as confirmation I was alright but Shane still moved on tentatively. If the man noticed the exchange between Shane and me, he didn't show it.

The attitude of the stranger's comment caught me off guard, ironically putting me on the defensive.

"How unfortunate for you." My matter-of-fact comment was delivered with a level stare. "Trinnian is probably one of the most genuine and respectable men I've ever met."

His eyes narrowed, ignoring my defiant standpoint, "I can see why he likes you. You are a very passionate and beautiful woman." With a pause, his demeanor softened but carried a cynical edge, "It is a shame you feel the need to defend somebody you obviously do not know very well."

5

I studied the man's face, unable to deny the truth in what he said. Realistically, I didn't know Trinnian. Knowing how you perceive someone, or even how you feel about them, doesn't mean you actually *know* them. After all, I only met him the day before. How much could you possibly know about somebody in two days? My spontaneous tirade suddenly felt irrational and childish. Not that I cared what this man thought of me. Still, I wasn't quite ready to dismiss him. I couldn't help but wonder what motivated his negative attitude toward Trinnian. Besides, maybe if I found out he had a darker side it may help bypass the depressing feeling of rejection that began to settle in on me.

"It sounds as if you have something on your mind you'd like to share...I'm sorry, I didn't catch your name."

I tried to sound indifferent, despite the fact that I was curious to hear what he could possibly have to tell me.

"Silas." The name took on a serpentine quality in my mind though it was spoken innocently enough. I struggled to appear unfazed by it, the mere utterance of which turned basic curiosity instantaneously into fervent interest. Claire could've married Scott right then if it would've kept her from coming back and ruining my chance to hear what Silas had to say. "And you are?"

"Jacquelyn." My response remained calm, much to my relief. "So, how do you know Trinnian?"

"I met him through our mutual friend, Collin, many years ago..." he explained, until my puzzled look stopped him mid sentence.

"I thought Collin was his brother?"

"No, he is not...is that what Trinnian told you?" He looked confused as I nodded my head, my suspect response humoring him. "Huh, I can barely even complete my first train of thought before his true nature starts to come through." Silas shook his head in disbelief, examining my skeptical expression. Apparently not the response he wanted, because when he spoke again he almost seemed wary. Perhaps he conceded to the fact that I wasn't going to be easily convinced. "Look, I know it is really none of my business, but you seem like a good person. I know how he works. He could charm the pants off the Devil himself. That is how he gains his power over people, he is a control freak. Do not mistake his charismatic appeal for something it is not. The man is manipulative, deceitful and possessive to the point of obsession."

I felt Claire settle back onto her stool next to me. Silas stood up as if her return was his cue to leave. He reached in his pocket and tossed a crumpled bill on the bar.

"Trinnian is dangerous, and if for some reason you do not believe me..." The doubt created by his comment must have been obvious enough to change the direction of his cautionary advice. His defeated eyes considered me as he continued, "Just watch your back."

I mulled over his words, watching him slip through the crowd and step out into the night. Silas was no less of a mystery than the first time I heard his name. Worse still, nothing he said seemed to soften the feeling of rejection.

"What was that all about?" Claire asked.

"Actually, I couldn't even tell you." That was the best answer I could come up with.

I finished my drink while Claire gave me the scoop on the Scott situation. He was seeing someone he met at work and was very happy. The news didn't seem to bother her. On the contrary, she actually seemed relieved. Maybe she finally realized she'd been wasting her time, as I tried to tell her for practically a year. Normally, I would've been on the verge of dancing for joy but my long day caught up with me. Exhaustion hit me like a ton of bricks, and by the time we returned to Claire's place, much needed sleep swiftly followed.

*   *   *   *   *

The heart monitoring machine interpreted its static message, beeping in time with Karl Novak's mending heart. Silas stood at the end of Karl's bed, considering the weak pathetic being that slept before him. He never could understand Trinnian's desire to interact with such inferior life forms—well, any more than required. From his point of view, the day Collin released him from his temporary existence into his current god-like state of being, the only purpose they could possibly serve was sustenance. Once in a while you came across one that stood out amongst the herd. Those were so few and far between.

His thoughts returned to Jacquelyn. There was something about that one that Trinnian clearly saw as well. She was not the typical sniveling female 'victim', no, that one was vigorous. Even as her female pride waivered with Trinnian's indifference, how defiantly she defended his honor. He sensed through her thoughts that she would not be so easily manipulated, and not even due to Trinnian's persuasion. She had already decided for herself who Trinnian was, which put Silas at a loss. If Trinnian merely claimed her mentally, Silas would have lured her away from her friend and drained her.

For the first time in his immortality, Silas could not decide what to do with that one. So he simply backed off. She could possibly come of use later.

This Karl, as it turned out, would have to do. His murder would send the message to Trinnian that his mortal puppets were not safe. Their deaths would grab Trinnian's attention, denying his attempt to ignore Silas and he would realize that exile would be tolerated no longer. Silas would die trying to bring down Trinnian

CHAPTER FIVE

if he had to. Better die fighting as a man than to bow to somebody's wishes like a dog.

*   *   *   *   *

I slept restlessly on Claire's couch. Sleep didn't travel alone, it brought along a familiar guest. The prior night's dream started off exactly the same. It played on as vivid and intense as before. Once again I sat upon the table, my body clamped tight to Trinnian's while his silky lips made their tormenting journey to the front of my neck. Only this time, as his hand eased its grasp on my hair enough for me to look into his eyes, the intense stare was the same but the eyes were bright crystal blue. I struggled against his restraining grip until the pain of my effort brought what little progress I made to a halt. Still it was enough to answer my unspoken question. Trinnian was not the man with which my body was entwined. The confused panic that paralyzed me gave Silas a disturbing air of satisfaction. His wicked smirk proof that he reveled in the fact he wasn't who I expected.

My eyes flickered open in recognition of the email alert on my cell phone, thankful for the interruption. Morning was in full swing judging from the commotion out on the city streets. I grabbed my phone off the table next to me, curious as to who could possibly require my attention before noon. The email came from Glenn Edwards. Apparently I managed to sleep through his two prior attempts to call. Dread washed over me. Sitting up on the couch, I swung my feet onto the floor and buried my face in my hands, well aware of the nature of my luck. The email was probably about to inform me that I would have to track down Trinnian to have him sign something I missed for the first time in my career. I winced as I opened the message.

Jack,

Call me as soon as you can.

Glenn

43

Oh God, kill me now!

Glenn is not the most social person on the planet, so it was pretty safe to assume there would be an awkward meeting with Mr. Talbott in my future. Maybe being asleep wasn't so bad after all?

The cell phone in my hand felt as heavy as a brick, all I could do was stare at it since the thought of actually using it made me nauseous. Lost in my own little purgatory, I never even heard Claire enter the room. When I finally looked up from my phone, she stared at me curiously.

"I dropped my cell phone in the toilet once but I didn't bother to fish it back out," she muttered dryly.

Was the look on my face so traumatized? I wouldn't have doubted it.

I told her about the early email and my dark prediction behind its meaning. She managed to convince me that it was possible there were other reasons he could want to speak to me. So I took a breath and reluctantly dialed the number. Glenn sounded distant when he answered. I knew immediately this had nothing to do with my foolish suspicions, which only made my stomach sink lower. His voice was hollow as he spoke.

"Karl's heart gave out around four this morning. The nurses could not revive him." His voice broke with the last bit of information. I felt the pain in his tone physically, as if someone punched me in the chest. He cleared his throat and continued, "I will keep you posted on the funeral arrangements."

I heard myself tell him that if there was anything I could do to call me, then there was silence.

The couch shifted, it took me a second to realize that Claire sat down next to me. I told her what happened, my voice sounded dull to my ears. When she asked if I needed anything, all I could do was shake my head. She suggested I spend the day with her. I nodded unconsciously, staring down at the floor.

A haze engulfed me from which I couldn't break free. The day passed by while I watched from the couch. When night finally descended on the city, I lay down and surrendered to the deep, dreamless sleep that eluded me for hours.

CHAPTER FIVE

I woke the next morning to the smell of Claire making breakfast. It reminded me I hadn't eaten since the Chinese takeout prior to attending the gallery opening. I was famished. Relieved to see me up and about, Claire confessed she'd been worried about me. Otherwise conversation came sporadically as we ate. When we finished, I helped her clean up the kitchen and took a much needed shower. I felt human again, just worn out. Thankful the haze was gone, I decided to head home.

The remainder of the week passed along rather uneventfully. Amazing enough, even my sleep remained dream free. Gloria sent me an email Thursday to let me know that Karl's funeral would be Sunday afternoon. It surprised me to see she sent it from the office. To my knowledge, she was the closest friend Karl had aside from Glenn.

I kept myself busy, not wanting to let my mind dwell on the events from earlier in the week. My time was spent working around the house. It received a much needed cleaning, literally from the attic to the basement. By the time I finished my cleaning frenzy late Saturday afternoon, I ended up making three fully loaded trips to the Goodwill.

Later that evening, I curled up on the sofa with a book, ready to relax. I assumed the day's hard work would prompt me to go to bed early. However, my mind started drifting. I found myself staring at the first page, reading the same paragraph over and over. The words unable to hold my attention, I began to think of the funeral the next day, perhaps dreading it would've been a better description.

The last funeral I went to was for one of my best friends that I met just out of high school. Janette died suddenly from an aneurism. It caught us all off guard. The heartbreak I felt was nothing compared to being at the funeral, watching her mother and father simply try to make it through the service itself. Absolutely gut wrenching. I never wanted to have to feel, much less witness, the agony of loss so intimately again.

I brushed off the feeling of sadness that came with the memories as I adjusted the book in my hand and made another attempt at the first paragraph. This time my focus was lost to thoughts of Trinnian. I hadn't heard from him since Tuesday night and his peculiar goodbye. Did I scare him off with my overzealous comment about his lack of competition? Was it because I didn't try to stop his 'forward' advance? What was the deal with Silas? If Trinnian was the bad guy, why does his circle seem so uptight about Silas?

The book closed in my hands. Something occurred to me that I never even questioned before. What was Silas doing sitting next to me at the pub in the first place? If you take into consideration the population of New York City alone, what were the chances of him ending up in that very chair next to me? My eyes stared vacantly at the cover of the book I held, calculating the odds until I noticed what exactly I'd been trying to read. It was one of my mother's mystery novels she left behind on her most recent visit. Annoyed by the absurd irony of it, I tossed it on the coffee table and stomped into my office to reorganize my filing cabinet.

The last few mourners were arriving by the time I got to the funeral home Sunday afternoon. I couldn't seem to coax myself out of the SUV. The viewing was one of the worst memories I had from Janette's funeral. The thought of that being the last way I saw Karl terrified me.

A light tapping startled me, it was Gloria. I rolled down my window.

"Hey, Jackie, you might want to bring your coat, it's pretty chilly in there."

The slight smile on her lips was more than I would've expected, though I was not surprised to see that it didn't touch her eyes.

"Thanks, Gloria...but I think I'm just going to head on to the cemetery, I don't handle viewings very well," I confessed. Tears started to glaze my eyes.

"I understand," she whispered with sympathy, suddenly fighting back her own tears. "I'll tell Glenn, he was saving a seat for you with us." I must've looked as embarrassed as I felt. She quickly added, "Don't worry, he'll understand."

My thank you was barely audible. She nodded and headed back inside.

For the first time since I found out Karl passed away, I cried. The deluge that waited patiently, knowing I couldn't ignore its existence forever, broke free with a vengeance. When the last of the sorrowful tremors shook my body, I reluctantly looked in the mirror and attempted to deal with my red blotchy face.

The funeral home sat directly in front of the cemetery. When I walked around the building, I could see the tent set up for the burial. The plot was situated toward the center of the cemetery, slightly off one of the paths. As I got closer I noticed a bench nearby that faced in the direction of the tent. I made my way to it and sat down. The late afternoon sky was overcast, though the forecast didn't call for rain. The gloomy weather seemed appropriate. Sunshine wouldn't feel right today.

The stone next to Karl's plot caught my eye. It simply read 'Julia Novak Beloved Wife'. She was his college sweetheart. They had gotten married while still in school. Julia died giving birth to Julian, their only child. He never remarried—unless you count the firm.

If I felt alone when I first got to the bench, I didn't notice it until that moment. The stillness of the cemetery, along with the silence, started to make me feel uncomfortable. My mind played tricks with my senses. I thought I heard someone walking through the grass somewhere close in front of me. A closer examination of the monument strewn lawn ahead yielded nothing to justify what I heard. I was still the only person in the cemetery. The unease I felt was obviously the result of my surroundings. I rose from my seat after I decided to return to my SUV until the burial ceremony began. A familiar voice stopped me short in my tracks.

"Jack." Glenn's hands rose up from his sides, prepared to steady me as I teetered backward a step, shaken. "I'm sorry. I didn't mean to scare you." My heart raced from his sudden appearance. "I was just coming to check on you. The indoor service is over. Everybody will be heading out shortly."

"I'm ok, thanks for looking out for me."

His concern for me and the sadness in his eyes made for a tragic blend.

The rest of my work family joined us under the tent. I became lost in the rich cherry wood grain of the casket. The words spoken around me couldn't penetrate my abstraction. Only when the casket was sluggishly lowered into the earth was my trance broken.

As the precession started to break up, I was finally able to give my condolences to Julian, Karl's son. He was holding together better than I would have. I couldn't imagine having to be in his shoes. It appeared he'd taken on the role of comforter for the day. That was probably how he'd been holding up so well. He was too busy consoling others to have time to allow himself to grieve.

Gloria weaved through the departing crowd toward me. I knew everybody was invited to Julian's house for dinner but I hoped to slip out unnoticed before the carpooling assignments started. As dear to me as they all were, I was ready to go home and be done with the day. My plan was scrapped as I found myself committed to going to Julian's, courtesy of Gloria's power of persuasion. At least she allowed me to drive there all by my lonesome.

It was almost dark by the time I got to Julian's. From the amount of people that showed up I figured one full circle through the mourning crowd should be sufficient. I milled around the guests, determined not to have my plan foiled again, skillfully avoiding Gloria as tactfully as possible.

At last, the front door was in sight. No one appeared to notice as I gathered up my coat and headed directly for the door. Tunnel vision set in. I reached blindly into my purse, digging for my keys. With barely ten feet to go, the door opened to admit another guest.

Trinnian Talbott stepped through the doorway. He looked even more handsome than the last time I saw him, if that was even possible. Maybe elegant would be a better description of him in a black suit, tailored to perfection. He scanned the crowd as he walked into the room. I forced myself to turn away before he saw me and think invisible thoughts while I put my full attention into finding my keys.

"Jacquelyn?" I looked up and there he was, the only thing that stood between me and the door. "How are you?"

His concerned tone caught me off guard.

"Ok," I said, trying to keep things short. Although I'm not sure for who's benefit. Was it to relieve him of any feeling of obligation to talk to me? Or so I wouldn't have to suffer through another one of his strange goodbyes?

I started to dig through my purse again for my keys as an excuse to not have to look directly into his eyes.

"Are you leaving?" he asked.

For some reason he found this odd, judging by his tone. I'd been staring at my keys by that point and knew it was time to give up on my charade. I pulled the keys out of my handbag and reluctantly met his gaze. Disappointment clearly clouded his face. I misunderstood his tone completely. The discovery only added to my confusion initiated by his original concerned behavior.

"I don't do this funeral stuff very well. I really just want to be home." Frustration set in. I felt the tears starting to fill my eyes again. My gaze dropped down to the keys in my hands, hoping he didn't notice. "It was good to see you."

The words were barely a mumble as I pushed past him and through the door. Half way to my SUV, I heard footsteps behind me.

"Jacquelyn, please wait." His pleading request stole my will to take another step. He planted himself firmly between me and my destination. "I want to apologize for the other night."

My experience in dealing with men left me totally unprepared for this. Wasn't he supposed to pretend nothing was even vaguely odd about his behavior that night? He looked off into the night behind me, as if trying to collect the right words to fulfill his purpose.

His eyes started to transform while I studied them fiercely, hoping I would be able to tell the difference between sincerity and bullshit. First I caught what appeared to be confusion, which was abruptly cast aside for anger. His entire body stiffened at the same time it dawned on me, he wasn't deep in thought. He was looking at something. My attempt to turn and look behind me at what could possibly be the cause of his distress was thwarted by his unyielding grip on my upper arm. Not before I saw a figure in my peripheral vision. Trinnian's face was the picture of serenity when my eyes returned to his, like I imagined his change in demeanor. Even when he spoke, it was as if nothing happened.

"Jacquelyn, I would really like to talk to you but this is not the place."

He gave my arm a tender squeeze before his hand returned to his side.

The uncertainty of what just happened, combined with the lingering confusion of the other night, resulted in my manner being more abrasive than intended.

"Actually, I don't live far from here. If you don't think it is too 'forward' you can come to my place," I said.

6

When we arrived at my house, I watched in my rearview mirror as Trinnian emerged from his Mercedes. Part of me felt badly about my snide comment before we left Julian's. His reaction caught me off guard. You'd have thought I'd slapped him in the face from his wordless response. The small part of me that felt a justifiable satisfaction in his reaction faded away fast when I noticed he still wore an expression of discontent. I'd never been one to take pleasure in hurting people, even if I felt they deserved it.

I invited him into my house, thankful for my week of over-enthusiastic cleaning. He passed over the threshold absorbing his new surroundings. My amusement was evident upon realizing I studied him the same way I discovered he'd been studying me the other day in his foyer. When he turned to speak his warm irresistible grin disarmed me.

"Your home is very peaceful. I appreciate your invitation even more now that I am here."

His strange heartfelt comment was oddly comforting.

"Please, make yourself at home. I can hang up your jacket for you if you like," I offered.

He thanked me, removed his jacket and handed it over while loosening his tie. I hung his jacket on the coat rack by the door. His scent clung to the cloth, clean and masculine. A voice in the back of my mind suggested devilishly that it wouldn't be too terrible if he perhaps forgot to take it when he left.

While he settled into the couch I asked if I could get him anything. He declined my offer graciously and gestured to the space next to him. The simple polite motion stirred up a feeling of apprehension within me. There would be no buffering small talk as suggested by his resolute manner. I couldn't help feeling guarded as I took the seat next to him, not knowing what to expect.

He chuckled in his familiar carefree way as he critiqued my posture.

"For all your concern about my comfort, you do not look very relaxed."

Trinnian's assessment was embarrassingly accurate. Under the scrutiny of his gaze, I unlocked my arms that were crossed defensively in front of me. I hadn't even realized they took up their own protective stance preparing for his explanation.

"Jacquelyn," he said, his approach forced all joking aside, "I have something I need to deal with in my life right now. There are things happening that I would rather not get you involved in or make you have to play second fiddle to. My more logical side tells me it would not be fair to you to drag you into something that will only make you miserable. My selfish side is fueled by the desire to have you near me. The other night...it was never my intention to hurt you. I just wanted to avoid having you getting caught up in any repercussions that may come from the decisions I have made." His demeanor softened as he continued, "I know I am being selfish but I enjoy your company and nothing could possibly make me happier than to be able to spend more time with you. I realize that we barely even know each other but..." He seemed to struggle briefly, his brow furrowed in thought. "I do not want to sound cliché but I cannot find the words to describe the way you make me feel...I feel alive when I am with you and I believe in my heart that you feel the same way."

He sat in silence, exploring my eyes intently for a sign of affirmation. His words were so straight forward and open that I couldn't help feeling overwhelmed. I was speechless.

The week had been like an emotional rollercoaster for me. My vulnerable state wasn't the place for decision making. I didn't want to jump into something I would normally let develop with time. It was more like Claire to make hasty decisions about men, not me.

Trinnian rose from the couch tentatively. The uncomfortable silence that resulted from my lack of response no doubt forced him into action. The sadness I saw earlier returned as he spoke.

"I am sorry, it was wrong of me to make such assumptions on your behalf. Today has been difficult enough for you without my arrogance added to it. Please forgive me."

Apology offered, he walked toward the door. His wounded expression prompted me to my feet. Or maybe it was the panic I felt at the thought of him leaving. Whatever the motivation, it was my turn to plant myself between him and his destination. I stubbornly blocked his exit but couldn't find the words to enforce my resolve. None of the phrases in my head sounded right. They were either too cheesy or too desperate. All I could do was stare into his dark patient eyes.

Hesitation was cast aside, as if he understood exactly what I couldn't bring myself to say. In response, his cool hands carefully cradled my face. For a brief moment his eyes searched mine, perhaps offering me a last chance to escape. My heart beat fiercely in my chest until I felt the force of his lips on mine, then I was no longer aware of it beating at all. I kissed him back brazenly, grabbing his shirt to pull him closer. Trinnian's reaction was instantaneous. His restraint shattered, accepting my aggressive response as unspoken consent. Primal enthusiasm surfaced with a vengeance.

I heard his hand slam against the door frame seconds before my body, his action spared me the crashing impact while his other hand braced me firmly by the back of my neck. I became practically fused to the door while his mouth feverishly tormented the exposed flesh of my neck and chest. Pleasure numbed me to my surroundings only to intensify my awareness of his sensuality.

It took me a minute to fully grasp the feeling of weightlessness I experienced until I felt my body delicately being placed onto my bed. The recognition of the change of venue quickened my pulse and faltered my breathing.

Trinnian pulled back in respect to the change in my body. His eyes once again searched mine for a signal to stop. My hands answered for me, impatiently fumbling with the buttons on his crisp white shirt. Taking a cue from my actions, he slipped off his tie in one quick motion before turning his attention to his shirt. Which he handled with even less patience than I had, popping off the bottom two buttons in the removal process.

His smooth pale skin accentuated his lean muscular torso. My hands moved fluently over his chest as he leaned in to kiss me with even more vigor than before. Fingertips skimmed down my arms to my waist, loosening the tie at the front of my black wrap dress. He sat back, pulling me forward by my wrists to sit up in front of him. Tenderly, he slid the dress over my shoulders, down my arms and gently freed me from the garment. The lace demi-cup bra that hid beneath the dress was carefully removed and tossed to the floor.

There I sat under the scrutiny of his dark eyes. Never before had I felt so exposed, yet so at ease. He pulled me back into his arms. Our naked flesh pressed together deliciously while he kissed me with a hunger I had never known. I felt his hand slide up my spine until his fingers tangled in my hair. Easing my head back, his lips explored the curve of my neck. A breath caught in my throat with the familiarity of the action. It was the same motion that preceded the panic educing events of my dream. I unconsciously braced myself for something dreadful to happen. But this wasn't my dream and nothing dreadful happened.

"I cannot spend the night," he said. I'd been lying against him with my head on his chest and my arm draped across his stomach. His hand stroked my hair, which had me on the verge of sleep. That was until his comment, which came as the equivalent of an alarm clock. "I have obligations at home to tend to tomorrow."

"Oh...I understand."

I kept my head on his chest to prevent him from seeing the disappointment on my face.

"Jacquelyn, it is not like that," he said, attempting to put me at ease. I knew he was on to me. He heard it in the tone of my voice. "Please look at me." I lifted my head to look into his eyes and was met by an equal measure of sorrow and disbelief. "Please believe me when I say I really do not want to leave. I have to," he continued with a more optimistic tone, "I plan to see you tomorrow and would be honored if you will allow me the pleasure of your company."

The genuine sentiment that backed his words emulated in his eyes. I studied his face for a moment, waiting for my gut to tell me what to say. It responded as I hoped it would.

"I would like that," I said.

His warm smile encouraged my own. I laid my head back down on his chest and his hand returned to stroking my hair.

After the events of the last few hours, since we excelled quickly past the polite 'getting to know you' phase into the more intimate realm, I figured I could bring up a more familiar topic.

"I met an acquaintance of yours the other night," I said, gingerly testing the waters.

"Really...who would that be?" He asked casually.

I rolled onto my stomach so I could look at him while we spoke.

"He said his name was Silas."

"Where did you meet him?" His inquiring gaze almost made me regret bringing it up. But part of me felt like I kept something from him by not mentioning it.

"It was at the pub around the corner from Claire's apartment the night of the gallery opening. Claire asked me to go with her after you dropped me off." I didn't feel the need to go into detail as to why she asked me to go with her. "He happened to sit in the stool next to mine shortly after we had gotten there and heard me mention your name."

"I see." He appeared to be deep in thought. "Well I am sure that was an interesting conversation."

"With Silas or Claire?" I smirked in an attempt to lighten the mood.

Trinnian considered what I said momentarily before he answered, "Both." He grinned. "Silas and I have never gotten along. I tolerated him because he and Collin were friends, otherwise, I personally would have never associated with him."

It comforted me that he didn't feel the need to defame or vilify someone he didn't care for as Silas did. Should I really have expected any less? Trinnian was a gentleman. He could even be diplomatic about someone that he obviously knew didn't extend him the same courtesy.

"I suspected as much. It seemed like there was more to it than he tried to put off. In fact, it was almost like he desperately grasped for something that would turn me against you." He looked perplexed by the concept. So I elaborated, "He said you lied about Collin being your brother."

He laughed to himself, "He got me there. Collin is not really my brother." The skepticism I felt in repeating Silas's declaration melted into disappointment at Trinnian's confession, which wasn't lost on him. Instantly his eyes softened and he affectionately took my hand, "Is an adopted child no less a brother to his siblings?" His gentle smile made me feel foolish. "Would you like me to help you clarify anything else?"

I shook my head. The fact that I even considered the possibility that Silas could've been the one who told the truth flooded me with shame. It's amazing the lengths the subconscious mind will go to protect the fragile heart.

His eyes lit with inspiration and he unexpectedly sat up.

"I have an idea." He looked at me mischievously, pulling me into his arms. "Since you are no longer employed, you should go pack a bag and come stay at my house. That way Silas cannot come and steal you away from me in the middle of the night," he said with a persuasive smile. "You do realize that is probably why he felt the need to say such terrible things to you about me. To turn you against me and claim you for his very own?"

I arched an eyebrow deviously, "Silas did warn me that you were possessive."

He kissed me as he spoke. "Did he really?" he purred in my ear. His lips skimmed across my collarbone, a tingling wave of pleasure spread across my skin.

"Yes." My response sounded more like a gasp. I quietly cleared my throat before I continued, "To the point of obsession."

The words were barely a whisper. His lips made their way up my neck and stopped just below my ear.

"That sounds terrible," he replied, feigning offence. Without warning, he slid me onto his lap. The abrupt movement conjured a surprised squeal from me. "So what you are saying is that I should help you pack so I can start practicing being possessive?"

I nodded submissively, realizing the packing would have to wait.

By the time I was packed and ready to go, it was well after midnight. Being unemployed sure had its advantages. Although, I did tell Glenn that I would make myself available if he should need me to help with the clients Karl left behind. That actually worked in my favor. It gave me an excuse to bring my vehicle. Not that I was concerned that I could be making a mistake. Or that there could be a microscopic possibility that Silas may be right about the possessive control freak thing. It is just good to be able to fend for yourself—especially when making rash decisions with a man you barely knew for a week. Even if you did feel that wanting to be with him was becoming more of a compulsion than a choice. Still a choice you would indisputably make.

I would never hear the end of it if I didn't call Claire, regardless of the hour. My thought that the late hour would keep the conversation short and sweet missed the mark completely. In fact, we were almost to Trinnian's place by the time I had gotten off the phone and her scream still echoed in the cabin of my SUV. She absolutely went insane when I told her where we were headed and how it all came about.

Honestly, I was still a bit astounded by the whole thing myself. For one, I wasn't an impulsive person. I'd always made boring, well thought out, level headed decisions. This was much more reminiscent of one of Claire's stunts. I wasn't one to fall into bed with any man. There had to be at least some sort of basis for a relationship before sex was even a consideration. This wasn't like me at all. So why wasn't I more bothered by my behavior? Why was I still en route to Trinnian's house? For some unknown reason, it *felt* right.

I looked in my rearview mirror and could see his Mercedes cruising in the distance behind me. He thought it would be a good idea if he followed me, in case he had to impress me with his mechanical skills. I'm sure he knew he was beyond having to impress me. He had my attention from the moment I first saw him. It was all like some bizarre dream, and at any minute, I would wake up.

We rounded a bend in the road so tight his headlights left my line of vision. As he disappeared from my mirror, I glanced back to the road.

A man stood in my lane. I jerked the steering wheel impulsively to the right, much too hard. In a blind panic I tried to correct my fatal error. It was too late. The tires of the passenger side hit the gravel on the shoulder of the road as I tried to compensate for my overcorrection. My SUV slid sideways. The guardrail did nothing to stop my progress as it broke free upon my impact.

At the same time I slid through the broken barrier, my vehicle turned enough to face the man in the road. Silas smiled as he saw the horror spread across my face. His smug response to my predicament disappeared from sight as my SUV violently flipped down the steep embankment.

Glass exploded all around me the first time the roof came into contact with solid ground. The structural integrity of the vehicle groaned in protest with each compromising jolt encountered between earth and metal. The cabin closed in tighter with the force of each jarring impact, threatening to crush me while shards of glass sliced brutally at my flesh. My body jerked viciously to a halt as my smashed tomb of leather, metal and glass collided with its final resting place. I heard glass and other small broken bits of debris settle around me while they too came to a rest. Silence engulfed me. My blurred vision submitted to the absolute domination of unconsciousness.

7

Allowing a comfortable distance between them, Trinnian followed Jacquelyn to his house. He would have felt better if she had not been so determined to take her own vehicle. Not wanting to rouse suspicion or make her uncomfortable, he did not try to change her mind. He knew Silas was near but doubted he would be foolish enough to try to get to her with him so close. Silas may be crazy but he was definitely not a fool. If there was anything Trinnian knew for certain in his elongated life, it was the fact that Silas absolutely lost any ounce of sanity that he may have possessed at one time. When Trinnian made the decision to ban Silas from their lives, he had a feeling it would come back to haunt him.

Trinnian, Olivia and Collin built a peaceful life in upstate New York. The three of them were one of the more stable families of the regions immortal population. There were others like Owen and Augustine that were considered part of the family, even though they led a more independent existence. They chose to live a life less confined but frequently returned to New York. Other than that, there were the city dwelling immortals. Well known, established immortals that existed comfortably alongside those that came and went as they pleased with little or no affiliations. Most of these 'transient immortals' were left alone so long as they respected common sense that has helped the species persevere.

The only conflict Trinnian's family ever had within their ranks occurred when Silas was brought into their circle. Yet for all the turmoil he caused, he had been given a choice: to leave their territory or forfeit his existence. This practically gave him the run

59

of the world, with the exception of the physical boundaries in relation to his former family. If ever he sensed one of them near, he was to make way providing a wide berth. Anything less would be considered disrespectful.

The day that Collin told Trinnian that Silas was back, he knew immediately it meant trouble. Collin tried to assure him that Silas would never venture closer than New York City and that the city was big enough for everyone to hunt. Trinnian specifically laid down the law and his request was not vague in any way, shape or form. Silas knew his mere presence breached the terms of his exile and it could only be taken as a hostile act on his part. Trinnian was well aware that, to this very day, the mere mention of Silas's name made Collin cringe. He was sympathetic to the fact that Collin truly felt he could never make up for bringing Silas into their lives.

After all, Collin created Silas. He had been out hunting alone when he was drawn to the scent of fresh blood. On a deserted stretch of New England beach, he discovered Silas drunk, stabbed and barely clinging to life. When Collin saw what was in Silas's mind, he was intrigued with his story. Silas considered himself a pirate. As opposed to draining him and finishing the job, Collin thought that he would be an interesting addition to the family. There was no way for him to have known that he could not have been further from the truth.

What originally attracted Silas to the life of a pirate was the rebellious nature of the job. Take anything you wanted without asking. Instill fear into society and command respect through that fear. All Silas ever knew was anarchy.

When he joined their family, Silas acted on his best behavior. That lasted for a few years until his self-centered destructive nature blazed through completely. His impulsive reckless actions endangered the life Trinnian and his companions built. Silas had to move on before he compromised their existence, which would force them to eliminate him as a threat.

The punishment Collin imposed on himself for subjecting his family to Silas banned him from ever creating another immortal soul. So for Collin's sake, Trinnian would try to let whatever Silas was trying to do slide for the moment. He figured Silas would be gone shortly, merely trying to test his boundaries. Especially once he realized he could not get a rise out of anyone. The general consensus, give him no need to stay around and no need for conflict by even acknowledging his presence. That seemed the best way. He was young in immortal terms and not strong enough to view as anything more than a menace. Still no immortal wants to have to destroy their own. Even if they seemed to have a death wish or even quite literally ask for it.

The night of the gallery opening was the first night Trinnian laid eyes on Silas in decades. He felt his presence and when he looked out the window into the night, Silas stood in the shadows across the street, staring fixedly at him. Trinnian assumed it was his attempt at defiance against the judgment that had been placed upon him. So he decided to turn his back on him not perceiving him as a threat. In doing so, Trinnian tested the theory that if he ignored him, Silas would simply go away. It was childish really. When dealing with the mentality of someone like Silas, childish is just as safe a bet as any. However much Trinnian would have preferred to have flown through the door and snap Silas's neck with his bare hands, it was definitely the wiser choice at the moment. He was enjoying himself that night and did not want to ruin his evening by having to kill one of his own. Whether or not he felt they deserved it.

In retrospect, Trinnian understood that his decision to ignore Silas was the death of Karl Novak. If only he stuck to his original feeling that Silas was in violation of his exile and knew the consequences of his actions, Karl would not have died merely to get a rise out of Trinnian. Recalling the conversation that Jacquelyn had with Karl's client at the gallery, he knew that was when Silas's plan was set in motion. They established Karl's connection to Trinnian and discussed the hospital he was in that very night. He never entertained the thought that Silas would dare provoke him. They both knew who the victor would be in a one-on-one confrontation. Suicide mission or not, Trinnian knew it was definitely a mistake to underestimate the hatred Silas harbored for him.

Karl Novak's funeral slipped into Trinnian's thoughts. He no longer wished to stay away from Jacquelyn, having tried the best he could. The funeral would allow him the opportunity to once again see her. Perhaps from a distance or maybe he would risk everything to talk to her once more. What started as a self-centered indulgence paved the way for the shameless confession from Silas. Thankfully, Silas was tactful enough to get his message to Trinnian unbeknownst to Jacquelyn. Hidden by the shadows that surrounded Julian's house, Silas boldly staked his claim to Karl's death. Which begged the question, if Silas wanted to get his attention so badly, why did he not go after Jacquelyn? Now that Trinnian knew he had the opportunity. Why would he have approached her and allowed her to survive the encounter?

From the recounting of the event through Jacquelyn's mind, she stood up to Silas for Trinnian. As he recalled that night, he gave her no reason to do so. The memory of he and Jacquelyn standing on the stairs to Claire's apartment building replayed itself in his mind. Trinnian allowed himself to get caught up in the moment. Temporarily ignoring the fact that Silas was in the city and Trinnian's affectionate behavior would surely sign her death warrant if they were discovered. She would not be protected once he left and he was certain she would have declined an invitation to stay with him that night at Owen's place. The facts gave reason the upper hand, instantly snapping him out of his unwise advance. He had to walk away, no matter how much it hurt her—or him. Her life would not be put in danger due to his arrogance. So against his own wishes, he walked away. Perhaps it was the indifference of his actions that saved her from Silas? Or maybe he had other plans for her?

Jacquelyn had been an unexpected gift in his life. Her integrity, principals and tenacity intrigued him. He found it refreshing that even though she was naturally very pretty, she did not use it to her advantage. To her, wit was a much better ally to her than looks. She was not immune to his attraction. The ability to attract prey is one of a vampire's most lethal skills. Even though she felt the attraction, she did not feel the need to throw herself at him. She did not immediately try to figure out how to seduce him to gain his estate or even plot out other ways as a means to trap him.

It can be quite disheartening to be able to read mortal's thoughts. But Jacquelyn's thoughts did not disenchant him. Her mind had quite the opposite effect. She looked at his estate as an architectural marvel. Not trying to imagine herself residing in it. Her appreciation of their antique collection was genuine. Jacquelyn knew what she was looking at but she was not appraising the monetary value. She was admiring the pristine condition of each piece and the way the different time periods flowed together seamlessly. That was when he realized she was different. He listened more intently to the things that motivated her thoughts. She was not driven by power or money, nor did she care for people that were.

Although Jacquelyn was a refreshing change from his usual experience with her gender, she was still so undeniably human. The thought evoked her scent, the warm feel of her naked flesh against his and the amount of restraint it required not to feed from her as she took him inside. Even in memory his body shivered and his blood surged at the thought. It might not be a bad idea to have a repeat performance when they got back to his place. Not only to appease the desire that was building at the mere thought of once again taking her but to ensure she would sleep through the day until he could emerge at dusk. He did not want to think about what was in store for him in the coming hours or days. Especially how he would have to figure a way to explain to her why she could not leave his house because her life was in danger. Right then, all he wanted was to enjoy his moment of…happiness? The very idea of which seemed foreign to him.

Here was someone out of the blue that brightened up his world, a world that over time crept deeper into depression. The routine his life fell into gave him too much time to think. Maybe that was the reason Owen chose a life that never tended to stand still? Trinnian's assessment of his life as an immortal started to darken with the passing decades. Unknowingly, he seemed to dwell more and more on the loneliness that dominated his immortality than anything else. He hid it well. Collin and Olivia inevitably looked up to him being the oldest of the three. Seniority has always meant something to immortals, the older the vampire, the stronger the blood. Although he did not necessarily want to be anyone's leader, he did not want to let them down either. Showing weakness, or letting them sense it, would bring upheaval to the peaceful happy existence they achieved.

Owen was actually the oldest, at least in their immediate family. He had Trinnian by almost a thousand years. Regardless, he was rarely around, too immersed in his own way of life as the consummate traveler. The world was his reason for existing. Once, Trinnian asked him if he had not seen the whole globe yet. Owen simply replied that he was not actually sure, since even the familiar places changed so much with the passing of time.

His place in Manhattan was not his only hub. Owen kept a few other places around the world that he regularly made his rounds to. He did not use travel as a way to avoid attachments with others. When in town, he enjoyed his time spent with his New York family as much as they enjoyed his company. It was simply not in his nature to settle down. Owen knew he was welcome to join Trinnian and the others whenever he was ready to stop exploring. Who could actually predict if that time would ever come? Silas was the only reason he remained in town so long this time. Owen felt the need to monitor the delicate situation closely, should it require the intervention of higher ranks.

Silas was up to something, Trinnian could only assume. That something involved Jacquelyn. Getting her away from Julian's was the best thing he could have done. If she would not have been in such a fragile state, maybe he would have actually tried to explain it all to her. In all honesty, the truth would have been more dangerous for her in her mortal status. And he had not had enough time with her to allow for her human comfort zone to become attached to the point where he could tell her he was going to kill her for her own good, and she would be fine with that. That only left him one option. He needed their relationship to move along quicker. Trinnian needed to gain her trust and some level of attachment to him—not that he did not *want* to engage her in a sexual manner. He knew she did not take the act of sex lightly and

64

hoped her moral side would not have a problem with the expedited time table.

So in a way her vulnerable state did work in his favor. If nothing else, he managed to avoid having to charm her into doing his bidding. She meant much more to him than being his tool and he was not willing to put her in that position, even if it meant saving her life. He had more respect for her than that. In light of the contact Silas made, Trinnian did not regret his actions in the least. On the contrary, he felt even more justified.

They were almost to his place. The familiar surroundings should have comforted him, but now that they were so close to their destination, the distance between him and Jacquelyn bothered him. Trinnian watched her Volvo disappear around the sharpest bend on their route to his home. As he rounded the bend, he was gripped by an overwhelming feeling that something was not right. He felt the hair on the back of his neck stand up and the scene before him came into focus. Silas stood in the middle of his lane, staring at a breached section of guardrail. A cloud of dust hovered over the road. It slowly diffused like a ghostly apparition into the light breeze. There was no SUV on the road in front of him as there should have been.

Fury rushed through Trinnian unchecked. His grip tightened on the steering wheel, threatening to snap it off. He slammed on his breaks. The squeal of his tires drew Silas's attention away from his source of amusement. In the blink of an eye, Silas ran toward the woods, having lost any tinge of gratification on his face.

The Mercedes barely came to a stop when he jumped from it and sprinted to the broken rail. Silas already disappeared into the tree line on the opposite side of the road. When Trinnian got to where the rail should have been, he looked down the embankment and froze. Jacquelyn's SUV was upside down, cruelly wrapped around a tree. Her arm hung lifelessly through the driver's side window, streaked in crimson and bent in a disturbing angle. The smell of blood hung thick in the air, even from where he stood, he knew it was bad.

Going after Silas was not an option. Trinnian shot a glare back toward the trees where Silas vanished. Growling a curse under his breath, he conceded.

Jacquelyn's heart still beat faintly but she needed help *immediately*. Within seconds, he was down the embankment, carefully removing her from the twisted heap of metal. The succulent aroma of her blood threatened to drive him mad with thirst. He willfully disregarded it, cradling her gently in his arms while he assessed her injuries. She was alive although not by much. There was no time to get help.

Even if he got her in his car right now, she would not make it to the nearest hospital. He could make it if he ran. Would the doctors act fast enough? He shuddered at the consequences the hospital staff would suffer from his rage if they were not. Faced with the facts, there was only one option. She would have to understand he had no choice.

Trinnian brushed her tangled bloody hair back from her face and neck. Her expression was as serene as it had been while she lay against his chest earlier. His jaw clenched as the memory ushered forth more images. He remembered her captivating smile as she stood by the table in the wine cellar and watched him collect bottles of wine for her selection. How beautiful she looked as she studied Augustine's paintings, giving them her undivided attention. Her riveting deep aqua eyes, gazing into his as they lay together in a tangle of limbs on her bed instead of packing her overnight bag.

This was not how he wanted it to happen. Not everybody saw immortality as a gift—especially when forced upon them. His jaw unclenched as the memories faded. The desolate feeling of sorrow and resentment pushed aside. He pulled her compassionately to him and whispered an apology in her ear before his teeth pierced the flesh just below it. His measured bite penetrated enough to release the weak pulse of blood that moved beneath the skin.

With the rush of the blood came the flood of life, snippets of experiences that surge through the mind in death. Trinnian supposed it was what people referred to as their life flashing before their eyes. The memories flicker and flutter like an old movie on a reel-to-reel projector when witnessed by an outsider. This was the normal view of a victim's life. That, along with the thoughts plucked from their vicious minds prior to death, was all he ever needed to reinforce his resolve that he chose his prey wisely. This situation was different. This was not the usual immoral fiend that he normally fed upon. This was the woman that brought him back to life.

The visions became brighter and more fluid. Trinnian made the conscious effort to see and understand the images playing out before him. He witnessed landmarks in Jacquelyn's life, things that held importance to her at the time of their happening. At first he was not surprised at the things she was reliving. Things like her first role in a school play, getting her driver's license while keeping her father's car intact and passing the real estate examination on her first try. The random images kept coming, even as the timeline slowed their pace. His curiosity peaked as visions of him seeped into her mind. Seeing himself from her point of view seemed so insignificant compared to a lifetime of experiences.

His attempt to understand was disrupted by the fading of visions. This was the signal to stop drinking because it meant death was only a breath away. He grudgingly withdrew. Her peaceful face was void of color and her lips were almost gray with the lack of blood. His teeth sliced his lower lip superficially and he affectionately kissed the wound left behind on her throat. The flesh mended at once, leaving no sign of the lethal puncture. He gently repositioned Jacquelyn before using his thumb nail to slice clean through the skin of his neck, allowing the current of blood to cascade from his carotid artery. Trinnian pressed her mouth to the wound. After what seemed like an eternity, she swallowed weakly. Relief passed through his tense body when he felt her voluntarily feeding on the blood her body desperately needed.

8

Trinnian sat motionless in the chair next to his stately four poster bed. His eyes fixed on the pale auburn haired beauty nestled amongst the evergreen silk brocade bedding. He could have been praying for her the way his chin was propped up by his folded hands, his elbows resting on the arms of the high backed chair in which he sat. His mind dwelled far from any merciful thoughts and he knew Jacquelyn was not the one in need of divine intervention. She would awaken to her new life as an immortal being. However, Silas should be making peace with whatever god he chose.

Collin and Olivia were close to the house, he felt their approach. As soon as he had gotten Jacquelyn into his car, Trinnian called them to erase the accident scene for him. The last thing he needed to deal with at this point was the authorities and missing person's investigation. He knew Jacquelyn told Claire where she was headed and it would not take long to turn suspicion on him should her vehicle be discovered.

Reluctantly, he rose from his chair, smoothed the back of his hand across Jacquelyn's cheek and left the room. The front door opened as he descended the stairs into the foyer. Collin and Olivia entered without a sound, he could smell that they both fed as he requested. Collin assured him that there remained no sign of the accident and that they dumped the crumpled SUV into an abandoned water-filled quarry well off the beaten path. There was no doubt in his mind that everything he asked of them had been done. Trinnian trusted them both with his life.

CHAPTER EIGHT

He thanked them and approached Olivia with purpose. She swung her long, straight caramel hair neatly over her shoulder and tilted her head in the same direction to fully bare her delicate neck. Her skin slightly flushed from her recent feeding, the scent enthralling. Trinnian drank enough to fill the void left behind from having fed Jacquelyn and then some, knowing he was about to do it all over again. He wanted to make sure Jacquelyn would be strong, so he intended to assist the process as much as physically possible. If she ended up resenting him for what he had done to her, at least, he hoped, he could make her strong enough to defend herself. Just because she was no longer human did not mean she was safe from Silas. Collin was not very old when he made Silas and that was not very long ago in immortal terms. The strength his blood lacked would not matter if Silas came up against an average newborn immortal. Despite not knowing who Silas had been slumming with, Trinnian could tell that he was not much better off in strength than when he had been banished from their lives.

Returning to his room, Trinnian sat on the edge of the bed. He picked up Jacquelyn's hand, running his fingertips over the soft skin of her forearm. Her innocent expression remained unchanged as she slept. He raised his wrist to his mouth, puncturing the flesh, freeing the blood Jacquelyn's healing body so desperately needed. She drank vehemently. Instinct led her hands to seek out his arm and cling to it tightly. He started to pull away when she drank enough. Her eyes flashed open and locked on his defiantly. Her piercing turquoise glare endangered his will to want to make her stop. It took more force than he would have thought to free his arm from her steely grip. As soon as the connection broke, her eyes shut, leaving no sign that they had even been open in the first place. She returned to her healing slumber.

Trinnian settled back into the chair beside the bed, his mind churned. Jacquelyn would have to understand, he thought as he studied her serene face. Could it even be possible for her to resent him for saving her life? His thoughts grew pessimistic, tainted by the memory of a similar situation. It being the only other comparison he could come up with at the moment and it kept repeating itself over and over in his head. Owen once saved a young woman's life for selfish reasons, the consequences of which still haunted Trinnian.

Olivia's approach brought his troubled thoughts back from the past. She peeked into the room, waiting for permission to enter. Trinnian's nod her silent invitation. A connection existed between them that went beyond the fact that he sired her. Their bond rivaled any other immortal link either of them had with another. Whether it stemmed from the centuries spent together or the uncomplicated way they always related to one another, neither of them could say.

Placing a comforting hand on Trinnian's shoulder, she knew something bothered him and exactly what plagued his thoughts. She gestured to the bed, he nodded, his eyes never leaving Jacquelyn's face. Olivia respectfully took a seat on the edge of the bed next to Jacquelyn. She turned her concerned gaze to Trinnian and spoke.

"I imagine she will be out for a while." Olivia's voice was low, as if she could wake Jacquelyn before her body was ready. "From the amount of damage you described, it could take her a few days to fully transform." He showed no sign that she even spoke. Undiscouraged, Olivia continued, "I do not mind sitting with her for a while if you would like to take a break."

He shook his head. Trinnian looked exhausted, definitely an accomplishment for an immortal. Olivia could not bear to see him like this and knew him well enough to know that her tip toeing around the issue would not accomplish anything.

"Trinnian." Her tone broke his trance. His eyes met hers, more through reflex than response. She was not one to raise her voice or to command attention, his incredulous look evidence of that fact. "You are needlessly torturing yourself. I know the reason for your brooding silence and you should know the two situations cannot be compared. First off, Jacquelyn was not suicidal. Second, I would be willing to wager on the fact that she was in love with you—which, in itself, is a hell of a lot more than I can say for Margaret the night she met Owen."

CHAPTER EIGHT

Irritated with the fact that Olivia could read him so easily, he changed the subject, not wanting to discuss the situation she referred to.

"It was not supposed to happen this way."

"But it did!" Olivia exclaimed, refusing his attempt to redirect the conversation.

They stared at each other in stubborn silence, she felt confident that she could get through to him. She chose her words carefully before she continued.

"Collin was not given a choice and he seems to think you saved his life," she offered in a more composed timbre.

"That is not true, I offered him—"

"I am familiar with the story, Trinnian," she said, cutting him off. "The advanced stages of blood loss you discovered him in, I do not consider any decisions he would have made at the time from a proper state of mind."

"Regardless, that was an entirely different situation," he replied defensively.

"How so?" Olivia asked, unwilling to disguise the frustration in her voice. "Because you cannot find a way to blame yourself for his mortal demise or because you were not in love with him?"

Trinnian flinched as if the words stung him. His stare returned to Jacquelyn. Olivia knew she hit the mark completely with both statements. Between his lack of rebuttal and the way his jaw muscles clenched, she needed no further evidence.

"I realize how difficult this must be for you. You are always so in control of yourself and your surroundings. There is not much you can do about the helplessness you are feeling except put a little faith in the woman who rendered you so."

Once again, Trinnian's eyes met hers, a glimmer of hope shown in them that had not been there when she entered the room. She stood to leave, halting when she heard him chuckle, only to find him watching her skeptically. Her eyes narrowed, searching his as she tilted her head in curiosity.

"Would you consider me a control freak?" The thought seemed to amuse him.

"Hmm, how would Switzerland answer such a question?" Olivia pondered with a giggle, trying to encourage his lighter mood. Her warm smile apologetic as she continued, "No, I only meant you normally have a firm grasp on your life. I did not mean anything negative by it."

"I was not necessarily referring to your comment, Silas tried to warn Jacquelyn that I am a control freak."

Olivia's reaction reminded Trinnian that he had not had a chance to fill her and Collin in on all that he learned earlier that night. All he had a chance to tell them was that Silas caused the accident. He knew he needed to bring them both up to speed. Though reluctant to leave Jacquelyn, he followed Olivia out of the room in search of Collin.

They assembled in the living room where the seating area converged around the fireplace. Trinnian explained all that transpired over the past couple days. Olivia and Collin both agreed that Silas had to be up to something to pass up Jacquelyn for Karl. They also felt that Trinnian's intention of bringing Jacquelyn to the manor was the right thing to do. Like Trinnian, neither of them would have suspected Silas to try something so bold, especially with Trinnian so close.

"Obviously he was confident enough in his plan to not worry about a confrontation. I find it difficult to believe he came up with this one on his own," Collin noted suspiciously. "Silas tends to act before thinking."

"It embarrasses me to say that it really was not *that* clever," Trinnian countered. "My ego did not allow for the creative inspiration of contempt."

"It could have happened to any of us, Trinnian, stop acting like something got by your all seeing eye," Olivia groaned. Her sympathy for him started to wear thin, "If Jacquelyn would have made it here unscathed you would have been gloating about the fact that he would have never had the stones to attempt an attack."

Trinnian's level stare met Olivia's defiance. "Well, I suppose we will never know, will we?"

CHAPTER EIGHT

"You two can sit here and bicker amongst yourselves. I am going to look for Silas," Collin said, getting to his feet. Before he could take a step, Trinnian blocked his exit in a blur.

"Silas is mine!" he growled savagely through clenched teeth. His eyes shone like black ice as his brutal glare relayed the severity of his position to Collin. Satisfied he made his point, Trinnian stalked off toward the stairs.

Even with shutters that allowed no trace of light to enter the room, all immortals instinctively knew the position of the sun. Dawn approached. Trinnian knew he needed rest. It had been a while since he last slept, and converting mortals to immortals uses a lot of energy. His underestimation of Silas got to him once. He would not extend to him another advantage. Climbing into bed next to Jacquelyn, he allowed himself one more glance at her tranquil face before he closed his eyes.

Scattered images started to piece themselves together as his mind gave in to a deep slumber. The result of the uniting fragments was a dream. When Trinnian did dream, it was usually a replay of events or a time he experienced. What unfolded in this dream was a time he would rather not experience again, the very memory that tormented him all evening. And as luck would have it, the whole dreadful scenario would play out from the beginning.

Margaret studied the rope that hung from the rafters as she had over the past few days. She would sit on the edge of the bed, her eyes surveying the rough twisting fibers. How harsh and brutal they looked, even as an empty noose. The chair that sat patiently beneath was merely menacing. But the rope, that was pure violence. Some nights, tears would fall, her cheeks offering them no resistance. Some nights she stared through clear empty brown eyes, knowing she could end all the loneliness and pain. One day she would and she would know when the time came.

Owen would watch her through the window. Each night her decision sat precariously on the fence. One night, she would decide she had enough. That would be the night he rescued her from herself. Until then, all he could do was wait. It did not seem fair to make the decision for her, being so fragile. He wanted to

73

make it all better. What he thought would be better, and then he would be her savior.

The first night he saw her, Owen knew he had to have her. To him, she was like an angel fallen from heaven. He survived enough lifetimes to know what true beauty was. There in the window at the top floor of the Inn lingered one such goddess, pure of heart, mind and body. Margaret was the daughter of a wealthy merchant. She was only weeks away from marrying her childhood sweetheart, Frederick, when a fall from a horse tragically brought his young life and their future together to an end.

All Margaret had left was her empty rented room, a noose and an old wooden chair. Owen knew tonight would be the night. For the first time since he started watching her, Margaret stepped up onto the seat of the chair. Her radiance not lost to the way the sadness twisted her face as she defiantly thrust her head through the noose. Ash blonde hair hung in rippling waves to her waist, blowing gently in the breeze from the window that she left ajar. There was a storm moving in, and for whatever reason, Margaret thought it was perfect timing.

Tears slid in rapid succession down her face while she stared unblinkingly at the ceiling, mumbling fiercely. Owen could easily hear her beg forgiveness from God for what she was about to do. Margaret avowed she could not bear another day on this earth without her Frederick. She swallowed hard and kicked the chair away with as much force as she could muster into her quivering legs.

The glass shattered with a crash of thunder when Owen burst through the window. Margaret was safe in his arms before the rope fully stretched beneath her weight. She lost consciousness sooner than the chair could even hit the floor, fear so consumed her. One tenth of a second more and the rope would have snapped her neck, rendering it impossible to transform her. Injured is one thing, dead is another.

He freed her limp body from the noose and laid her carefully upon the bed. Her innocent face streaked with tears. For the first time in days, the sadness no longer contorted her lovely face. Her features were relaxed in her state of unconsciousness.

Owen tenderly caressed her face as if to confirm the exquisite beauty his eyes beheld. His day finally came, Margaret was his.

Lightning flashed across the sky, followed closely by the swift clap of thunder. Her storm arrived at last. His thoughts froze in unison with his body when, without warning, Margaret's eyes flickered open. She peered through confusion, her eyes flashed from his face to the rope and back, staring deeply into his. Recognition led to acceptance. He gasped, caught off guard as he understood, Margaret thought she died and Owen was an angel. His mere presence convinced her that God heard her prayers and sent an angel to escort her to her Frederick.

Owen's familiarity with the healing powers of the immortal conversion made him confident her broken mind would be healed. He told her she would have no need for Frederick anymore and that she was free. She looked at him incredulously, shaking her head. Owen ignored her refusal to believe his words as he bent his face to her neck, holding her down to the bed by her shoulders. Her fragrance assaulted his senses, intensifying with her struggle against him. The more she struggled the harder her heart beat, threatening to render him powerless. A low guttural moan escaped his lips as they parted to expose his teeth, all too eager to discover the source of the pulsating aroma.

Night passed by, indifferent to what transpired between them. A dense veil of rain masked them as Owen carried her through the city. They reached his place well before dawn. He placed her affectionately in his bed where she could transform undisturbed.

When she awoke the next night she barraged him with the curiosity of a newly immortal mind. The questions he expected, what he was not prepared for, was the sadness that lingered. So the blood could completely heal a broken body but not the mind? He did his best to hide his disappointment, thinking maybe, eventually, it would pass.

Over the next few months their companionship grew naturally. He could still feel the sadness that did not release its claim on her completely. Even as their friendship developed and they became even more intimately involved, it seemed she would never entirely be his. Part of her would always belong to her dead fiancé.

As the years passed, bitterness grew in Owen. At the same time, Margaret became more and more frustrated, trying to get him to settle down like many of his other friends. On a trip to New York, Owen pulled Trinnian aside and begged him to please make Margaret happy. He tried with all his being to accomplish just that but finally gave up. All that remained was an overwhelming resentment for his failure and at her for her wasted suffering for the past. Owen confessed he could no longer conjure up the patience to deal with her but knew Trinnian could. He believed Trinnian could offer her a better life than he was willing to and in the process she might even put an end to Trinnian's loneliness. To Owen, it seemed the perfect solution, leaving Trinnian no reason to refuse him.

The first few nights after Owen left had been awkward for everyone. Collin and Olivia tried to be hospitable as usual. Margaret attempted to be social, only to end up feeling out of place and spent most of her time in her room.

Trinnian went to check on her one night about a week after she arrived. He lightly knocked on her door, unintentionally causing it to swing open. He could hear her crying as she lay on her bed. Tentatively, he entered the room and made his way to her. He stood at the edge of the bed. His heart silently breaking for the beautiful woman he barely knew while sobs sent shudders through her body. She looked up, as if she had suddenly realized he was there, pushing herself up against the headboard. As she sat upright, she timidly looked into Trinnian's eyes ashamed of her behavior. He sat next to her in consolation, to let her know it was alright for her to feel what she was feeling.

Margaret wiped the tears from her eyes and pulled Trinnian closer to her. He stroked her hair from her face as she pulled him closer still. Her teeth penetrated his neck. He gasped, clutching her tighter to him. She drank passionately, her nails clawed at his skin, leaving welts behind. Trinnian felt every stinging puncture and scratch. To a vampire, during the intimacy of blood exchange, the line between pain and pleasure blur. Driven by his mounting desire, Trinnian grabbed Margaret by her hair, pulling her lips from his neck. He kissed her ravenously, licking his own blood from her mouth before eagerly sinking his teeth into the base of her inviting neck.

A connection forged between them that night. They each understood the other's emptiness. The common thread found brought them close, turning them into more than lovers. Margaret came out of her shell and became a part of the household. Trinnian never brought up Frederick—or Owen for that matter. It seemed she finally adjusted to the life of an immortal.

Almost five months passed since Margaret's arrival. Collin and Olivia went to hunt in the city. Trinnian stayed close to be with Margaret. She claimed she was not hungry and sent him to hunt alone. He returned to the strong scent of immortal blood. Almost insane with terror, he searched the house, braced for battle. He burst through Margaret's door on guard.

Unprepared for the scene that awaited him, he stumbled back into the door. There in the middle of her bed lay Margaret. Her throat and wrists were sliced open with deep gouges. The gaping hole in her chest could be attributed to the monstrous dagger that she weakly clutched in her right hand. Blood oozed slowly from her wounds coating her flesh, soaking the bed linens and making her once white nightgown resemble battlefield dressings. Her tear filled despondent eyes settled unashamed on Trinnian. She begged for him to end her life, her voice a ragged rasp forcing itself through her damaged vocal cords. He slid down the door, devastated, knees too weak to hold him up any longer. Trinnian stared in revulsion at the disregard she had for herself and groaned in agony at the request she made of him. How could she ask such a thing of him? Was the love she professed to him nothing but a lie? Trinnian's promise to take care of her that he made to Owen echoed in his head, mocking him viciously. This decision was not his to make. The only one who could grant her wish was her maker. Anything else would be a slap in the face to Owen, regardless of her predicament.

Margaret, not pleased with the news but confident that Owen would give her what she wanted, seemed convinced he would do anything to be rid of her for good. Trinnian reluctantly mended her wounds and allowed her to feed from him. He felt betrayed, angry and heartbroken. A small part within him almost regretted having to wait for Owen. But he knew it was only the hurt that surfaced from the love he had for her. Having done all he could, he left her to rest for the night. Not before he warned her that if she did anything to herself like that again, she would be left to suffer in her self-inflicted disrepair until Owen showed up.

Olivia and Collin returned from their hunt well before day break. When they arrived at the manor, Trinnian sat on the front steps waiting for them, head in hands. He relayed the story of what occurred in their absence and sent them off to put the word out that Owen was desperately needed back in New York.

A few nights later Trinnian returned home from hunting when he felt Owen's sudden advance. Trinnian waited for him outside to explain the situation. Owen could not disguise his wrath as he burst into the house and nearly flew up the stairs. Trinnian heard the door to Margaret's room splinter off its hinges as Owen broke into her room. Owen's expression was murderous rage as he passed Trinnian with Margaret in tow. Neither of them spoke a word. The last memory Trinnian had of Margaret was of her being escorted from the house by her wrist, wearing a strangely smug look of satisfaction as she and Owen disappeared into the pitch black woods.

_9_

Trinnian woke late the next evening, amazed he slept so long. Obviously his body required more rest than he anticipated. Despite his dream of Margaret, he felt a little more at ease about his situation with Jacquelyn. She remained unconscious, his blood having shut down her system to focus all her available energy on healing. He knew Olivia's assessment was accurate. Jacquelyn would not experience rebirth today, the extensive injuries to her mortal body would take precedence over immortal changes. Today he would take Olivia up on her offer to watch over her and go hunt.

Darkness staked its claim on the city thoroughly. Prey was ripe and ready for the taking. Trinnian indulged his hunger and headed toward Owen's apartment.

Owen greeted him, looking as stylish and contemporary as ever. He was the most resilient and progressive immortal Trinnian knew. He enthusiastically embraced the changes that came with each new age, no questions asked. Like a nocturnal chameleon, Owen blended into the city displaying the latest designer collections straight off the runways. Their nearly identical stature and pale immortal complexion was the only similarity between him and Trinnian. Owen's meticulously groomed short golden hair had a soft natural wave with highlights that echoed the sun ironically. Beneath his strong brow, his cobalt blue eyes held their own, possessing a piercing air of authority. He did not expect to see Trinnian so soon, having heard about his unfortunate encounter with Silas.

"How is our newest addition to the family coming along?" Owen asked when they settled into the living room.

"She is still unconscious. I do not expect her to wake until tomorrow evening at the very earliest, her injuries were quite extensive."

Trinnian never really felt comfortable in Owen's place. The stark, modern furnishings had a cold impersonal feel. It was more like being in an art gallery than a living room, the sparse seating area respecting form and structure more than comfort and function.

"Silas has been sticking to the edge of the city for the past two evenings," Owen said, analyzing Trinnian, trying to determine his motivation in coming all the way to Manhattan to hunt. Trinnian nodded absently, his gaze drifted to the sliding glass balcony doors. Their vantage point offered a dramatic, unimpeded view of the city. "What do you plan on doing?"

"I have not decided," Trinnian answered, his eyes never left the city skyline. "Whatever it is, it will result in his death."

The response did not faze Owen. As Trinnian's maker, he knew him well enough to know what to expect from him.

"You plan to do this tonight?" Owen asked.

"No. As much as the idea appeals to me, something just does not feel right. I need to make sure I know what I am up against. Something Collin said has made me consider the fact that Silas is not acting alone."

His stare was still intent on the city as if the conspirators could show themselves at any moment.

"Well, then assuming you have no other enemies, we shall only have to strike down a shoddy army of anemic zombies he may have created," Owen said dismissively, scoffing at the mere thought.

The sarcasm of his comment stole Trinnian's attention away from his scrutiny of the Manhattan skyline. Trinnian's stare met Owen's. When he spoke his words came devoid of humor.

"You cannot think of anyone who may support him in his mission to vex me?"

CHAPTER NINE

Owen's eyes narrowed and his brow furrowed for a split second as he contemplated the question. Although his expression relaxed, his gaze retained a subtle intensity that filled his pause with more than silence.

"Not particularly. Although I cannot be sure my enemies would not be willing to use you as a means to get to me."

He seemed more confident with his anemic zombie theory than the latest admission.

The journey home was simply a passing occurrence in comparison to the chaotic symphony of thoughts that clanged about in Trinnian's head. He needed to make sure he was not about to stumble blindly into an ambush, the sole purpose being his demise. There had to be a way to find out exactly what Silas was up to.

A new day gave the earliest signs of its impending presence when Trinnian arrived at the manor. He found comfort in the fact that everyone was home and accounted for. The only thing that made him feel more grateful, at the moment, was the gift that Owen gave him before he departed for home. They agreed that Jacquelyn required as much strength as possible to discourage Silas from any further attacks. Owen gave Trinnian his ancient blood, knowing he would want to feed Jacquelyn when he returned home. Trinnian could feel it course through his veins like liquid energy. Those with blood the strength of Owen's were not necessarily rare, however, they were not exactly common either. Immortality, it seems, may only turn out to be a rough estimate for some. If it came with a label, the fine print would read: Eternal existence barring lethal intervention.

As Trinnian tended to Jacquelyn, he was pleasantly surprised by how much stronger she had become in the last twenty-four hours. The possibility of her awakening tomorrow night came with a bitter sweet mix of excitement and fear. Fear, not being an emotion immortals were familiar with, understandably flooded him with a disturbing level of discomfort. It was all he could do to scour his mind free of all thoughts and surrender to sleep.

Trinnian's eyes opened at dusk. Even to his highly perceptive observation, Jacquelyn appeared to not so much as flinch since the prior night. But the change in her astounded him. She no longer smelled human. The luminous perfection that would mark her as immortal upon sight to others of their kind veiled her skin. Tonight would be the night of her rebirth. The continuous administration of the oldest, strongest immortal blood available worked miracles beyond anybody's predictions. His pulse quickened in response to the sudden resurgence of fear he experienced the night before. He rolled onto his side to watch her tranquil profile, looking for any signs of consciousness.

As he waited, questions that plagued his thoughts for days bombarded his mind. How would he tell her what she had become? What would he do if she ran off fueled by anger and hatred for him? Would she blame him for dragging her into his quarrel in the first place? If she asked, could he grant her request if she preferred death to being a killer? There was no way for him to prepare for what lie ahead. The knowledge of which did nothing to ease the dread that crept up on him. And the fact that Jacquelyn stirred, signaling her awakening, allowed that dread to crash down completely.

$$* \qquad * \qquad * \qquad * \qquad *$$

The perfume of night unfolded to my senses like the bloom of an exotic flower, each petal offering forth a new secret fragrance, yet never hinting at an end to the extent of its bouquet. Some scents identified themselves without question while others teased on the periphery with mere suggestions of their origin. Water flowed nearby. It carried the fresh green aroma of the moss that clung to the rocks scattered in its path. The clean crisp fragrance of pine traveled on the gentle breeze that meandered through the woods.

My mind could have puzzled through the mysterious onslaught endlessly, delighting in each new recognition as if it were its own reward. But the sounds that accompanied the scents begged to join in the game. The rustle of the wind and gurgle of the water played as background noise to the animals of the night that were on the prowl. Deep in the woods an owl screeched and a bat navigated through the trees using its sonar. A fox stalked a mouse on the forest floor. I could see it all in my mind with such clarity, yet I felt an overpowering urge to open my eyes.

I wasn't in a forest as some of my senses may have led me to believe, I was actually in a large four poster bed. Its luxurious, overstuffed makeup almost gave the impression of floating. The bed was housed in a large chamber, heavy dark velvet drapes blocked out any intrusion from the moon and stars. Not one single lamp that adorned the area contributed light into the space, yet I had no trouble making out even the smallest details of the room. Such as the intricate patterns of a vase on the fireplace mantle, the titles of the books that lined the shelves across the room or the Roman numerals on the face of a porcelain clock that sat on an antique writing desk.

Though I felt safe here, I couldn't recall ever being in the room before. The latter being the final piece of evidence earmarking the realm of dreams. I was sleeping. The lucid world that surrounded me made perfect sense now. Even the sudden feeling of being watched didn't seem out of place, much less the knowledge of the exact direction of the stare.

Propping myself up on my elbows, I glanced to my right. There, nestled in the bed next to me, was Trinnian. The sheets draped deliciously across his stomach, exposing his smooth, pale chest. He lay on his side, observing me with an unfamiliar expression. I said nothing while I studied his face as if I saw him for the first time. Had I ever really noticed the smooth, flawless texture of his skin or the strong set of his jaw? His eyes were so dark they were almost black, yet seemed to absorb and refract light simultaneously. I could've lain there in his gaze forever...lost in that moment.

His expression reanimated and his lips moved to form a word. I silenced him before he could interrupt my musing. I felt his disappointment, the look in his eyes compelled me to lean toward him and gently kiss his lips. He responded instantly. His lips moved in sync with mine. My body quivered with sensation, building a deep and passionate hunger within me. The hunger started to consume me, it possessed me. Images flashed through my mind too quickly to pin down any particular thought. Something about the images quickened my pulse. My blood burned as it raced through my veins. The burn but a shadow to the ache it preceded. It spread slowly from my core until it filled me completely.

I broke out of the spell long enough to realize I had climbed upon Trinnian and held him down by his wrists. My body trembled with exertion, my hands stiff from their white knuckle grip. Releasing him along with the breath I'd been holding, I sat up.

The expression Trinnian wore did little to reveal any reaction to my behavior. Even if he thought nothing of it, I couldn't help feeling a bit taken aback by my own conduct. I was about to speak when I suddenly became distracted. Inhaling deeply, my eyes drifted closed, breathing in the most alluring, succulent aroma I had ever encountered in my existence. Words failed to do any justice as they raced through my mind. Their feeble undertaking of the task made for a diluted comparison to the salty, sweet, rich, warm, tangy, earthy…to be able to pin it down exactly would've certainly brought me to tears. The scent intensified the aching hunger and the burning in my veins flared white hot.

Motion from Trinnian opened my eyes. His intense stare commanded my attention while his hand made its way up to his throat. With one smooth motion across the front, his hand came away leaving behind a deep red scratch. Still too enraptured by the scent to fully grasp the concept of what I just witnessed, it wasn't until I saw the scarlet fluid seep out of the laceration, trickling into the hollow at the base of his neck that I became fully aware of his action.

My breath caught in my throat and my hands lingered in uncertainty by my thighs, frozen. Then scent hit me harder than it had the first time. I breathed it in deeply, my eyes locked on to the blood pooling in the indentation. In the blink of an eye, I was on all fours, inhaling the intoxicating scent. Trinnian didn't flinch or protest while my curious tongue lapped gently at the blood collecting below his shallow wound. I pulled away, letting the syrupy elixir coat my tongue before I swallowed. A tingle left in its wake continued down my throat, prompting an excited chill to surge through my body. Much to my surprise, it tasted even more exhilarating than its scent, making my mouth water. That was when I realized Trinnian was watching me. His expression appeared more at ease, a small smile played on his lips. He pulled me back to him, allowing me to lick his flesh clean, leaving me greedily awaiting more.

Trinnian entertained my obsession until I was finally satisfied. Not a mark of evidence remained as proof of what occurred between us. Oddly enough, the savagely primitive act didn't begin to disturb me until I laid back into the pillows. It reminded me of analyzing a dream that made perfect sense at the time but, in reality, the bizarre happening left you gaping in awe of the perversions of your subconscious. The fact that I wasn't waking up started to become disconcerting.

The flash of images that assaulted me earlier returned. This time they played out slower.

Driving in my SUV, swerving to avoid hitting Silas. Sliding off the road, flipping over and over. Trinnian holding me and apologizing for something. Then came darkness. Trinnian beside me holding my hand. His blood. Repeatedly drinking his blood.

Slowly sitting up from the pillows, the images continued to come. I couldn't have ignored them even if I wanted to.

Olivia next to the bed talking to me. Trinnian again offering me his blood.

These things happened to me. *All* these things happened to me.

The persistent visions began to dissipate, but the need for answers left in their absence couldn't be denied. I turned to Trinnian to ask him if it was all true and if I really was awake. The words vanished on my tongue when I saw the guilt in his eyes he could no longer conceal as he looked at me. A sickening unease took root and the strangeness that clung to the room started to close in on me physically. Darkness pressed in, reminiscent of tunnel vision. I groped the light on the nightstand, desperately searching for the switch.

The brightness seared into my eyes painfully. It seemed I couldn't back away from its blinding presence fast enough. I was off the bed, stumbling blindly backward helplessly. My body clumsily slammed into the writing desk, splintering it between myself and the wall. The antique clock that perched on its edge smashed to the floor, sending shards of porcelain and glass slicing into my skin. I slid to the ground still cowering, shielding my eyes.

All this occurred in the split second it took Trinnian to turn the light off. I shook uncontrollably, weeping against the wall. Trinnian approached me cautiously. Nothing made sense. I teetered on the verge of panic.

A soft tinkling sound broke me out of my impending hysteria. Trinnian knelt next to me, his hands out in front of him as if to deflect a possible attack or debating whether to try to comfort me. A strange sensation drew my attention to my shins. The shards of glass that impaled them stung as they were being forced out of my skin. The punctures left behind tingled, healing right before my eyes. The sound I heard was the expelled glass falling to the floor. I couldn't look away until the very last nick healed.

Trinnian's hand on my shoulder startled me. His guarded expression remained unchanged, surveying me without a word.

"What is happening to me?" I managed to whisper hoarsely.

"You had an accident and you are healing."

"So flipping my SUV wasn't just a nightmare?" I asked. Trinnian slowly nodded, his eyes never leaving mine. "How long ago was this accident?"

"Three days," he said, almost reluctantly.

None of this added up. I felt fine. My eyes returned to the fragments of the shattered clock that littered the floor around me, the majority of which were encrusted with dried blood. I shook my head, meeting his gaze.

"I don't understand...it's not possible...I..." The words fought any attempt to form them into a coherent thought. Trinnian stood up and offered me his hand. I looked at it for a moment before I allowed him to help me up.

CHAPTER NINE

The house was quiet as he led me to the front door.
Somehow I knew that Olivia and Collin were somewhere within.
The feeling that led to this knowledge was similar to the feeling of
being watched, but knowing who watched you while at the same
time being able to identify them individually by their essence.

We passed through the door into the night. It had the same
tantalizing effect as when I experienced it earlier with my eyes
closed. But now, as it physically surrounded me, I felt completely
saturated by it. I can't say for sure how long I stood in that spot
absorbing all that the night wanted to show me. Trinnian merely
stepped aside and allowed me to surrender to it. When I finally did
escape its wonder, he was waiting patiently.

"I am going to lead you through the woods, do not be
afraid. There is something I need to show you. Can you trust me?"
he asked.

With all the bizarre things happening to me, trusting him
almost seemed the least of my worries. I nodded, much to his
relief.

We were off in a blur, running through the trees. The
forest whipped by us as if even the hundred year old trees stepped
aside for our passage. The astonishing speed at which we traveled
was absolutely effortless and I felt no fear whatsoever.

It barely took a minute to arrive at our destination. The
woods gave way to a sizable clearing that surrounded a long
abandoned limestone quarry. Trinnian led me to the edge, still
holding my hand. It was about a twenty foot drop to the surface of
the water. My crippling fear of heights gave no protest, even when
my bare toes hovered at the brink. Was there an end to the
inexplicable oddities of the day? The wind flicked at the knee
length, charcoal silk nightgown I wore, but I couldn't tell the
difference between the temperature of my skin and the evening
breeze.

"There." Trinnian pointed at a black mass lying in the
depths of the crystal clear jade water. My puzzled look forced him
to elaborate. "It is your vehicle." My gaze returned to the
deformed black object at the bottom of the quarry. A sickening
feeling gripped my stomach as I tried to find the familiar pattern of

my SUV in the black form. "Come, I will show you." That being said, he casually stepped into thin air and dropped like a rock into the water. Quarries were notorious for being very deep and cold, neither of which sounded very appealing. Trinnian's head broke the surface, "You do not trust me anymore?" His voice was relaxed and even, not the clipped speech that is forced through cold, chattering teeth.

Without allowing myself a second to think about it, I plunged into the water. It was cooler than the evening air but by no means uncomfortable.

The crumpled mass of Volvo sat about fifty feet below us. Much to my delight, swimming was as enjoyable as running. There wasn't a panic filled need to surface for air, which was good for me since the instant I recognized my SUV all the air vacated my lungs at once. The Edwards & Novak logo in the center of my rear bumper was all the proof I needed and pretty much all the proof I had. There were no license plates or personal effects amongst the crumpled wreckage. Morbid curiosity prompted me to look in the driver's side window. The top of the seat was forced into the roof and the upholstery was unmistakably stained with blood. Nobody could've lived through such total devastation without even a scratch.

No longer able to bear being near the devastated heap of metal, I swam to the surface as fast as my body would propel me. The second I broke the surface, I was on the verge of hyperventilation. Trinnian appeared next to me, he took hold of my shoulders, trying to get me to calm down. I thrashed like a wild banshee against him, trying to break free of his grip, all the while screaming for him to let me go. The churning water gave more of a reaction than he did.

"What have you done to me?!" My screams echoed back off the steep walls surrounding us. "What is happening to me?!"

I screamed and fought against him until the futility of my actions convinced me to stop. Defeated, I buried my face into his chest and wept. He wrapped his arms around me and kissed the top of my head.

"I will explain it all when we get back to the house." His calm voice subliminally reassuring me that everything was going to be alright.

He gently placed my arms securely around his neck and scaled the quarry wall.

We traveled in silence the whole way home.

10

The air felt heavy as Owen made his way through the dark streets. Even though his journey would take him to the other side of the city from his apartment, he welcomed the walk. He needed to clear his head. This situation with Silas that started as a simple annoyance was quickly turning into a problem. Collin's concern about the possible involvement of others echoed Owen's own suspicions. A theory nagged at him that he needed to put to rest.

Arriving at his destination, Owen ascended the steps of a small apartment building. There was nothing about the building that stood out in any way from its neighbors. He approached the keypad next to the door and punched in a code. His request for access was instantly granted, allowing him to pass into a hallway with a single metal door at the end. The hall held no décor, no mailboxes, no pictures and no signs. Mounted to the ceiling next to the metal door was a camera. As he came within reach of the door, he heard a distinct buzz and click as it unlocked mechanically. He passed through the sturdy metal door into a lobby. There was a small seating area to the left with a coffee colored leather couch and chairs that bordered an intricate oriental rug. To the right was a reception area reminiscent of a lawyer's office.

Behind a large cherry finished desk sat a stunning platinum blonde. Her short pixie hair framed her delicate features and managed to make her smoky gray eyes even harder to look away from. The tight black cashmere cardigan she wore was unbuttoned far enough to allow for an unimpeded view of her ample cleavage. Plump, sensual lips broke into a devious smile as she rose from her chair and smoothly rounded her desk to greet him. Owen shook his head with a slight laugh, wondering if she had help getting into the black patent leather pencil skirt that appeared to be painted on.

"I knew I put on my lucky panties for a reason!" she sang triumphantly as she threw her arms around his neck and hugged him.

"How on earth did you fit panties in there as well?" he asked, holding her at arm's length and surveyed her ensemble in awe.

She laughed and slid her hands up to his shoulders, closing the space between them.

"I get off work at four if you really want to find out," she purred in his ear.

"I am not so sure my decorator would like that after last time, Lisette." She arched an eyebrow at him as he continued. "She had to replace the whole living room."

Thrusting her chin in the air, she sauntered off to sit on the edge of her desk with her arms crossed.

"Your loss," Lisette sulked, eyes flickering to Owen to see whether or not he would give in before returning to their examination of the ceiling.

"As much as I would love to continue our conversation, I really need to speak to Petrus. Is he in?" Owen asked.

Lisette sighed in defeat. She picked up the receiver cradled on the desk beside her, placing it to her ear and hit a button. While she waited for Petrus to answer, she shamelessly eyed Owen up and down, giving him a wink as the other end finally picked up.

"Owen Smith is here to see you...yes, sir." She hung up the phone. "He will see you now."

Sauntering to the double doors next to her desk, Lisette theatrically opened them and stepped into the hall beyond. Owen followed her lead. They walked along the corridor, passing numbered doors that lined the hall on both sides. This was not his first time there so he knew it was to his advantage to concentrate on something to avoid the thoughts of the mortals within the building. With his current view, distraction would not be an issue. His gaze held captive by the sway of Lisette's curvaceous hips as she strutted ahead of him in her platform stilettos. Lisette peeked over her shoulder to ensure he was appreciating the view she displayed for him. The sly grin she wore in profile showed her approval, having caught him admiring her backside.

At the end of the hall they entered an elevator. Lisette's deceptively delicate hand reached out to press the button for the top floor. Her long candy apple red fingernails conjured up memories of the night that made his decorator threaten to quit working for him. He felt a subliminal flutter of pleasure pass through him before he abruptly forced the recollection from his mind. As appealing as her earlier invitation sounded, he was there on business and the information he sought may very well lay claim to the rest of the night.

With nothing to distract him, his mind wandered. He was instantly assaulted with human thoughts.

I deserve it. I have been so very, very naughty. Thank you... one man thought as a paddle smacked against the flesh of his naked buttocks rhythmically. *Oh yes, yes, yes! The ball gag...* another squealed in his mind with joy. *"Mommy, hold me..."* cried one that wore nothing but a cloth diaper in an oversized crib.

Owen's disgusted gaze met Lisette's indifferent expression. She rolled her eyes and shrugged her shoulders.

"What can you do? They pay good money. Who are we to judge another's fantasies?" she asked. "Who knows what they would get themselves into out there in society if Petrus did not provide them with an outlet."

She had a point. He was well aware of what Petrus provided there but he still could not help the fact that the majority of it repulsed him. The most unusual part, the clients rarely requested actual sex. Role playing, discipline, foot worship, etc... but sex, that could be found anywhere.

The elevator doors opened into a penthouse suite. Lisette gestured for Owen to enter. As he passed her, she informed him that she would refrain from making other plans in case he changed his mind. Purely carnal intentions reflected in her expression as the elevator doors closed between them.

The elevator landing was separated from the living room by a partition. As Owen stepped deeper into the space, nonthreatening neutral colors and contemporary furniture seemed at odds with the business that went on in the rest of the building. Adding to the discrepancy, a large, muscular tank of a man that sat on an 'L' shaped sage couch. His head was shaven bald and he wore a Fu Manchu mustache. The boldness of his features along with his black facial hair and dark brown deep set eyes gave him a sinister edge. He acknowledged Owen, motioning for him to sit and returned his attention to the football game he had been watching on a massive television.

When Owen rounded the couch, his eyes were drawn to a woman's body at Petrus's feet. It looked as if she lay where she had fallen.

"What the hell is that?" Owen asked, nodding at the body on the floor.

Petrus paused his recorded game to see what Owen referred to. He nudged the woman with his toe before answering.

"The crazy junky tried to stab me in the back ally when I returned from hunting. I was about to kill her when she offered to make it up to me. So I brought her up here and allowed her to show off her mediocre talents as an amateur prostitute. When she was done I realized I was still hungry, so..." Petrus explained, absently waving a hand in her direction.

"Thankfully for you we are not susceptible to disease," Owen grimaced. "I would like a moment of your undivided attention. But first, could you please remove that?" He requested, pointing at the corpse.

Petrus reached down, grabbed the deceased junky's ankle and dragged her limp body from the room. Owen could hear his grumbled complaints about having his game interrupted and the squeak of the kitchen garbage shoot opening as Petrus proceeded to stuff the corpse inside.

The building belonged to Petrus. His loyal employees, both human and immortal, did not mind taking care of the less desirable tasks for him. He had always been good to them.

Petrus returned to the couch ready to talk. When Owen asked him if he knew about what had been happening with Silas, he claimed ignorance. Owen proceeded to fill him in on the situation.

"I cannot think of anyone that would form an alliance with that one," said Petrus. "Silas is a walking time bomb."

"Has your business partner been in town lately?" Owen asked.

"She is too busy with our sister shop in Germany." Petrus looked at him in disbelief. "You think Mistress Scarlett may have something to do with this?"

"Mistress Scarlett," Owen mumbled to himself, shaking his head.

"Why would she associate with the likes of Silas?"

"I need to look at this situation from all angles and she is not my biggest fan." His gross understatement of her feelings toward him made Owen laugh to himself. "It would not surprise me if she felt the need to make my life miserable for a bit. Anyway, to your knowledge, she has not made any arrangements to come here any time soon?"

"No, not that she has told me."

"Well, I will be in town until this gets resolved. So please let me know if you even hear anything that might be of interest. This situation has started to get pretty intense and it would be good to know if this is going to turn into some type of war."

"I will," said Petrus. "Have you fed? I can arrange to have something brought up."

"Still charming your clients to sample from I see," Owen observed, walking to the elevator.

"It is not always easy to make sure the girls get a proper lunch break," Petrus said.

"I fed earlier, thanks." He stopped, turning to face Petrus. A sly grin slid across his lips, "But I will have a little something to go…that is if you do not mind letting Lisette off a little early."

Owen caught a cab with Lisette in tow. While they made their way to his apartment, Owen thought about his meeting with

CHAPTER TEN

Petrus. Although he did not think Petrus lied to him, still he could not put his suspicions behind him.

When they arrived at Owen's place he warned Lisette to mind the furnishings. Despite her noncommittal response, he set out to discover if she really did manage to fit a pair of panties under that skirt.

11

I sat on the floor in front of the living room fireplace. My skin absorbed the warmth from the fire that crackled and danced before me. The edges of the logs gave off a shimmering amber glow that fed the flames, encouraging their restless motion. My attention never left the fire, even as I felt Trinnian wrap a towel around my shoulders and settle on to the floor next to me. He waited for me to speak. I didn't even know where to start. Each time I felt like I had a starting point the logical side of me rejected it, doubting the experience or feeling had even occurred. Tears of frustration welled up in my eyes as I began to question my own sanity. Had I hit my head so hard in the accident I completely lost the capacity to distinguish fact from fiction? Or perhaps I slipped into a coma and would be trapped in this dream for months? Maybe I was dead and this was my bizarre twist on the afterlife? Blinking back the tears, I went with the least significant item that invaded my thoughts.

"Where is the place from Augustine's paintings…the dark island with the dead forest?"

"There are theories but nobody really knows for sure. Those among us that claim to have ever been there are convinced the sea swallowed it long ago," Trinnian answered, his voice dull.

"I dreamt of that place. It was so vivid I could feel the salt of the sea in the air and smell the rotting vegetation…" My words trailed off into silence. Out of all the opening statements I passed up, this one suddenly sounded the craziest. Especially when spoken out loud. What made it even stranger was that Trinnian knew exactly what I referred to. I turned to face him. He too was lost in the churning glow of the fire. "What do you mean, 'among us'?" I asked.

When he turned to me, I could tell by the look on his face that he struggled over his answer. His reaction brought back the uneasy feeling in the pit of my stomach, making time stand uncomfortably still while I awaited his reply.

"Jacquelyn…before I answer your question I want you to understand something." He paused to make sure he had my undivided attention as if to relay to me the importance of what he had to say. When he seemed convinced he had it, he continued. "I could not stand by and watch you breathe your last breath knowing I had within me the power to save your life. I felt…I *feel* I had no choice but to decide for you." Once again he paused, perhaps to silence his inner turmoil that played out behind his eyes. "Vampires are what I refer to when I say 'us'."

I faced him, silent and stunned, unsure of whether to laugh, cry or scream. Trinnian was not joking. At least he believed what he said to be the truth. Unable to decide which was worse, I felt every hair stand on end all over my body. At a loss for what to do, I sat there trying to act like what he said didn't shock me in the least. My gaze returned to the fire while I ran through all possible scenarios and options in my mind. Panic told me I needed to get out. Where was my cell phone or my clothing for that matter? I could call Claire and she would come and get me. I just needed to get back to the main road. Trinnian knew I wasn't alright with what he told me, I wasn't fooling anyone.

As discreet as possible, I looked for the closest weapon I could find. There, about three feet from my left hand, stood a fireplace poker.

"Jacquelyn, talk to me." Trinnian got to his feet, watching me suspiciously.

"I…um, I just need a minute," I managed. My mind frantically calculated the odds of being able to reach my only available means of defense before he could stop me.

"You do not believe me, do you?" he asked, taking a step toward me.

Not sure what to make of his advance I felt instinct kick in, self preservation the focus.

"I don't know."

No sooner did the words pass my lips, I grabbed the poker like a baseball bat and was on my knees swinging for his shins. The poker connected with the bone in a loud crack. Trinnian collapsed to the floor, howling in pain, reaching for his leg. I stood over him braced for his attack until I noticed the unnatural angle of his left leg. I stepped back in shock, the bent poker slid from my grip, my hands clasped over my gaping mouth.

The poker skittered across the floor at the same time Collin appeared out of thin air. He stood between me and Trinnian as if to protect him from me. Olivia crouched on the floor next to Trinnian, explaining to him she needed to make sure she could get the bones to line up. I tried to peek around Collin, at least as much as he would allow. Olivia straightened Trinnian's broken leg while he growled curses through his clenched jaw. Collin was looking down at me. His expression was blank, yet somehow terrifying.

"If you will please have a seat, Olivia is going to need my help," he said.

I lowered myself onto the couch behind me. Collin took Olivia's place and held Trinnian's leg in the position it should've held on its own. Olivia stepped over Trinnian and kneeled by his head.

"He is going to be fine, Jacquelyn," she said with a quick smile, ironically trying to put *me* at ease.

That being said, she slashed her wrist and put it to Trinnian's mouth. A gasp escaped me before my hands once again clasped over my mouth. He clutched onto her arm, suckling on the wound. The scene that unfolded in front of me threatened to be the last thing my overloaded mind could bear for one day, until the scent hit me.

I didn't notice I'd been leaning forward and practically off the couch until I became aware of the three faces staring at me, all sharing the same look of concern. Their apprehension meant nothing to me, all that mattered in my own little universe was that scent. I couldn't help myself as I lunged for Olivia's wrist. My impact with the floor snapped me out of my fixation. Collin held me down by my throat, limiting my field of vision to the ceiling. Even in my shame I was thankful that I didn't cause him to lose his hold on Trinnian's leg. I couldn't explain my actions. All I could think about was how badly I wanted her blood.

"You can let her go now, it is safe," Olivia reassured. She held up her completely healed wrist to prove her point. When Collin let go of me, I sat up staring at her wrist, torn between confusion and disappointment. "Collin, could you please take Trinnian up to his bed to rest and finish healing? He should not put any weight on that leg tonight to be sure it heals correctly. Jacquelyn and I are going to go for a walk," she said, smiling at me as if I didn't just maliciously break somebody's leg.

Collin didn't look comfortable with the idea, though it was Trinnian that spoke in protest.

"Olivia, I did not really get to explain things to her. We need to finish our conversation," he said. His eyes met mine for a moment until I looked away, suddenly intent on the area rug beneath my feet.

"I think I can handle it," she said, turning her attention back to me. "We will be fine, right, Jacquelyn?"

I nodded, keeping my eyes to the floor still caught up in the shame of my actions.

Even as Olivia escorted me to the door, I focused on her back. I could feel the weight of Collin and Trinnian's eyes on me. She opened the door, stepping aside for me to walk through. Dreading the disappointment I would see on their faces, I couldn't bring myself to look back.

We emerged into the night. This time it felt different, or maybe I did. Olivia strode into the woods, never offering me a backward glance to make sure I was still with her. We traveled in the opposite direction of the stone quarry. I could tell that, once again, we approached water. This time the trees gave way to a vast lake. Its surface appeared smooth as glass in the absence of the breeze that stirred earlier in the evening. Olivia lead me down a pier that jutted out into the water, far enough to give the illusion you would end up in the center should you walk its full length. We sat at the very end, our feet dangled over the motionless water. I no longer felt the panic or shame that had overtaken me at the manor. With Olivia, I felt more on the level, regardless of the fact that I knew so much less about her than I knew about Trinnian.

"So are you a vampire too?" The question sounded so absurd, an uncomfortable chuckle quickly followed.

"Yes I am. Luckily for me sometimes they take pity on the downtrodden," Olivia mused to herself.

"You sought them out? You chose to become…one of them?" I asked, not sure I understood what she tried to convey.

"No, I was not looking for them. I never even knew they existed aside from myths and tales. However, I was fortunate enough to have one find me and offer me hope. And I was shameless enough to ask for so much more."

"You don't regret your decision?" I asked. My curiosity outweighed the unease I should've felt.

"No, and I never understood those that do. If you are granted the ability to live forever, what could you possibly have to regret? The world is your playground and you get to see history play itself out before your eyes. Sometimes you even get to help write it."

"Do you mind if I ask how old you are?"

"I trust you mean how many years I have roamed the earth? I am approaching the six hundred mark." My explicative reaction amused her completely, her laughter made the night seem a bit brighter. "Such words from a lady?!" she chided playfully.

"You've been around since the fifteenth century?" My question was more incredulous than accusatory.

"You do not believe me? Perhaps it would help if I told you the story of how I came to be immortal?" she asked.

Studying her expression, I found nothing but pure open honesty.

"I would like that very much," I replied, a smile of appreciation spread across my face.

*   *   *   *   *

CHAPTER ELEVEN

A small, black beetle crawled across Olivia's arm, silent as the sunrise. She lay prone on the clammy stones that made up the floor of her prison cell, watching it make its clumsy, aimless journey along her skin while the morning sun climbed the sky. Her torn and stained shift did little to protect her skin from the intensity of the chill held by the stones. She welcomed the numbness the chill provided. It numbed her to her very womb, which still ached fiercely. Two whole days passed since the wretched old crone penetrated her with a crude stick, barbarically removing her unborn child. It was what her father wanted and whatever his highness wanted was given to him without question—even human life.

Olivia knew her father chose her cell intentionally. So she could see her lover, the father of her unborn child, hang in his infamous gallows outside her only window. His name was William, the captain of her father's guard. She stood powerless behind the bars and watched William escorted by his own fellow guardsmen to the gallows. His back straight and his head high as he walked, even as the crowd spat and cursed at him. He would die a traitor in the minds of the witnesses, choosing his own personal dishonor above Olivia's. Their eyes met one last time before the floor gave way beneath his feet. His look relayed more to her than words ever could. That was the day before they murdered her child, the last part of her and William. There was no more they could take. She had nothing left to give.

The beetle fell off her arm flailing on its back to right itself. Its weak desperate attempt angered her. She clenched her jaw, balled her hand into a tight fist and smashed the beetle. Her eyes squeezed shut, forcing the last tear she would cry for her life to drop on damp stone floor.

Her father's angst was not without merit, in his eyes anyway. He arraigned a marriage between Olivia and one of his conquest's sons. She was only a pawn in his stomach churning game of acquisitions. Her mother was merely a whore in the eyes of his council, a lowly serving wench that conveniently killed herself after Olivia's birth. Consumed with the depression of being shunned by society even though she gave birth to royalty, she jumped from the castle's towers. Anyone who believed her demise to be anything except murder was on the royal payroll or a buffoon.

Olivia's beauty and poise made many of them forget that she was not legally of royal descent. Exceptions could be made in empires if you had bargaining chips. Unfortunately for Olivia, her actions botched her chance to escape her brutal fathers grasp. Her would be husband took her leaked pregnancy as a personal affront to his manhood and wanted nothing to do with an immoral whore. She naively believed that her father would forgive her and understand her love for a common man. It was then that she was told the true story of her mother and father.

The clip clop of hooves interrupted her thoughts and brought her painfully to her feet. She stiffly made her way to the window, cold bare feet just managing to keep her upright. A portion of his guard escorted her father from the castle. Olivia snorted with the realization that her incarceration and death of all she loved did not put a damper on his hunting trips.

As if he felt the daggers of her glare, he looked up at her. He wore a stony expression of indifference. Olivia mustered up what moisture she could from her dehydrated body, she spat vainly out the window at him, grasping the bars with white knuckles, launching forward for momentum. Unaffected, he turned away from her pathetic display of defiance. Her body shook in anger but it was the lack of food and water that finally took its toll on her. Even though her knees gave out, she refused to relinquish her grip on the bars. Seconds passed and the room blurred while she hung from the bars, determined not to let them see her curled up on the floor, a pathetic beetle flailing on its back.

Days gave into weeks, morphing into months. The two to three day bread and water schedule and her father's bimonthly hunting trips became the only constant in Olivia's life. They were helpful in marking the passing of time.

Night approached as she shared her bread ration with the rats. The formally loathsome creatures were fast becoming her only friends. Human contact came in the form of shameless groping from prison keepers and the occasional violation from the more brazen ones. In comparison, the rats were the least revolting of her companions.

It seemed as though something had them on edge that night. In unison, they looked down the hall before returning cautiously to their bread. Moments later they disbursed as if they were never even there. Their sudden retreat unnerved Olivia. She immediately stood and flattened herself to the wall next to her cell door, listening for any clue to their hasty exit. The only sound she heard was the loud thud of her heart.

She inched her way to the door with her back pressed to the rough stone wall and strained to hear whatever drove her guests away. Her stomach became queasy with the thought of one of her bold captors coming to pleasure themselves against her wishes. Fingertips tentatively led the way until they found the doorway, stopping her advance. She cast her eyes toward heaven and took a deep breath as she chanced a peek down the hall, craning her neck to see around the corner.

Shock instantly replaced curiosity. Though she heard not a single foot step, someone stood outside her cell door. She easily recognized the man that stood outside but his was the last face she expected to see.

"Trinnian?"

Her voice sounded foreign in her ears. William's only true friend in the guard stood before her. A year or so before William was falsely accused and hung for treason, Trinnian had been sent with a select few of the guard to travel with one of her father's scouting vessels to guard its captain.

The way he looked at Olivia could have broken her heart in another life but she was not that person anymore.

"Yes, Olivia, it's me." The way his voice broke on her name, paired with the pained look on his face confused her. "I am so sorry I failed you...but if you can trust in me, I give you my word, I will get you out of here."

"I do not understand." Her brow knit in confusion, searching his face for answers. "How did you fail me?"

"William never told you?" Trinnian glanced down, shaking his head before he continued, once again meeting Olivia's confused stare, "Why would he?" His silence lasted long enough for a slight feeling of nausea to set in. "William asked me to look after you should anything happen to him. He knew there was no chance of a future for the two of you but he loved you too much to care about his own well being. Any time he could have with you meant more to him than his own life. He wanted to be with you no matter the cost."

Olivia swallowed hard against the lump that formed in her throat, an automatic response to the memories of William that Trinnian's words conjured up. Though keenly aware of the ache in her heart that came with the memories, Olivia had no tears left to cry.

Trinnian's eyes were full of shame as they surveyed her. He immediately dropped his gaze to the floor under her stare. She then understood the pain in his manner as she too took in her own appearance. Her body was gaunt and filthy, barely covered in rags. She brought her hands up to discover her hair matted and tangled. What a fright she must look. No wonder he suffered so in her presence.

Something down the hall broke Trinnian from his uncomfortable study of the stone floor beneath his feet. Unable to hear a thing, Olivia studied his profile as it hardened beneath her gaze. When his dark eyes returned to her, they glistened with a sinister elation.

"One of the guards is coming to demonstrate his skill as a lover to you," he said. "What good fortune for me. Please do not be afraid, I will never let you down again."

He vanished in the blink of an eye, raising gooseflesh on her arms. She strained to look down the hall in either direction, but he simply disappeared. Olivia tried to feel reassurance in the protection he promised her. In his absence, it became difficult to believe he had even been there in the first place and the distinct sound of footsteps approaching her cell became even more discouraging.

The heavy footfall alone named the approaching guard, they called him Murphy. He was the roughest of the lot and the first to force himself upon her. If she did not hallucinate Trinnian's presence, she worried for his safety. Murphy was twice his size and very strong. She had seen him fight off two prisoners simultaneously that tried to overpower him. Hopefully Trinnian could catch him off guard. She would do her best to keep him distracted. Anticipating the arrival of her tormentor, she backed away from the door.

Murphy's hulking frame nearly filled the doorway. His eyes searched for her in the dark shadows of her cell. Thin, greasy hair clung to his filthy scalp. A predatory grin exposed his rotting teeth. When his eyes grew accustomed to the murky darkness, he finally made out her form. The sound of metal sliding against metal broke the silence surrounding them when his key unlocked her cell door. Olivia braced herself for the worst, still unsure about the existence of her protector. The door creaked loudly on its hinges as it swung open.

Confidently, he strode into her cell. She could see Trinnian standing behind him. Any feeling of relief became lost to the fact that Trinnian held no weapon or means of defense. A fearful gasp escaped her, alerting Murphy of something behind him. He spun to face the source of Olivia's alarm, unsure what to expect. Upon discovery of the fact that he faced what he considered a pretty boy, well dressed, half his size and unarmed, he laughed deeply. Olivia took advantage of Murphy's distraction, quietly sliding herself into a dark corner of the cell closer to the door. Her new vantage point put her in a better position to fight or flee as needed.

Murphy's laughter was cut short, his eyes bulged as his hands grasped at his nose. Blood seeped between his fingers and trickled from beneath his hands, dripping off his chin. He winced in pain and confusion, not having seen the blow that obviously broke his nose. Olivia understood as she noticed Trinnian's hand relaxing out of a fist, though she had not actually witnessed the strike. Her suspicion confirmed by the content smirk spreading across Trinnian's face.

His actions were not lost on Murphy. He would not be shown up by a fop in front of Olivia. He needed to maintain the fact that he was the man of these prisons. His confusion and pain was forced aside as his big lumbering frame lunged at the pretty boy. His attack appeared to be deflected by an invisible force, accompanied by a loud crack as Trinnian spun easily out from under his advance. This time Murphy's large grimy hands clamped over his mouth in a desperate attempt to stem the blood flow that now doubled. He turned to face his assailant, even more confused than before, his hand cupping under his chin as he spit his front two teeth into it.

"You won't get a penny of ransom for her," Murphy spat, a nervous smile twitched painfully at the corners of his mangled mouth. "His highness knows she's nothing but a used up whore."

Trinnian raised his fist to his chin. His eyes drifted closed, breathing in the scent of the glistening blood that covered his knuckles. His tongue flicked out like a serpent only to withdraw slowly, savoring the taste euphorically.

Nervous eyes darted to the cell door, not exactly sure what to do, Murphy knew his attacker was too fast and agile to allow himself to be locked in the cell. He attempted to lunge at Trinnian once again. Trinnian spun to face Olivia. Murphy stopped dead in his tracks, his horrified eyes staring into space. Trinnian opened his clenched fist to produce Murphy's tongue.

Dropping to his knees, the most pitiful, gurgling wail escaped between Murphy's blood soaked fingers. Trinnian turned to face him, his full on glare sent Murphy skittering backward to cower against the stone wall a few feet from Olivia.

Not convinced that she had not completely lost her grip on reality, all Olivia could do was to stare dumfounded at her protector. She glanced from one man to the other, mystified by how wrong she had been in her initial assessment of the situation, backing away unaware that she stepped out of her dark corner in the first place. Olivia watched in disbelief while Trinnian approached Murphy. He crouched lower the closer he drew to the trembling man, moving with the grace of a stalking cat. Murphy braced himself against the stone wall, whimpering and shaking convulsively. Once Trinnian was mere inches from him, well within reach, he dropped Murphy's tongue between them.

Never breaking his gaze from the pathetic wreck of a man, Trinnian spoke, "Turn away, Olivia," he hissed. "You do not need to see this."

12

Olivia appraised the dark sky. Her pale green eyes shone like peridot in the moonlight. The hint of sadness that tried to influence her delicate features could do nothing to mar her timeless beauty. I waited patiently, eager for her to continue her tale. When she finally turned back to me, it seemed as if she forgot I was there.

"Forgive me." A half hearted smile tried to tug at her lips. "I cannot remember the last time I really thought about my mortal life...you have a question?"

"A few actually but I would rather let you finish, if you don't mind," I replied.

"We really need to head back, I can finish while we walk."

While we made our way to the manor, she went on to explain how they staged her cell to look like a lantern fell onto the shabby straw mattress, burning both her and Murphy alive. Then, how they escaped her father's towers and took shelter in the royal crypt as dawn approached.

The next evening, Trinnian allowed Olivia to sleep while he went to hunt. He understood how long it had been since she had a decent night's sleep with a full stomach. When he returned, he brought her a change of clothes, along with some more food and water. They escaped the kingdom, taking advantage of the dark moonless night. But traveling by foot took its toll on Olivia. They needed to find a place to stop and rest. Trinnian knew of an old

108

abandoned cottage in the woods nearby. The root cellar would provide him ample protection from the sunlight.

When they arrived at the cottage, Trinnian knew he could not put it off any longer. He needed to explain exactly what he was to Olivia. After all the things she witnessed since he came to her in the cell, she knew he was no longer human. Her awareness was not lost on Trinnian. As he spoke, any fear of him she may have harbored became eclipsed by fascination. Olivia knew he would not harm her. She also realized she could not expect him to protect her forever, her solution, to become what he was. They spent the rest of the night arguing over the pros and cons of transforming her into a vampire. Just shy of dawn, he finally started to wear down. She attributed this to her closing argument that he was all she had left in her life. Anybody that knew her assumed she was dead. He could not leave her alone and defenseless in this world. Trinnian reluctantly promised that if she felt the same the following night, he would grant her request. But she had to take a day to make sure that is what she wanted.

The day passed dreadfully slow for Olivia. To her, it almost felt like being back in her father's cell. In contrast, Trinnian slept peacefully in a dark corner of the cellar, never once stirring in his sleep. Olivia sat on the steps, transfixed by his sleeping form as she tried to imagine what it would be like to possess his power, stealth and endurance. The past few days she spent with him were filled with so many things she could not explain. His encounter with Murphy alone had been awe inspiring in itself but then there were the other things. Like the blinding speed with which he navigated the palace halls, carrying her in his arms, never once showing hesitation. Or the ease with which he scaled the wall that surrounded her father's kingdom while she clung for dear life to his back. What would life have in store for her if she could live fearless and free? It took every scrap of self control within her not to wake him. Her excitement and restlessness building as the shadows lengthened. The sun could not have set fast enough for Olivia. She had not changed her mind, and Trinnian was obligated to keep his promise.

The following evening, Olivia emerged from the protective cocoon of the cellar a vampire. Trinnian explained to her the prior night that she would immediately be aware of her hunger when she woke. The intensity of it was different for everyone. Those made by older vampires did not tend to be hindered by it. Since he was only a few years old, there was a bit of concern on his part she may find herself overwhelmed. She told him what she felt seemed comparable to how she felt for months while imprisoned by her father. More than anything, it felt like extreme dehydration intermittently overshadowed by hunger pangs. Far from anything she could not handle.

They set out for her first hunt. He told her the first time would be the toughest, so it was best to just get it out of the way. She understood without having to ask him to explain. The trade off for her immortality would be human lives. Although one did not have to kill to survive, it made it easier in a way to only have to search for one blood source a night. She saw Trinnian feed a couple of times, even though he requested she turn away. Her curiosity got the better of her on both occasions. The thought of actually doing it herself was a bit unnerving. However, her apprehension drifted away when she closed her eyes and felt her newly acquired strength surge through her body. It pulsed to the symphony of the mystical night. The blend was nothing short of divine.

Making their way through the woods in search of prey, he shared with her the philosophy his maker passed on to him about how to select victims. Thieves and murderers were the best choice since they were less likely to be missed by anyone and you were actually doing society a favor. Just because they required blood to survive, it did not mean they had to be night dwelling fiends. Vampires have also been known to feed from animals in a pinch. They do not taste as good as humans and it usually takes more of them to satiate hunger. Sometimes immortals fed from each other. This could be done for many reasons, although regular infusions of fresh living blood are still a necessity.

One of the most useful tools in a vampire's arsenal was their ability to read human minds. All they needed to do was peer into the mind of their prey to find the information needed. He cautioned her of the fact that mind reading did not work on vampires, due to the complexity of their thought process. Their minds are too occupied filtering through the constant assault of information to their heightened senses to truly get a fix on any particular thought. Other vampires can be 'sensed' with proximity but like mind reading, it requires practice to develop the talent. The closer the bond the clearer the signal, thus, a vampire's bond with their maker is usually the easiest to sense at first. Bonds can weaken over time with distance. The link with one's maker does not fade easily.

Olivia absorbed everything he told her avidly. She tingled with excitement, anxious to put her new skills to the test. Before long, they came across a fresh camp. Trinnian guided Olivia as she made her first attempt at mind reading. Frustration attempted to sabotage her resolve. She pressed on, determined not to disappoint her maker. Once he got her to relax a bit and not let the scent of their blood distract her, she caught her first images. Even with her novice ability, she could see that they were not a collection of evil men. These men were merely hunters.

Trinnian was about to suggest they move on when Olivia's attention locked on to one of the tents. This was her father's hunting party and he was alone in his tent across the camp from where they stood, hidden in the dark woods amongst the trees. She took a step forward. Trinnian stopped her dead with his vice like grip on her upper arm. Her head whipped around to face him, her eyes were wild as she let out a low hiss. Not at all naive to the things her father did to her, Trinnian reminded Olivia of the fact that not long ago she was human and he saw it all in her mind. However, part of being a vampire was being discreet in your existence. You could not just walk into a camp at least ten men strong and slay them all without raising suspicion. One or two was another story. He promised she could take her father down but she would have to do it his way.

They waited for the camp fire to die down before they made their move. When they were sure everyone slept, they made their grab. They managed to extract her father from the campsite without raising alarm and took him deep into the woods. He begged and wept like a coward for them to spare his life, groveling on pudgy hands and knees until he made out the familiar features of Olivia's face. His face blanched and he stared wide eyed at her in complete disbelief. He started to mutter incoherently about ghosts and curses.

In his rattled state, he tried to shuffle backwards out of their reach until a tree stopped his retreat. Fear set his beady eyes darting around the terrain, desperately searching for a way out. He was well aware that his bloated pampered physique would not take him far, his only option came down to buying his way out as he did so many times before.

"Olivia, my sweet girl…I can give you money…more than you could ever imagine. I will never let on that you still live. You can go wherever you please and not worry about pursuit. The council made me lock you away. They feared others would not take my rule seriously if I allowed your betrayal to go unpunished. It was for the good of the kingdom and our people," he bargained, mopping beads of sweat from his face with his shirt sleeve. "Oh how it broke my heart to think of you locked away—"

"Enough!" The word echoed off the trees and silenced the forest. Olivia's father could only gape in disbelief at her insolence, too stunned and afraid to dare speak a word. She sauntered toward him, lowering herself until their eyes met. "Today it seems fortune is on your side, father. You see you do have something I want."

Relief relaxed his tense expression that tightened with her proximity.

"Anything, my sweet girl, take it, it is yours!" he exclaimed, almost before she finished her sentence.

He clamored awkwardly to his feet, brushing the dirt and leaves from his night clothes. Olivia followed his lead, raising slowly, her reassuring smile relaxing him further.

"The extent of your generosity will never be forgotten," she assured with a slight inclination of her head.

The predatory glint of hunger hardened her eyes, backing him into the tree towering behind him. Olivia grabbed her father by his terrified face, pinning him to the trunk of the tree by the side of his head. He clawed blindly at her, unable to distract her from the pulsing artery in his neck. His frantic struggle made his heart beat furiously, disbursing the scent of his blood into the air surrounding him. Restraint was no longer of interest to Olivia, her teeth sliced through his skin and she took the only thing he had that she wanted.

*   *   *   *   *

Olivia and I emerged from the trees that faced the manor. A slight twitch of a second floor curtain alerted me to the fact that our arrival didn't go unnoticed. I stopped in my tracks, turning to her.

"I don't know if I can face him yet," I whispered, avoiding looking back at the manor.

Any questions I had for her vanished in that instant. Olivia squeezed my hand and gave me a small smile.

"There is a guest room next to our room, why not sleep there today? You have much to process." Before I could even form the question, she answered it, "I will let him know you need a little space to sort it all out."

"Thanks, Olivia...does the fact that you just read my mind mean I am still human?"

"No, but human nature takes a while to shake off."

That being said, she turned and entered the house. I stood there for a moment, working up the strength to walk through the front door as leisurely as she had. The gray predawn sky became all the motivation I needed. Its influence made it difficult to resist the urge to seek shelter. As my panic started to escalate in anticipation of the sunrise, any lingering denial abandoned me. It was true. I was a vampire. Something deep within me knew Trinnian was telling me the truth. I chose not to believe it.

Taking a deep breath, I walked through the front door, closing it quietly behind me. I could feel Collin at the foot of the stairs before I turned to ascend them. He wore the same blank expression as earlier but this time his eyes held nothing that terrified me.

"Olivia requested I show you to the guest room," he said in a calm, level voice before turning to head up the stairs. I followed him down the long hallway to the second door on the right. He politely opened it and gestured for me to enter. "Sleep well, Jacquelyn."

I passed by him into the room. He was shutting the door when I stuck my hand out to stop it. He let go of the knob and faced me.

"I am truly sorry for hurting Trinnian. I was afraid…"

"Why are you apologizing to me?" he asked, his expression remained unchanged.

"Because I don't think he is the only one I've managed to hurt today," I replied.

"I owe Trinnian my life. If it is within my power, I will protect him," he said, his eyes taking on a lethal gleam, "even if it costs me my own life."

He left the doorway of the guest room in the direction we came. I heard the door we passed on the way open and softly close. I stood at the guest room door, debating whether or not to go check on Trinnian. The uneasy feeling that accompanied the thought confirmed the fact that I wasn't ready to face him. Besides, he needed his rest and it was almost dawn. Reluctantly, I closed the door and crawled into the massive bed.

More than anything I wanted a long hot bath but I never felt exhaustion like I felt at that moment. My limbs were so heavy and my eyes fought stubbornly to shut. Even my thoughts were shutting down. I couldn't have processed my day if I wanted to. The last thought to slip through my brain was how horrifying my dreams were going to be…assuming vampires even dream.

13

A soft knock roused me from my deep slumber. It took a moment to orient myself. I was in the guest room at Trinnian's place, nestled comfortably in the lush covers of a huge antique bed. With a stretch and yawn, I sat up against the headboard. Under normal circumstances, the knock would've set me scrambling to make myself presentable, assuming it was Trinnian. However, after the prior day's leg smashing, I doubted he could ever look at me again with any sort of interest.

I closed my eyes to see if I could identify exactly who was at the door. From what Olivia told me, I should have no problem with this. At first I saw nothing. Undeterred, I focused on the presence that stood on the other side of the heavy wooden door. What I received in return was similar to a memory briefly triggered by a scent. Olivia's face flashed in my mind. A shiver of excitement flowed over me in anticipation of the correct answer.

"Come in," I said.

Olivia poked her head into the room. Her presence encouraged an enthusiastic smile, a small celebration of my new found ability. Even though I did have a one in three chance, it was still exhilarating. She entered the room carrying my bags.

"Good to find you in such fine spirits today." Her tone carried a touch of concern. "How are you feeling?" She paused by the bed, waiting for my reply.

"Better than last night but extremely thirsty, I guess that shouldn't surprise me. Is it normal to feel like all your energy has been drained in an instant when the sun starts to rise?"

"In your situation, yes, because you have not yet fed on living blood. So after tonight, when you prepare to turn in for the day, the effect will not be so extreme," Olivia stated in her matter-of-fact way. She placed my bags at the end of the bed, continuing on to a door opposite the one she entered. It took me a second to realize what she meant. Today would be the day. There would be no putting it off. I would feed from a live human. If she noticed any change in me she ignored it. "I figured your things may come in handy. We will be leaving shortly to go to the city." The door she opened swung inward to reveal a spacious bathroom. "You will find fresh towels in the cabinet to the right of the sink along with a decent selection of toiletry items you will need. The majority of the ones you brought with you did not survive the accident."

Her instructions played as background noise. My mind was still stuck on what the trip to the city entailed. The thought of 'hunting' a human sent a terrifying chill down my spine. In the same breath, it stirred a hunger in the pit of my stomach. When the time came, which sensation would win out?

"What if I can't do it?" I asked. Tears started to fill my eyes as I imagined someone cowering at my feet, begging for mercy. "What if I can't get past taking a human life?" Olivia approached the bed, her demeanor filled with sympathy.

"You will not have any say in it, really. Once you catch the scent, instinct will take over. Remember how compelled you were to get to my blood?" I nodded. "It will be like that."

"But it didn't seem that way for you," I pointed out, my voice thick with emotion. "You seemed to have control over yourself."

"I was not allowed to wait so long and revenge is a substantial motivator. You will be fine. We will be there for you."

Olivia's reassuring smile helped to ease my uncertainty, if only a little. Even though I knew I was in good hands, I still wasn't entirely comfortable with the whole idea.

"Thank you for everything," I said, successfully blinking back the tears. "You've really helped make all this a bit easier."

"You are welcome. Remember, you are family now. We have to look out for each other. Oh, speaking of which." She fished my cell phone and charger out of the pocket of her long belted taupe cardigan, considerately plugging it into the wall. "I trust you will not be tempted to call the vampire police," she said with a wink, heading for the hall.

She almost made it to the door when I finally built up the courage to ask one more question.

"Olivia?" She turned to face me as if she had known I wasn't through. "How's Trinnian today?"

"One hundred percent healed," she replied, her answer seemed to amuse her. "Sorry, I do not mean to come across as cold hearted but your situation made living with him almost unbearable. So in a way I was not exactly displeased to see him brought down to earth…literally."

Her laugh did little to ease the shame for what I'd done to him.

"I don't understand," I confessed, feeling a bit lost.

"He had himself convinced that you would hate him for what he had done to you. Never once did he think you would ever understand or forgive him for the choice he made the night of the accident. He spent most of the time you were healing wallowing in self pity, fixed to your bedside. It was terrible." Her voice sounded flat by the end of her explanation. "On that note, I will leave you to ready yourself. You have a big night ahead of you." Off she went, back to her normal cool and collected self.

Olivia's words replayed themselves in my mind while I crawled off the bed and headed for the shower. I stepped into the soothing hot spray, my brain still sorted through all the questions and thoughts that plagued it. Did I forgive him? Could I blame him? How exactly was someone supposed to feel toward the person that made them a vampire? More specifically when they had no say in the matter from the start?

It was then that I realized my first immortal slumber was not dream free. The accident replayed itself in my mind in the form of a dream even more lucid than my mortal ones. I knew without a doubt I should've died in that accident. Trinnian saved my life. If anyone deserved my hatred, it was Silas. I had seen his face, clearly amused by what he'd done. He intended to kill me, not Trinnian. If the situation had been reversed, would I—could I have let Trinnian die? The answer either way was no. His anguished apology echoed in my mind, 'Forgive me, but I do not have the strength to let you go.' Without a doubt, I would've done the same thing.

Wrapped up in a soft, plush white towel, I crossed the bathroom to the sink. The steam that coated the mirror distorted my image into a fuzzy apparition. With a swipe of my hand, my reflection came into view. The breath caught in my throat. I took a step back. This was the first time I'd seen myself since joining the ranks of the immortal. My skin was flawlessly radiant, like the rest of my...family. What really grabbed my attention was the color and clarity of my eyes. They were a brilliant, shimmering jade. I wondered if my mother and father would be able to tell the difference. Or even Claire for that matter.

The familiar ring of my cell phone tore me away from the mirror. I got to it before the first ring completed. Speak of the devil, it was Claire. I lowered myself onto the edge of the bed, my brain kicked into damage control mode. With all else that happened in the past couple of days, I'd not prepared myself to deal with my old life. I was still stumbling through my new one. What on earth would I say? At least we weren't about to talk face to face, she had a knack for telling if I was lying.

"Hey, what's up?" I asked in my attempt to emulate Olivia's cool, calm style.

"Are you serious?" Claire wasn't trying to emulate anything. Her irritation was obvious. "I haven't heard from you in days after leaving you messages and that's all you can say? I was really getting worried. In fact, I almost called your parents instead of you."

"Claire, I'm sorry, I just found my charger before I jumped in the shower. I hadn't even realized my phone died." *Which wasn't entirely a lie?* "I was going to check my messages when I got out."

"So you're ok then?" she asked, sounding a bit calmer.

"I'm fine, I guess I just lost track of the days." *Which was also not entirely a lie?* "I haven't even checked my email, since I didn't bring my laptop with me."

"Oh, so you're still at his place? Wow, this is the longest sleepover ever!" she jabbed. As irritating as I found her comment, it was always a good sign when she started joking again. My sigh being the cell phone equivalent of eye rolling prodded her along. "Then I won't keep you, but please do check in every so often so I don't worry, ok?"

After I reassured her I wouldn't drop off the grid again, the call ended. I placed the phone on the night stand, staring at it suspiciously. Either I got through that way too easily or I was just being paranoid. A knock at the door reminded me I needed to be getting ready for the evening.

"Be down in a second."

I stood up to resume my preparations when the door opened slightly.

"May I come in?" Trinnian asked.

The sound of his voice knocked the wind out of me, turning my limbs to stone.

"Sure." The word was scarcely a whisper.

He entered the room, closed the door behind him and stood against it for a moment. Was he waiting for me to speak? That would be one way to get out of going to the city. Provided he'd be willing to wait that long for me to say something, because honestly, I really had no idea where to begin. In a way, he let me off the hook by speaking first.

"It would be nice if I could read your thoughts right now," he said. The remark followed by a small uncertain smile.

"I'll bet that would've been even more important yesterday," I countered, barely able to maintain eye contact.

He walked toward me. The towel I still wore seemed to shrink with each step he took. The closer Trinnian came the more exposed I felt.

"I cannot blame you for what happened yesterday. My method of explanation was substandard to say the least," he said rather frankly, his comment easily regained my full attention.

Was I seriously hearing him correctly? Not only did he not hate me but he actually thought he could justify shifting the blame to himself? If this was his attempt to make me feel better, his plan was backfiring miserably. Releasing me from blame somehow made the guilt even more painful. He stood close enough to touch. My arms crossed in front of me, ensuring I would resist the urge. I thought that if I touched him it would be the same as admitting it *was* his fault, the solace of physical contact being my way of forgiving him.

"Are you crazy? *I* attacked *you*! *I* broke *your* leg! How can you not blame me?" I exclaimed.

Again I felt the sting of tears in my eyes. I turned to head back to the bathroom in hopes that he didn't notice. He grabbed my arm, redirecting me with little effort. His eyes were like pools of melted dark chocolate, locking me helpless in his gaze.

"Because *I* did this to *you*!" he insisted, his voice raised enough to emphasize his point. He took a breath and continued in a calmer tone. "The only thing worse than forcing you into an eternity of darkness and blood lust is that I could not even find the words to tell you what I had done."

"Trinnian, you saved my life. I'm just sorry I didn't realize it sooner."

Tears that hovered on the rims of my eyes spilled over. His hands cupped my face and his thumbs wiped away my tears. The innocent touch sent a wave of arousal through my body, the likes of which would usually accompany a more intimate caress. I released a shuddering breath as he leaned in to press his supple lips against mine. My arms relinquished their standoff and slid around his body. The tenderness of his kiss swept away the sadness and guilt I'd been feeling. Fear of what the night held for me dissipated into a distant memory. Thirst and hunger pushed to the surface with the scent of the blood that pulsed beneath his skin.

The change in me didn't go unnoticed. His hand slid to the back of my head, gently pushing my mouth to the base of his neck. Before I could talk myself out of it, my teeth broke through his skin, liberating the source of my desire. The world around us vanished, all that mattered was his blood. It dominated my very existence. Every nerve ending throbbed in time with rhythmic surges of the flow. The more I drew on the source the more intense the sensations became.

My blissful moment of ecstasy started to dwindle as if being pulled back from a warm, bright light source at the end of a cold, dark tunnel. I opened my eyes, unaware of the changes that took place around me. We were in the bed. My towel had been abandoned on the floor next to the pile of clothing Trinnian wore when he came to the room. He pulled me away from his throat and finally released his grip on my hair when I was far enough away to make eye contact. I sat up, well aware of the fact that I was astride his naked body. A drop of blood fell from my lip to splatter onto his smooth muscled chest. Trinnian's nostrils flared, taking in the aroma emulating from the drop. His hungry eyes watched my tongue skim across my lower lip to catch any more that may have lingered.

Almost too quick for me to even register, our situation reversed. The drop of blood was now above me, I craned my neck to lick it off him when his teeth sunk onto my exposed flesh. My head fell back into the pillow and my back arched from the onslaught of pain and pleasure surging through me as he fed. When it seemed my excitement could peak no further, he entered me. Our bodies moved in a synchronous dance, escalating sensuously toward mutual climax.

How we ended up in the shower may always be a mystery. Quite honestly, it didn't matter. Still coming down from the most intense sexual experience of my life, I had no interest in such trivial things.

Trinnian left me to get ready for the evening with a deep, passionate kiss and promised a repeat performance later if I agreed to move back into his room. Without a word, I handed over my bags to take with him. His sly grin marked his victory, shutting the door behind him.

The four of us loaded into Trinnian's black Mercedes and headed to the city. We arrived sooner than I would've preferred. My anxiety made itself known again when the car was parked and the motor shut off. Trinnian reached over, giving my hand a reassuring squeeze. We were in the parking garage level of Owen's apartment building. Collin explained on the way that he spoke to

Owen earlier and, though he looked forward to meeting me, he wouldn't be home until later. His statement prompted Olivia to lean forward and whisper in my ear something to the effect of, 'God forbid he skip a night of sampling the local play things.' My surprised reaction received a quiet chuckle from Trinnian and a grin from Collin.

It occurred to me as I looked at Collin in the rearview mirror that had been the first time I ever saw him smile. He stared out into the night. The amused expression lingering on his face softened his normally stern features. I silently hoped he would start to warm up to me soon now that all seemed to be well between Trinnian and me.

Our plan was to hunt first and meet back at Owen's afterward. We approached the bustling sidewalk that bordered the parking garage. I found myself having to concentrate to keep from becoming overwhelmed by the deluge of sensory distractions. Trinnian's arm wrapped around me and, with a last minute nod of encouragement, he let me know that I would be fine as we stepped into the flow of foot traffic.

The warm fragrance of blood surrounded me. My back stiffened when I tried to imagine how much more difficult this would be if I'd not fed from Trinnian. The tension met with a gentle squeeze to my shoulder from Trinnian's hand. His attentiveness comforted me in light of what lay ahead.

We walked amongst the living with ease. Not a single soul seemed to notice anything out of the ordinary about our little group. Then again, we were shuffling along a crowded sidewalk in New York City, why would they?

The pedestrians started to thin out until it seemed we entered an abandoned shell that once was a thriving part of the city. For the most part, the people that were in this area barely gave us a second glance. These were the forgotten ones. The homeless, drug addicts and the mentally insane cast from society, forced to make a life where they could, away from the good people of the city. The streets there were strewn with garbage, few of the buildings still had doors and windows but all were covered in graffiti.

CHAPTER THIRTEEN

We approached a rundown apartment building. Olivia and Collin waited inside the door as Trinnian and I made our way down the litter filled hall. I could hear the people that dwelled within. Footsteps shuffled overhead. Voices whispered from the dark recesses of the vacant apartments. Vermin scurried along the hall in search of food. Trinnian stopped in front of the last door on the right, reaching out for my hand. I took it in hopes it would chase away the feeling of dread that engulfed me. The reassurance his touch allowed me was short lived as my eyes adjusted to the darkness of the room we faced.

Huddled in the corner of what had been a living room, a woman slept. Her greasy brown hair stuck to the side of her dirty face. Threadbare clothing suggested she wore them for some time. I turned to Trinnian with eyes wide, shaking my head. He couldn't expect me to drain this poor homeless woman? His eyes hardened as he spoke.

"Jacquelyn, you are not seeing clearly. Look again and this time, peer into her mind before you make your decision," he instructed.

His attitude caught me off guard but I did as I was told. I stepped into the trash heaped room, taking a closer look at the woman on the floor. Her exposed forearm covered with fresh and scarred puncture marks. She wasn't merely asleep, she was unconscious. The succulent aroma of her blood drew me closer. I crouched down and tried to see into her mind, using the same method that identified Olivia at my door earlier. The images that played out were awful.

For years, this woman had done unspeakable things to support her habit. Her memories confessed to everything from home invasions with her junky friends to armed robbery. The terrified faces of her victims flashed by, she held no remorse for any of them. The vision that horrified me the most was the night she traded her daughter, an innocent toddler, for a fix. She had been well aware that her dealer had child pornography connections but all that mattered to her was the heroin. Her daughter's big, soft brown eyes staring over the shoulder of the man that took her away was the last memory she had of her. This woman never laid

123

eyes on the child again and her only regret was that she hadn't held out for more dope.

My body shook from the anger that coursed through me. A low growl of fury broke from my clenched jaw. I stood, jerking her to her feet by her upper arm. The abrupt movement startled her. Her lethargic limbs struggled to stand upright but failed completely. I pinned her pathetic frame to the wall. Her eyelids fluttered, signifying she was still heavily under the influence of the drugs she injected.

The only remorse I felt at that moment was the fact that she wouldn't experience the fear she inflicted on so many. I bit into her flesh, being cautious not to crush her throat in anger. My measured bite was rewarded as her blood spilled slowly into my mouth. The living human blood had a different effect than immortal blood. What it lacked in sensuality, it made up for in strength. The result of which induced a euphoric state of weightlessness. The detailed images of her worthless existence were easily pushed aside, allowing me to immerse myself in the thrill of sucking the life she didn't deserve from her.

14

Trinnian disappeared into the upper levels of the rundown building to feed while I waited by the door with Olivia and Collin. My body hummed with a current of energy, attributed to my first hunt. It was all I could do to not fidget while we stood there waiting for him to return.

Certainly, regret would settle in for killing the woman I fed from. So far, I felt nothing. Nothing for her that is, her poor child was another story. I couldn't help but ask Olivia if she knew the fate of the little girl. She told me she wasn't sure but thought she may be able to find out something later. The drug dealer that carted her off was on her menu for the evening. When Trinnian emerged from the building, we made our way back to Owen's place.

The return trip was even more of a challenge. My senses were sharpened by the blood to the extent that I had difficulty simply focusing on forward progress. Everybody that passed by seemed to trail the scent of their blood after them. It hung in the air like incense. Trinnian had to put his arm around my waist to keep me in check. He saw the worry in my eyes and whispered in my ear that the first time was always the most difficult. Human blood wouldn't affect me this way forever.

Much to my relief, we finally arrived at our destination. Olivia and Collin were off to hunt with Augustine. Olivia informed me that it would be the last chance they would get to spend with their friend since his 'woman' was due to arrive in the city the next evening. The grimace that accompanied the word 'woman' told me all I needed to know about that situation.

Before they departed, Collin reassured Trinnian he didn't feel Silas's presence the entire time we had been in the city. The prior night, Owen noted Silas's absence as well. Each night that passed without a sighting gave them hope that he might have given up and left. Silas had never really been one for commitment, they agreed. Maybe he was content with the amount of suffering he did get to cause. No one knew for sure.

When we arrived at the door to Owen's apartment, Trinnian knocked, explaining that it was for our benefit almost as much as his. Trinnian's comment brought to mind Olivia's earlier remark about him 'sampling the local playthings.' I nodded in agreement. Even though I couldn't sense anyone inside, I guess it wouldn't be a bad habit to get into. When we received no response, Trinnian used his key to unlock the door and gestured for me to follow.

The space we entered was substantial, the layout of the apartment and its furnishings made it seem even bigger than it was. To the right was a large open kitchen. A long black marble topped island bordered with stools separated the kitchen from the entryway. Straight ahead was a dining area. The wall on the other side of the table displayed one of Augustine's extravagant paintings. The living room off to the left could've been the forerunner of the minimalist movement. Everything about it screamed expensive interior designer. Ironically enough, the most eye-catching thing about the high priced room was the view of the city through the balcony doors. This was definitely the living quarters of someone that spent no time here.

Trinnian tossed his keys on the island and grabbed my hand, turning me to face him. He wrapped his arms around me, hugging me close and kissed me softly on my cheek.

"You did great tonight," he whispered in my ear before kissing me again.

"I couldn't have done it without you."

Taking my hand in his, he walked me over to the couch, which turned out to be more comfortable than I anticipated. His arm draped around my shoulders, allowing me to rest against his side. I asked him about the place we went to earlier, if that was where he normally hunted. He told me it wasn't but it seemed to be the ideal place for my first time. The remote location offered a virtually witness-free, controlled environment and the semiconscious addict avoided the struggling victim issue. Her having been particularly nasty was an added bonus. I considered his reasoning. He couldn't have been more on the mark. If any of those things had been different, I might not have been able to do it.

For some reason, I couldn't ignore Collin's update on Silas. From what I could gather it seemed they had him under surveillance. Surely that wasn't for my benefit was it? Did he still pose a threat to me?

"Do you think Silas will try to kill me again?" I asked.

Trinnian withdrew his arm from around my shoulders, turning to face me.

"Where did that come from?" he studied my face, looking a bit surprised.

"It just seemed as if everyone has been keeping tabs on him, so I figured there had to be a reason," I replied.

"I doubt you are as tempting of a target in your current state. You were much more valuable to him as a human. His mere presence alone is reason enough to keep track of him. Remember when I told you that Silas and I have never gotten along?" I nodded. "It had pretty much been that way from the start between us. But what escalated our dislike for one another was when I banished him from our lives. To be more precise, he was forbidden to set foot in New York again. I had grown tired of his carless antics and blatant disregard of our most basic rules. He started to endanger our very existence."

"What rules?" I asked, thinking it might be to my advantage to know what exactly they were.

"No feeding where you sleep, cover your tracks and be discreet. Of course there are others but those are the everyday common sense ones he specifically could not adhere to. For future reference, being discreet can be more difficult than it sounds.

Making a conscious effort to watch your speed and strength around humans takes constant vigilance. People tend to…react…when you become a blur in front of them."

Another thing to keep in check…wonderful, I was beginning to understand the complex workings of the vampire mind. I seriously hoped it would all get easier with time. Even as we sat there, I caught myself having to ignore sounds and smells.

"What do you think he wants?"

"I do not know. But the only person he seems to be targeting is me," Trinnian said.

"Revenge?"

"Most likely."

"So you think he tried to kill me to get to you?" I asked and he nodded. "If he was using me to get to you, he could've killed me the first night he met me. Why didn't he do it then?"

"I asked myself that same question the night you told me you met him," he said absently.

Something about the way he answered my question made me rethink his statement. Like there was more to his comment than I originally picked up on.

"You wondered why he didn't kill me? What made you so sure he even considered killing me?"

He looked as if I asked the one question he didn't want to answer. His gaze shifted to his hands, answering my question without looking at me.

"Because he killed Karl that night instead of you," he whispered.

My heart sank. Silas killed Karl? The night I met Silas replayed in my mind. I could remember the strange conversation I had at the pub with him but couldn't recall anything about it that would have spared my life. For whatever reason, Silas chose to kill Karl Novak instead of me. Poor Karl, I couldn't imagine anyone wanting to hurt him. He was a kind and gentle man. Silas was nothing but a cold blooded killer. How cowardly could he be to go after the humans in Trinnian's life simply for his own warped satisfaction? I watched Trinnian for a moment. His gaze still hadn't returned to me, his eyes were far away, perhaps somewhere else entirely. Maybe the cowardly actions of Silas had been enough to get to Trinnian. If he blamed himself for what happened to me, I could only imagine how easy it was for him to convince himself he was responsible for Karl's death.

"Trinnian, look at me." He lifted his head, meeting my eyes reluctantly. "You can't shoulder the blame for everything bad that happens in this world."

"I should have dealt with Silas the moment Collin told me he dared to set foot in New York," he said. "If I would have just listened to my gut instinct…"

"I'm not going to sit here and listen to you beat yourself up over things you can't change. Regret is a poison that kills over time. The only thing that can be done at this point is to make Silas atone for all the terrible things he's done. That will just have to do. Karl is dead, you can't bring him back. And just so you know, it's impossible to think that you can save everybody," I told him.

His furrowed brow started to relax. Perhaps he took my words to heart. I leaned in to kiss him. He gently kissed me back, pulling me closer. I wrapped my arms around him, happy to oblige. The phone ringing in the background wasn't enough to break up our little make out session. That is, until the answering machine picked up and a very angry female voice spoke loud and clear:

Owen, if you have something to ask me, ASK ME! Did you honestly think Petrus would not come to me about this?

Trinnian froze in my arms by the end of the first sentence but stood by the end of the second. Disbelief riddled his face, staring toward the phone in the kitchen.

And do not dare be angry with him. His motivation to say anything about this to me was strictly concern. Yes, Owen, there are actually people out there that worry about things other than themselves! I suppose it should bother me that you believe me to be so petty and shallow, however, I actually do not give a damn what you think of me! But, do not drag my name into your silly little territorial pissing battles.

The caller on the other end slammed the phone down and the line went dead.

By the time the call ended, Trinnian had walked to the edge of the island. His hands on the marble counter top appeared to be the only thing holding him up. He hung his head in silence. I didn't notice the man that stood just inside the door until Trinnian spoke.

"Margaret," Trinnian said. He turned abruptly to face the newcomer, betrayal seethed behind his eyes. The man shoved his hands in the pockets of his black slacks and nodded in defeat. "Why did you not tell me?" The sorrow in Trinnian's voice was heartbreaking.

"Because she asked me not to," the man answered.

"Did you know all this time?" Trinnian asked. He received no response. His jaw clenched, in three strides he was inches from the man's face, having grabbed him by his shirt. "Owen, tell me you did not know she was alive for the past two hundred years!" he growled.

Owen never flinched or moved a muscle, even his hands remained in his pockets. His calm manner resounded in his words as he spoke.

"Actually, I did not. I found out accidently on a trip to Germany about fifty years ago. She begged me not to tell you," Owen said.

Trinnian stared at him for a moment before releasing him and taking a couple steps backward.

"Is she still there?" Trinnian asked in a calmer voice.

"Yes."

"Did Olivia and Collin know about this?"

"No."

Trinnian rubbed his temples for a moment and took a deep breath. Something in his manner changed, he shook his head laughing and placed his hands on his hips.

"You know something, Owen? Of all the members in our family, you were the one that I have trusted the most. Is that simply because you made me? Perhaps...I am not entirely sure. Olivia and Collin show me honor and loyalty on a daily basis but it has always been *you* that I put my complete faith in. The one *I* trusted," he said. Trinnian's eyes narrowed and he took a step toward Owen, fixing him in his glare. "I'm done."

He pushed by Owen to the door. I stood up, not knowing what to say or do. Trinnian looked at me with his hand on the door knob. He cast his eyes down and stormed through the door, slamming it behind him. I almost made it to the door when Owen grabbed my wrist.

"Let him be," he said gently. "He will be back." Stepping over to the island, he picked up Trinnian's keys and shook them. "See? Relax, he will be fine."

Still at a loss for what I should be doing, I stood there looking at Owen. In any other situation, I might have been admiring his handsome features, thinking that I understood the reputation he apparently had with the ladies. But this wasn't the time for such things. If anything, Owen knew Trinnian much better than I did. So if he thought I should relax, that is what I would do. I walked over to the island, pulled out a stool and sat. Owen took my lead, sitting in the stool next to me.

"Is it safe to assume you are Jacquelyn?" He managed a slight smile.

"Yes," I replied. "Is it safe to assume what just happened is none of my business?"

"You have every right to know what is going on, in my opinion. But I am not quite sure it is up to me to tell you."

"Can you at least tell me who that was?" I inquired.

"That was Margaret, the last companion Trinnian had before you."

"Oh." Was all I could say. He has been single for two hundred years? Either Trinnian had the patience of a saint or something pretty bad must have happened between them. "Asking why he thought she was dead is probably out of the question?"

"I am sure you will hear all about it one day but today is not that day. You are too young to understand," he said, as if explaining something to a child.

His answer caught me off guard. Too young? There's one I hadn't heard in a while. Time must be the vampire version of a class system. I took a closer look at Owen's face. How old was he? Would it be inappropriate of me to ask? He had to have been in his very early twenties when he was made. His eyes fixed onto mine, deep blue as the ocean at dusk. The soft curves of his lips stood out against his strong chiseled features. I suddenly felt like a deer in headlights, quickly giving in to the urge to look away.

"Great." His tone suggested whatever he referred to was anything but. "They are here."

Owen's head dropped into his hands, propped up by his elbows on the counter top. It wasn't until the knock at the door I realized who he referred to. Olivia and Collin were finished hunting. Owen sat up straight before addressing the callers.

"It's open."

Olivia and Collin came into the apartment. Olivia's smile vacated her lips, taking in our faces. She looked around and exchanged a strange look with Collin before she spoke.

"Where is Trinnian?" Her question tinged with concern.

"He left." Owen knew he was not going to get out of this one easily. He exhaled before he continued. "Margaret called while he was here." Olivia and Collin shared an even stranger look than before. "Yes, she is still alive. No, I did not know the whole time, she insisted I not tell him," Owen said, as if he had told the story a million times already.

Olivia's glare appeared as if she were trying to set Owen on fire with her mind.

"How could you have done this to him, Owen?" Her voice cracked with anger and accusation. "And how could you have *not* known she was alive to begin with?"

Collin said nothing as he placed a hand on her shoulder, watching Owen intently. He wore the same blank expression from the night I broke Trinnian's leg, right down to the lethal glimmer in his eyes.

"Because, *Olivia*, I took her to Lattimer thinking he may be able to help her since I could not bring myself to look her in the eye and kill her. By the time I found out she was still alive, Trinnian was doing so much better. It was as if he had finally moved on. And as far as Margaret was concerned, she felt she put him through a lifetime of misery as it was. She could not bear the thought of ever hurting him again. So you tell me, what would you have done?" he asked, frustration echoed in his words.

Olivia was speechless, but it was obvious she considered the logic behind Owen's argument. Collin could've been carved in stone standing behind her. I too took in the information passing between them, quietly sitting on the stool. The story slowly pieced itself together in my head for the most part. The only part missing that I really cared about was whether or not Trinnian would return to Margaret. She must be pretty amazing to take one hundred and fifty years to get over. Was it selfish of me to be wondering about this? What would happen to me if he wanted to go back to her? I took a deep breath, trying not to panic. Three pairs of eyes were suddenly locked on me. Olivia finally spoke.

"Ok, Collin and I will go home to see if he is there." Her eyes flickered to his keys on the counter. "He may very well just be walking or running to clear his head since he did leave his car here. So, Jacquelyn, you stay here in case he returns. If for some reason he does not...at least you have his keys." She turned to Owen. "You...never mind, it seems *you* have done enough already." The look she gave him spoke volumes. Olivia headed for the door Collin held open for her, only to stop short of passing through. She turned to face me, "The little girl is dead. But justice has been served."

Olivia gave me a small nod before she continued through the door with Collin shutting it behind them.

15

My chin rested on my folded arms. Trinnian's keys sat in front of me on the marble surface, my unseeing stare settled on them. It was as if Olivia and Collin had taken all conversation with them when they left. I could swear I felt Owen's eyes, studying my profile, chin propped on the palm of his hand. But I didn't really feel a need to confirm my suspicions. I had enough buzzing around in my head. One thought in particular wouldn't leave me alone. It was the one question I had to ask. I sat up to face Owen, he watched me as I suspected. His attention triggered a self-consciousness that bothered me. Being the focus of people's attention, especially someone I didn't know, had never been one of my favorite things.

"Be honest with me, Owen, do you think he is coming back?"

My stomach sunk to actually hear it said out loud. Somehow vocalizing my fear made it all too real.

"I do not know."

"So you lied to me earlier?" I asked.

"If you could have seen the look on your face, trust me, you would have done the same thing," he answered.

His expression became pure honesty. I knew he was right. I probably would've done the same thing. A part of me knew he lied when he said it in the first place. But what else could I really have done? Helplessness and frustration closed in, but I refused to tear up in front of Owen. He wasn't going to see me cry.

"So if he doesn't return, what am I supposed to do?"

My words came out as level as I intended. I felt a bit more confident having discovered I was able to pull off the appearance of someone who could handle such things.

"We deal with that if the time comes," he said with a gentle smile.

Owen the ladies man...yeah, I could definitely see the attraction. The way his smile made his eyes light up was really not something I needed to notice right now. Or the way his black silk sweater clung to his muscular chest. That was especially not something that was going to help resolve the unfortunate events of the night. Dammit, what was wrong with me?

Owen's forehead fell into the palm of his hand, "Oh, you have got to be kidding me...not tonight."

I hadn't realized my whole body stiffened, thinking he somehow read my thoughts until I picked up on an immortal presence on the other side of the door. Relief spread through me instantly. Owen was already en route to answer it as I heard the knock.

The door opened to reveal a breath taking woman draped against the door frame. Her sable hair hung slightly past her shoulders, bangs cut straight and blunt. She wore a black trench coat that stopped at her knees, but her black stiletto boots continued further up as previewed by the way the coat parted to her upper thigh. The cigarette held between her fingers sent lazy ripples of smoke to the ceiling. Her expression bordered somewhere between bored and irritated.

"I flipped quarter with Lisette, she had tails, I had heads. I will cheer her up tomorrow," she stated in a thick Russian accent. A devious smile broke through her stony facade.

"Tatiana, this is not a good time—" Owen tried to explain as she pushed by him into the apartment.

Her expression didn't change while she considered me.

"I don't care if she joins us..." she said. Her eyes scanned me from head to toe. She untied the belt of her coat as she continued, "Lisette is the jealous one, not me."

Instantly dismissing me, she turned to Owen and took a long drag on her cigarette, blowing the smoke upward.

"You are not listening to me." Anger infused his demeanor, taking a step toward her. "Tonight is not a good night, Tatiana." The words came slow with emphasis.

"If it has been that bad, we should have cocktail," she said casually, like there wasn't an extremely pissed off vampire inches from her face. The trench coat slid down her arms, on to the floor, revealing black and gray tattoos sporadically covering her skin. Most of which seemed to be symbols of some sort. The black leather strapless mini dress she wore did little to cover much of anything. Unfazed by his anger, she turned her back to him, stepping over her discarded coat. She walked to the kitchen and stabbed out her cigarette in the sink. "Who wants drink?" she asked, yanking open the freezer and plucking out random bottles of liquor.

Owen looked at me, like I could do something about her impromptu visit. All things considered, maybe Tatiana was just what I needed right now.

"I'd love one, Tatiana." My voice sounded a hell of a lot stronger than I felt.

"Good," she said. Her black lined hazel eyes reassessed me. "You look like vodka girl like me, yes?" The right side of her mouth curved up in a half smile, her manner retained an air of menace.

"Yes, I am."

Owen relaxed a bit but still watched me with uncertainty.

Tatiana returned with two shots in one hand and a solo one in the other, which she handed to me. After Owen took his, she stepped back, looking at us.

"Don't look so serious, eternity is too long to carry burdens. Forget these things." She raised her glass, "Za Vas!" That being said, she tossed back her vodka and said, "Let's go out."

We set out on foot once again, blending in with the nighttime foot traffic. Owen's lack of concern for Trinnian returning while we were out only added to my feeling that he may not come back. I wasn't entirely sure if that feeling was strictly in reference to the current night in particular. Either way, the cell phone in the back pocket of my jeans gave me some small comfort.

Our trek only lasted a few blocks before we stopped in front of an apartment building. If we were going to Tatiana's place, after her earlier comment about me 'joining' them, I wasn't sure how comfortable I felt about it. She made her way up the stairs toward a keypad mounted by the front door. Owen followed on her heels until I grabbed him by the elbow, he turned to face me.

"Owen, I don't feel comfortable going to her place," I whispered, not wanting to offend our deadly looking companion.

His pursed lips were obviously stifling the urge to laugh. I could feel my jaw set and vision narrow while my anger showed its first signs. At least one of us was amused.

"Technically, it is Marco's place. Rest assured, you will leave with your virginity intact," he chuckled, no longer bothering to hide his amusement.

He trotted up the stairs to grab the door Tatiana held open for us. She passed into the building. Owen turned to look at me. He held the door patiently, still wearing the slight trace of a smirk. I tried my best not to stomp up the stairs, pausing in front of him.

"That was not my concern," I hissed, stepping inside the building.

Owen followed, letting the door close behind us. His soft laugh echoed down the hallway we entered. The dark gray carpet underfoot was as bland as the bare light gray walls. The hall came to a dead end with a door on either side and a camera mounted on the ceiling between them. Tatiana turned to the one on the right and pressed a button that resembled a door bell. There came a dull buzz followed by the click of a lock. The three of us entered another hall that ended at an elevator door. We stepped into the elevator. Tatiana hit a button and the doors slid shut.

"Jacquelyn, I have to make sure you understand something before we reach our destination," Owen said, all joking aside. "Not all immortals exist the same way you have experienced. Lifestyle preferences do not necessarily make one group better than the other. Just like humans, we each go about our lives in our own way."

Tatiana made a noise similar to a muffled grunt that could've been her version of a laugh, judging by the look on her face. I looked from her to Owen. Their expressions were polar opposites of each other. His look was serious in contrast, raising his eyebrows at me, waiting for me to acknowledge him.

"I got it...I'll be fine."

He didn't look very convinced but his expression relaxed. I could only assume that my earlier comment made me look like a closed minded prude or something. I faced forward, irritated at myself as the doors glided open.

*   *   *   *   *

Silas drifted in and out of consciousness. His entire body ached unbearably. Between the beating and the hunger that came with being drained of the majority of his blood, he wished he would die. He knew he was being kept somewhere underground, although he had no idea where. Damp earth was all he could smell, aside from his own dried blood caked to his body. He could barely make out muffled noises coming from somewhere but could not sense anybody through the layers of earth that separated him from everything. Whoever held him jumped him in an alley and had thrown a black hood over his head that still remained in place. The means in which he was confined consisted of a metal cuff around his neck and shackles on his wrists. Thick chains that attached him to the wall did not allow for much movement.

His weakened senses alerted him to the approach of an immortal he was not familiar with. A leaden metal door swung open with a loud groan somewhere off to his left. Heavy footfall closed in on him. He pressed himself against the rough stone wall his chains were secured to, his body trembling in his vulnerable state and fear of the unknown.

"I just wanted to make sure you were not dead," said his captor in a deep masculine timbre. "It seems there might be incentive to keeping you alive after all—at least while you are a guest here. As soon as I find out who you have managed to piss off the most, I do not particularly care what they do with you as long as the check clears."

The hearty laugh of his captor echoed off the walls as his footsteps retreated. Silas relaxed when he heard the groan of the door shutting the man out of the chamber. There came a small consolation in the fact that he was not going to receive another beating.

16

We stepped out of the elevator into another time period. At least that was my first impression of our surroundings. Off to the left was an old fashioned gas lamppost, a flame flickered behind its glass. A cobblestone sidewalk butted up to a pair of wooden double doors with stained glass windows leading into what appeared to be a weathered brick building. Above the doors a sign simply read, 'Marco's'.

In the style of a true gentleman, Owen stepped forward to open a door and stood aside inviting us in. The music that played within flowed out into the basement level faux street to welcome us as we entered.

The place could've been anywhere. In fact, the interior resembled many a pub found around the world. A stout, dark stained wood bar jutted out into the center of the room with stools on three sides. Booths along the walls had curtains that offered a bit of privacy to the parties that chose it. Vampires from all walks of life milled about the area. Obviously the city hosted more immortals than I would've ever guessed. I could smell humans here as well but I didn't see them.

Owen led us to one of the booths in a corner. It could've easily sat a dozen people comfortably, even with the small door in the wall that eliminated part of the seat. As Owen and I settled in, Tatiana excused herself, saying she saw someone she knew and would be back. She disappeared somewhere on the other side of the bar. Owen stared at me from across the table with an odd grin on his face, making me feel self-conscious again.

CHAPTER SIXTEEN

"What?" I asked.

"Tatiana scares you and you do not even know anything about her."

"Let me guess, I'm getting the wrong impression from her. She was a nun who spent her life doing charity work for disabled children before she turned into a blood thirsty seductress?"

Owen laughed so hard I thought he might have a seizure. His jovial outburst caught the attention of a man behind the bar who signaled he would be over in a minute. Not that Owen noticed.

"Oh...that was good. I will have to tell her that one!" Another wave of laughter struck him, resulting from the horrified expression on my face. Tatiana was the last person I wanted to piss off and I couldn't see her finding humor in my comment. Or pretty much any other. "I do not think I have the heart to tell you the truth about her now."

"Well, now you have to since you brought it up," I said, starting to get irritated again. "That is if you're finished laughing."

I folded my arms in front of me and sat back in the bench, waiting for him to speak.

"If you insist," he said, leaning forward. Thankfully his amusement faded. "Tatiana was a fourteen year old runaway. She ended up on the doorstep of the Russian mob. They took her in and gave her small tasks to do to keep her out of trouble. Though she started out as an errand girl, eventually she became one of their most feared assassins. Her nickname was 'Suicide' because her methods were so brutal, if someone discovered they were her mark they would often kill themselves for fear of what she would do to them. She ended up having an affair with a newer member of their ranks that was later discovered to be KGB. He disappeared without a trace. Her mob cohorts feared she talked so they put out a hit on her. Tatiana escaped and ended up being discovered one night by Petrus. She had been hiding out behind his establishment in Germany. He offered to save her, giving her immortality. She has worked for him ever since."

The man from behind the bar stopped at the edge of our table as Owen finished his story. I didn't know whether or not to believe Owen since he discovered how much fun it was to mess with me. So the distraction was welcome.

"Good to hear you are enjoying yourselves," said the man, placing his hands on his hips. His smile glimmered in his almond shaped, light brown eyes. "Who do we have with us tonight, Owen?"

"This is Jacquelyn, Trinnian's companion," Owen answered, in a matter-of-fact tone. I wished he wouldn't refer to me as someone's 'companion.' It sounded awkward and, in light of the events of the past few hours, a little overly committed. The thought carried with it a sting of rejection. I ignored it, putting a smile on my face.

"Marco," he said. Leaning in to shake my hand, a lock of his shoulder length, wavy brown hair swung into his eyes. He tucked the stray behind his ear, making it easier to admire his high cheekbones. His square jaw line and strong nose were enough to keep his features from being too delicate. "It is good to meet you, but unfortunate for me, it seems all the pretty ones are always taken." His comment accompanied a warm smile that lingered as he continued, "I hope I am not being too presumptuous but I could not help notice your reaction to Owen calling you Jacquelyn. Is there another name you prefer?"

I felt like saying, 'Anything but companion because that was what I actually reacted to.' Instead, I went with something a bit less confrontational.

"My friends call me Jax or Jackie...whatever is easiest for you to remember," I responded, feeling Owen's stare.

"I will keep that in mind, it is important to me that all my guests feel comfortable here," said Marco.

Tatiana slid onto the seat next to me, "Did we order yet?"

Russian mob, huh? It didn't seem like anything else *could* fit her.

"Not yet, we were waiting for you," Owen answered, his gaze cut to me.

What the hell have I done now?

"Good. Marco, have Diana bring three shots of vodka, please," Tatiana requested, ordering for us.

142

"She will be over shortly." Marco's eyes met mine once more before he closed the curtains on our booth.

"What is the significance of drawing the curtains?" I asked.

Owen seemed more at ease with Marco gone but it seemed something still bothered him.

"Because we ordered." His half-assed answer brought life back into his eyes.

Minutes later, a door in the wall next to me opened and a young girl, no more than a teenager, came out. The girl was human. She wore a black CBGB's t-shirt and frayed denim mini skirt. Her long blonde hair pulled to the top of her head in a ponytail. She carried a tray with three shot glasses. I could feel the excitement and apprehension flip flopping back and forth in her mind. Each of us received a glass. Tatiana repeated her toast from earlier and we drank in unison.

The shot we had at Owen's seemed to warm me but that was about it. I wondered if vampires could get drunk. After feeding off of the junky earlier, I was told that drugs and alcohol in the blood we consumed wouldn't affect us. If anything, it only changed the flavor of the blood. It would be interesting to see if this shot would do anything.

"Diana, put your tray down and come sit with us." Tatiana's voice was smooth as silk. Even her accent sounded soft and inviting.

Diana did as requested. She slipped past me and sat between the two of us. The scent of her blood made my body quiver. I imagined what she would taste like. My hands clenched together on my lap and I kept my eyes forward on the table. Out of the corner of my eye, I saw Tatiana take her hand, turn it over and gently kiss the inside of her wrist. Diana's heart lurched into a faster pace, her pulse drumming in my head. I tried to measure my breathing when I felt the weight of Owen's stare. His head tilted down but he peered straight ahead. His eyes boring into me from under his brow sent a shiver down my spine. He looked truly evil. Diana's scent alerted me to the fact that Owen wasn't looking at me but her wrist that she extended to me. One glance Tatiana's way clarified the whole scene to my naive mind. She was feeding on Diana's other wrist.

"Go ahead," Diana whispered to me with a reassuring nod.

I held her warm arm in my hands, instantly aware of the veins that were visible through her pale skin. Her fragrant blood surged beneath. I could no longer restrain myself. My teeth broke through her skin. The blood flowed into my mouth and danced on my tongue before I allowed myself to swallow. It was far sweeter and more vibrant than any blood I experienced yet.

Diana's thoughts were revealed to me. She felt a pleasure of her own in allowing vampires to feed from her. One day, if she proved herself, she knew they may turn her into one of them. They saved her from a brutal life on the streets. To her, offering blood to them was a small price to pay in comparison.

Something interrupted my blissful indulgence. There were hands on my shoulders, trying to pull me away from the girl. I wasn't ready to stop, but the intrusion ruined the moment and finally succeeded in breaking me away from her.

The booth came back into focus. Diana's eyes were closed and her mouth slack as she lay back in Tatiana's arms. Owen and Tatiana both gazed at the limp girl with worry in their eyes.

"Oh my god!" I murmured. My hands clamped over my mouth as I slid backward to the wall. "Is she dead?"

The concern on their faces melted away as they shared a chuckle over my reaction. Diana's hand raised, palm side up, her eyes popping open. They each pressed a wad of money into her hand. Diana sat up and gave me a hug.

"Sorry, I just can't resist a good initiation prank," she giggled, collected her tray and left.

"You guys are awful," I grumbled in embarrassment.

The comment only served to enforce the comedic value of their practical joke, bringing on another wave of laughter.

My cell phone rang, offering me a much needed distraction. It was Olivia. She was calling to let me know Trinnian hadn't shown up at the house. With sunrise only a couple hours away, she suggested I would be better off staying at Owen's. Reassured by the fact that she would let me know as soon as she heard something, I thanked her and ended the call. While I spoke to Olivia, Tatiana disappeared again into the crowd. I relayed the conversation to Owen. He let me know I could stay at his place anytime I needed to. Something in his expression reminded me of pity. It could've been my imagination. Regardless, I felt a need to change the subject.

"Where did Tatiana go? Off to arrange another amusing rite of passage for me?"

"I told her we were leaving soon. She said she was not ready to go and went to look for a friend of hers that has a place upstairs," he answered. A clever grin spread across his lips, "I can stop her if you would like her to return with us but I was under the impression that she made you uncomfortable."

The ridiculous comment couldn't even justify a response. I chose to ignore it, deciding my life would be made easier if I didn't let him get a rise out of me.

"So upstairs are vampire apartments?" I asked instead.

"Yes. Marco owns the whole building. He rents short term and long term to the immortal community. Most of our businesses are run out of apartment buildings. Especially here in New York, they tend to be invisible except to their residents. Since he does not rent to humans, it is the perfect way to hide in plain site."

I wondered how many places I walked by on any given day that were fronts for vampire affairs? It made perfect sense. After all, part of their longevity had to be attributed to their ability to adapt to their surroundings.

Tatiana swung back by to say she was going to join some friends of hers and bid us a good night. The crowd thinned out a little as we made our way to the exit. A hand on my shoulder prompted me to turn, coming face to face with Marco.

"I wanted to say it was good to meet you, Jax," he said, pressing a card into the palm of my hand. "There is a code on the back that will grant you entry if you would like to come by yourself sometime."

"Thanks, Marco."

With a smile, he made his way back to the bar. I stood for a second watching his retreat, sliding the card into my pocket.

Trinnian had way too many good looking friends, I thought as I turned, almost running headlong into Owen.

"Whenever you are finished here, I am ready to go."

The irritation in his words caught me off guard. What was that all about? I saw no point in asking him right there, we would be in the privacy of the elevator soon enough.

No sooner did the elevator doors slide shut then I rounded on him.

"What is your problem, Owen?" I demanded.

"I could ask you the same thing. Trinnian is scarcely gone for a few hours to sort out a devastating turn of events and you are practically throwing yourself at Marco!" he roared.

"What are you talking about? I did no such thing!"

"He made it a point to see you to the door. Are you planning to sneak out later? Just be careful the sun is not up, I would hate to have to give Trinnian a baggie full of ashes when he comes back."

"Oh, give me a break!" I stormed out of the elevator and almost pushed the door to the hallway off its hinges. His hand latched on to my upper arm as he swung me around to face him. "Let go of me!" I growled.

"I will not stand by and allow you to hurt Trinnian," he seethed, releasing my arm.

Me hurt him? Funny, I seemed to recall him walking out on me. Owen's statement came as an interesting concept that only served to piss me off.

"I'm sorry. I forgot hurting Trinnian is your department. God forbid I invade your territory."

His expression hardened. He shoved me up against the wall by my arms.

"How dare you speak above your status. It would be to your benefit to learn when to hold your tongue," Owen hissed. His furious glare eased up slightly, replaced by a fiendish smirk. "Maybe you should stay here with Marco, save Trinnian the heartache you will no doubt bring him down the road."

Releasing me, Owen stalked off through the door and into the night.

I slid down the wall, wrapped my arms around my legs and rested my forehead on my knees. The emotional reactions of the night I'd been desperately trying to keep in check shot to the surface all at once. Sobs shook my body. I sat on the floor, crying in the middle of the hall.

"Jacquelyn? Are you ok?" asked a somewhat familiar voice with an Italian accent.

I looked up to find Augustine crouched down next to me. His brow creased with concern, his eyes seemed to be scanning me for injuries.

"Yeah...kind of," I answered. "What are you doing here?"

"I live here when I come to town. Olivia and Collin called to tell me about Trinnian so I searched the city for any sign of him. I had just given up and decided to come home. What are you doing here?"

Someone busted through the door that led to the elevator. It was Marco.

"Is she ok?" he asked.

My heart sunk as I remembered the camera over the doors. He'd seen the whole thing.

"She seems to be, what happened?"

"It looked to me like she and Owen had words. At one point he shoved her up against the wall. I got up here as fast as I could," Marco said.

"Jacquelyn, what happened?" asked Augustine.

The thought of explaining it in front of Marco was nothing short of mortifying. My trembling hands wiped tears from my face as I tried to stand up. Marco reached out to assist from one side as Augustine helped from the other. I felt silly but didn't want to seem ungrateful by resisting.

"I spoke above my status, I suppose," I answered with a weak smile. "If you both don't mind, I would really prefer not to talk about it right now."

Augustine and Marco exchanged a look of acceptance, neither attempted to force the issue.

"I will take her up to my place. Violet and I can take her home tomorrow," said Augustine.

"Only if you are certain it will not create a problem between you and Violet. I know how she can get. There is plenty of room at my place," offered Marco.

Augustine looked from Marco to me, perhaps rethinking his invitation in light of Marco's comment.

"I don't want to be any trouble, Marco, do you have any vacant places? I don't mind paying for a place," I said.

"Absolutely not!" he insisted. "It is not your fault you have found yourself in this position."

"She can stay at my place. Violet will understand," said Augustine. He almost sounded like he was trying to convince himself.

As much as I would've preferred another choice, Marco wasn't even an option. The last thing I wanted was to have Owen up in Marco's face for trying to help me.

I silently wished the vodka would kick in now.

Thanking Marco for his help, I followed Augustine up to his apartment. It was neat and tastefully decorated, much smaller and more inviting than Owen's place. He gave me a tour, shuttering the windows against the predawn sky as we went. Last stop on the tour, he showed me to the guest room that hosted a comfortable looking queen sized bed and private bath.

He bid me goodnight, shutting the door behind him.

I took my cell phone out of my pocket and sat on the edge of the bed. Something on the floor caught my eye. I reached down to pick it up. It was the card that Marco had given me. It must have fallen out of my pocket when I retrieved my cell phone. I looked at it for the first time. The front said 'Marco's' in the same lettering used on the signage of his bar. Hand written on the back of the card was a numeric code to access the building along with a phone number.

Placing the card on the night stand next to my cell phone, I laid back into the pillows. My eyes drifted closed.

The night replayed itself to me in fast forward. It was hard to believe the course of events that brought me to this point. I found it laughable that the part of the night I most dreaded was almost the easiest part. Compared to the rest of my night, the hunt

was a piece of cake. The review of my day cut short as sleep came
for me.

17

The brisk pace Owen kept did not slow as he made his way home. He marched on, head down and the collar of his wool coat turned up against the chill of the night. Although the cold did not touch him, there was the ever present need to fit in. Even if he could feel the cold, the anger that surged in his veins would have been enough to keep any chill at bay. He was fed up. Everybody seemed to be trying his patience. Most of all he cursed Silas. Things only came to this point because of him. If not for the turmoil he caused, Owen would have had no reason to question Petrus in the first place. Certainly Margaret would have never called him. Owen had not even spoken to her in decades and would definitely not have contact with her by phone. For his sake, Silas better be long gone.

No blame could be placed on Trinnian for his reaction. One of the images that would haunt Owen to the end of time was the anguish etched on Trinnian's face the night he came for Margaret. Heartbreak and regret could not begin to describe the look in Trinnian's eyes as Owen hauled Margaret out of the manor right in front of him. Trinnian's emotional capacity was truly a rare attribute amongst immortals that tend to harden over time. It was this compassion that Owen relied upon when he asked Trinnian to take care of Margaret in the first place.

The apartment was quiet as a graveyard. Trinnian's keys sat on the island exactly where they had been left. Owen tossed his coat over the couch and headed for his bedroom. He kicked off his

150

shoes and opened his laptop on his nightstand as he crawled onto the bed.

While he waited for the machine to power up he thought of Jacquelyn. Trinnian evidently did not explain to her the immortal chain of command. Owen understood that the women of these times carried themselves like men, demanding respect and equality. Still, here were traditions to be observed in their world that she needed to be made aware of. Women were not second class citizens, on the contrary. If she had been sired prior to him, Owen would have to show her respect as his elder. In his eyes, to have a newborn vampire show disrespect to him in front of others was the equivalent of a slap in the face. Marco's behavior would be up to Trinnian to deal with, but Olivia, Collin and Owen needed to watch over Jacquelyn while Trinnian was away. A companion that took two hundred years to find was worth protecting for Trinnian's sake.

The internet opened and he signed in to his email account. Nothing. He shut the computer, staring off into one of Augustine's paintings that hung in his bedroom. It was of Manhattan at night. Pinpoints of light dotted the skyline. Trinnian would return when ready and from the lack of further chaos, it appeared Silas had crawled back under his rock. Owen could do nothing more. He was ready to leave. The longer he stayed, the worse things seemed to get. He would speak to Olivia and Collin when they woke.

*   *   *   *   *

Blood surged into my mouth, I fed greedily. It didn't occur to me, at that moment, how odd it wasn't reading any thoughts from my prey. The heart slowed, beating its last few beats, bringing my gluttony to an end. I sat back against the concrete wall behind me, unable to make out the face of my victim. It was hidden in shadow, turned away from me. The back of my hand wiped any evidence of the deed from my mouth. My head swam in the euphoria of a fresh kill.

A familiar scent briefly touched my senses when my hand skimmed across my face. Recollection coming forth to confirm exactly what it was, my mother's perfume had a very distinct fragrance. Revulsion took hold of me. I shook my head in denial.

On trembling hands and knees, I crawled forward to turn over the body that lay before me. My mother's glazed over vacant stare fixed off into space behind me. Dead. I scurried back against the wall, trying to understand how I could have made such a terrible mistake.

Gradually, my eyes adjusted to the dark and more bodies were revealed behind my mother's. My father, Claire, Glenn Edwards, Karl Novak…the list went on. They all shared the same dead stare. I searched the wall behind me, desperate for an exit. The wall had no doors or windows. Hysteria built with each passing second I couldn't find a means of escape. Hesitantly, I turned back toward my victims to see if there was a way out beyond them. Every pair of eyes had their dead fixed stare locked on mine.

The blankets flew off me from the speed with which I sat up. It was only a nightmare. I was at Augustine's. Burying my face in my hands, I tried to regulate my breathing. Funny the comfort that came with the simple act of breathing. Olivia told me that with time I may not even bother with it, we really didn't have to breathe to keep functioning. For now, I still found solace in my human habits.

A new evening had descended. I made my way into the bathroom to clean up. Taped to the mirror, a note:

Jacquelyn,

I went to pick up Violet at the airport. Please make yourself at home. We should be back by 8:00.

Augustine

I peeked out into the bedroom. The clock said 7:40. That gave me about twenty minutes to shower and dress. No sooner did

I step out of the shower and dry off, I heard all hell breaking loose in the living room.

"Who did you say is here?" asked a woman with a thick French accent. Her tone more than a little bothered.

"I told you, Jacquelyn, Trinnian's companion," Augustine said, sounding a bit frustrated.

There it was again, 'companion.' I was really beginning to hate that word.

"Why the hell is she not with him then?" the woman asked.

"Violet, I refuse to repeat myself. You are not deaf, senile or stupid."

Crash! Something shattered against the wall. I picked up the pace of getting dressed in hopes of being able to defend poor Augustine.

"Do not call me stupid!" Violet screamed. "You should not say such cruel things to people!"

"I did not call you stupid, I said you are *not* stupid!" he yelled back.

"Did you fuck her last night? Is that why you are behaving this way?"

"*Sei pazzo!* Why would you even say that?"

"So now I am stupid *and* crazy?" Violet asked in heated disbelief.

This had to stop. Augustine was in trouble because of me. One last scan of the room to make sure I had everything, I entered the war zone. Violet held a vase above her head ready to launch at him when I stepped into the room. She froze and turned her attention to me. I got the once over from head to toe. Placing the vase back on the shelf it came from, she crossed her arms in front of her. Although petite, her attitude more than made up for her tiny frame. Her indigo eyes smoldered beneath naturally arched eye brows. Sleek brown hair hung past her shoulders, framing her perfect oval face.

"You are Trinnian's companion?" she asked in a surprisingly calm manner.

"Yes, I am. Please don't be angry with Augustine, he was just trying to help me. Trinnian left me in the care of Owen and we had a fight. He was—"

"So! Trinnian left you for another woman and Owen decided he did not want to sleep with you so you come after Augustine?" Her tone sounded confident, as if she had it all figured out.

Augustine rolled his eyes, mumbling to himself and shaking his head. Broken glass littered the floor around him.

"No!" I paused, "Well, maybe the one part about Trinnian but—"

"I think you should leave. You have caused enough problems here," said Violet.

She positively glowered at me. There would be no reasoning with such a person.

Like a switch tripped in my head, I could no longer find the restraint I clung to for the past twenty-four hours. Plain and simple, I snapped. My feet were in motion before I knew it. Violet took a step back, her eyes went wide. I stomped right up to her with my finger poking in her chest.

"In the past week, I have been killed, resurrected, broke someone's leg with a fireplace poker—on purpose, killed a junky, found out my coworker was murdered, had my boyfriend leave me for his ex and got kicked out of the only place I had to stay last night." With each point she received a jab for emphasis. "So quite frankly, the last thing I need right about now is any shit from you. Augustine offered me shelter last night and that is all. I don't give a flying fuck who you are, I will not stand here and have you accuse either of us of something we didn't do. Now, if you don't mind, I will be more than happy to leave as you have requested."

When I got to the door, I looked back before passing through. Neither of them moved an inch but both watched me leave. Augustine wore a small grin and Violet stood with her mouth hanging open as I pulled the door shut. I took a deep breath and headed for the elevator. About half way there I heard the glass smash against the wall. I figured Violet finally noticed Augustine's grin.

CHAPTER SEVENTEEN

Thankfully I didn't feel hungry, since I was apparently on my own. I left the apartment building and started walking. Why didn't I pocket Trinnian's keys? What could they have done, called the police and reported his car stolen? Maybe I should go to Claire's? No, that was just a bad idea waiting to happen. I may not be hungry now. However, I couldn't predict when it would hit me. Images from my dream flashed in my mind. Claire's dead stare in particular. With an involuntary shiver, I pulled my suede jacket closer. Besides, there would be no lying to Claire face to face, unless that was a new skill that came with being a vampire. I just wanted to be home. That was it, I would go home. I could run the whole way in theory, why not test it out?

The most difficult part of my journey was avoiding populated areas. But the further I got from the city, the easier it became. Although the run was amazing, there couldn't have been a more beautiful site, at that moment, than my house. I made it. It felt like adrenaline replaced the blood that rushed through my body. With a smile, I considered continuing on to Trinnian's house. I abandoned the thought, fairly certain that Collin would've convinced himself by then that Trinnian's leaving was my fault. Collin giving me the evil eye for the remainder of the night sounded about as much fun as going to Owen's place.

Under the third flower pot on the right hid my house key. Thankfully, years of locking myself out actually taught me something. As I slid the key in the knob, I thought I heard a noise. I paused to listen. Silence. Not willing to dismiss it to an over active imagination yet, I tried to prepare myself for the worst.

Quiet as possible, I entered my house, shutting the door behind me. The air hung with an unfamiliar scent of a human. A soft thud came from my room, confirming my suspicions. Somebody was in my house.

My jaw clenched and my fists balled up.

You have got to be friggin' kidding me!

The thought preceded another mental run down of the rotten events from my week, the same list I shared with Violet. It appeared being robbed would be added to the inventory.

With a sigh, I slipped out of my shoes, flattened myself against the wall and ascended the stairs. When I reached the top I peaked around the corner toward my bedroom. The beam of a flashlight bounced around the area. I leaned into the doorway and looked into my room. A man dug through my dresser drawers with his back to me. I took a couple steps into the room, being careful not to announce my presence. He pulled a pair of my panties out of the drawer, held them up to the light and shoved them into his pocket.

Shock came first, followed closely by disbelief as my gasp of disgust alerted him to the fact that he was no longer alone.

The man spun to face me, a complete stranger. Before I anticipated his move, he ran by me toward the stairs. I gave chase, pursuing him downstairs and into the kitchen. The back door stuck, like it usually does, delaying his exit. I grabbed him by the scruff of his neck. My thumb nail nicked his flesh. A trickle of blood ran down his skin.

The scent hit me, causing my attention to falter for a split second. It was long enough for him to reach my butcher's block. He grabbed the meat cleaver and spun toward me as far as he could, still locked in my grip. The momentum of his swing buried the cleaver in my left arm. I heard the bone crack before I felt the excruciating pain. A scream stuck in my throat. My own blood ran down my arm while my other hand squeezed onto his neck even tighter. With my left arm useless, I couldn't let go and risk him escaping. I had to stop him.

The intruder pulled the cleaver from my arm, intending to deliver another hacking blow. Once again, the heavy blade swung toward me. I lunged for his throat.

Our assaults were both successful. Mine was more overpowering. The frenzied sensation that came with his blood gushing into my mouth, countered the pain of the cleaver sinking into my arm again. The weapon clattered to the floor while he struggled against me, desperately trying to break free. I felt him weaken in my grasp. We both crashed to the floor, our feet slipping in the blood pooling beneath us. My tortured groan muffled against his flesh from our impact with the ground. His last breath escaped his chest and I collapsed on top of him.

The pain from my arm was agonizing. I had to get up and tend to it. The blood still flowed from the wounds. My right hand found the kitchen floor, as I tried to push up, I slid in the blood covering the hardwood floor. The impact from the fall jarred my mangled arm, my hand clamping over my mouth to stifle a scream that would surely wake the neighbors. I made another attempt to get to my feet. Having gotten to my knees, I leaned against the cabinets and grabbed the lip of the sink to pull myself the rest of the way. My left foot secured beneath me, next the right. It slid out from under me causing me to collapse on my useless arm. The intolerable shock of pain from the crash threatened my ability to remain conscious. Gingerly, I rolled over on my right side. Tears streamed down my face, blinking them away, I looked at my arm. It barely hung on.

Making another attempt to stand wouldn't be very wise. I lay on my back and fished my cell phone out of my pocket. Trying to deal with this alone wasn't an option. My choices were almost as bad as the thought of losing my arm. I brought the phone into my line of vision, stuck to the front of it with blood was Marco's card. His cell number faced me as if it were a sign. Owen could go fuck himself, I needed help *now*.

The blood that stained the card made the number almost unreadable. It took me a minute, but I was able to dial the number.

"Marco," he answered before the second ring.

"It's Jacquelyn." I managed to choke the words out between sobs and waves of pain. "I need help."

"Where are you?" he asked.

The calm yet urgent tone of his voice somehow reassured me he understood the severity of the situation. I gave him my address and briefly described my injuries. He told me I would be fine and to stay put, holding my arm firmly against my body. From my own experience with broken vampire limbs I understood why he requested I do this. Having to re-break the bone because it didn't line up properly while healing was not exactly a concept I wished to ponder at the moment.

"Please, don't tell anyone. You're the only one I can ask," I pleaded through tearful gasps.

"You have my word," Marco promised. In the background, I heard the revving of an engine coming to life. "I am on my way."

The cell phone slid from my hand. I reached across to my arm to try and hold it together. The pressure of my own hand sent stabbing pains down my arm at first and then the stabilizing hold actually seemed to take some of the edge off. My head rolled to the side, the dead man's vacant stare peered back at me. Flecks of red dotted his lifeless face. The dream from earlier came back to me. I turned my head the opposite way to find something else to focus on.

The oven door reflected my image back to me. My face smeared with blood and streaked with tears. I lay in a dark, glistening pool of gore, spreading out from my body. From what the reflection showed me, the whole kitchen appeared to be smudged or splattered with blood. I laughed softly to myself when all I could think about was how on earth I was going to clean this mess up.

18

There was someone in the room with me. My eyes fluttered open momentarily to identify the intruder. It was Marco. He was alone. *Good...*I remember thinking as my eyes slid shut and I attempted to smile. The small movement cracked the dried blood caked to my face. This odd sensation was the last thing I remembered before everything went black.

Tires squealing and gunfire was the next thing I could recall. They were the noises that roused me from a deep sleep. I sat up in my own bed, not quite sure how I ended up there. That is until I remembered calling Marco, which enabled me to put two and two together. My left arm was sore and hurt to try to bend. It bore a bandage that started at my shoulder and went to the crook of my elbow. Curiosity nagged at me to peek inside but common sense told me I should wait. The sleeveless white cotton night gown I wore had occupied the bottom drawer of my dresser, untouched for at least a year. That is when I noticed how clean I was. I had a bath at some point. It had to be a while ago since my hair felt mostly dry. All the blood drained from my face. Marco bathed me. The jury was out on whether I should be grateful or mortified.

The racket that woke me came from the guest room down the hall. Hiding out in my room from embarrassment wasn't going to change anything. I got up and made my stiff body venture to the other room. Marco lay across the bed. His Doc Martins hung off the edge. Good call on his part. He was propped up on his elbow engrossed in a movie.

159

"Die Hard, huh? One of my all-time personal favorites," I said.

Although my voice sounded a bit rough, I felt better than I would've expected. I attempted to cross my arms and casually lean against the door frame but only succeeded in the leaning part. My left arm protested at the suggestion, not quite ready to take requests. As long as I gave off the impression that I wasn't the slight bit bothered by the fact he'd seen me naked or touched my naked unconscious body. That's what I aimed for. He muted the movie before he spoke.

"Yippie-kay-yay," Marco said with a smile, turning the quote PG-13. Ok, maybe he was a gentleman and I was being silly about him bathing me. After all, we were grown adults, right? I was pretty sure he'd seen his fair share of women naked. "Come, sit down." He patted the bed next to him, scooting over to make room for me. "You will heal quicker if you allow your body to relax. How are you feeling?"

"A bit rough but I'm sure I'll live." I sat against the pillows propped up on the headboard. "I can't thank you enough for coming to my rescue."

"I would hope that someone would be there for me if I were in that situation."

"I'm sure you wouldn't be in that situation. You would've been in control from the start," I said.

"Just because you have the tools at your disposal does not mean you are proficient in the use of them. You are what, a week old?" he asked.

"I woke up like this about three days ago. I don't really know from what point you guys start counting."

"The exact number is irrelevant to my argument, which is how could you possibly expect to have mastered your new abilities in that short amount of time? This was not your fault, you are simply too young to be going around unprotected. The amount of blood you lost coupled with losing the use of an arm was enough to render you defenseless. You could have been killed tonight. Why were you here by yourself, if you do not mind my asking?"

"Because the thought of going anywhere else didn't particularly appeal to me, this is my home. I guess I needed to be in a place that brings me comfort and makes me feel safe," I answered.

"Where is Trinnian?" asked Marco.

I shrugged, "Nobody knows...Oh wait, where's my cell phone?"

"It is not working. When I got here it had been laying in the pool of blood beside you. It would not even turn on."

"Oh my god! I hadn't even thought about that. How bad is it down there? Is he still in the house?"

"I got rid of your 'visitor' and cleaned up the best I could. Trust me, months from now you will find blood somewhere. That's just a proven fact, happens to us all."

His back went rigid and his attention drawn to the window that overlooked my front yard. I heard a car door close. Just before a knock at the door, I identified the presence on my porch.

"It's Olivia and Collin," I said, heading off to let them in. Marco stood, following me to the bedroom door.

"It took you that long to decide who it was?"

"Yes," I replied, knowing already it wasn't the response he hoped for.

"Did Trinnian teach you anything before he left?"

I froze at the top of the stairs. He hadn't really taught me much of anything. If anybody taught me anything it was Olivia. Even that wasn't very much. But, then again, I wasn't her responsibility.

I glanced back at him over my shoulder, "Not really."

Descending the stairs on autopilot, my mind was set into motion. The hurt that should've come with Trinnian's decision to walk out on me finally surfaced with the awareness of his pre-departure neglect. Something I hadn't even realized until Marco brought it to my attention. I'm sure Trinnian figured we had eternity together to teach me everything. Right? I put on a neutral face and opened the door.

"Jacquelyn?" Olivia said with a touch of impatience in her tone. I could tell she caught the scent of blood in the air. "What the hell happened here?" Her focus immediately went to my bandage. Worry creased her brow before she returned her gaze to mine. "Who is here?"

She stepped into the house heading straight for the kitchen. I didn't see Collin behind her at first until he followed her inside. He carried the bags I left at the manor, setting them next to the door before following Olivia to the kitchen. I shut the door, turning to answer her. Marco was descending the staircase as Olivia and Collin were returning from the kitchen.

"It's only Marco." I nodded in his direction. "He came to my rescue earlier when I was attacked by a burglar."

"Are you ok? All I can smell is your blood," Olivia said.

"She is fine. Her arm is not completely healed yet but it should be by tomorrow night," Marco said, answering for me. "The intruder managed to get a hold of a meat cleaver. When I arrived her arm was only attached by about two inches of skin and muscle. I cannot believe she was allowed to be on her own with no instruction and no protection. She is too young for such independence," he offered in a timbre brimming with accusation.

Everything happened so fast. Collin pushed Olivia behind him with a gentle swipe of his arm. Marco stepped past me to place himself between me and them. The two men now stood barely a few feet apart.

"Is this your attempt at volunteering for the job, Marco?" Collin asked. He wore his blank mask of calm, as usual his eyes told another story.

"I have not abandoned her yet, so I suppose that makes me the best candidate so far," said Marco, casually crossing his arms.

Collin took a step forward before Olivia pulled him back, stepping in front of him.

"Marco, I would suggest you not express your opinion on a matter until you are aware of all the facts," said Olivia.

"The only fact I need to know is that this newborn could not even detect an immortal until they stood close enough to be detected by even a human. Being able to identify others of our kind to discern a threat is lesson one of basic survival. Why has she not been taught even the most fundamental skills? How was it possible for a human to almost get the better of her? Even one with novice skills could have easily taken down an unarmed human," Marco stated.

"I did not come here to stand in judgment for things that were not my duty. Nor do I feel the need to explain anything to you. I came here to speak to Jacquelyn," Olivia said. "If you will please step aside?"

The two of them stood, locked each other's glare. I tapped Marco on the shoulder telling him that it was ok. He looked at me in passing and sat on the couch behind me.

"What happened after we left you at Owen's last night?" asked Olivia.

Without any details omitted, I relayed the story of how the night unfolded after their departure. I even told them the part where Owen accused me of flirting with Marco, which received a muffled grunt of understanding from behind me. For some reason the spat with Violet appeared to amuse Olivia. If it would've been me and her alone in the room I may have asked her about it. The tension I could feel between Collin and Marco refused to let up, so I pressed on. My recollection of events continued through to their arrival not moments ago.

"Why did you stop here instead of coming to the manor?" Olivia asked.

"No offence to you, next to returning to Owen's, that was the last place I wanted to be."

I made it a point not to look at Collin. If she assumed my reasoning to be purely over not wanting to be alone in Trinnian's empty room that was good enough for me. Since it was part of the problem but, most of all, I didn't feel like explaining my suspicions of Collin's hatred for me. Especially while he stood right there glowering in my general direction.

"Is it safe to assume then that there is no point in trying to get you to return home with us?" Olivia asked.

"If she wants to stay here I will remain with her." Something about Marco's offer came across as a jab, Collin's subtle reaction to his statement being my only indication. A calming touch from Olivia made him refrain from comment.

"Jacquelyn?" Olivia raised a questioning eyebrow at me.

"I would like to stay here in my own house, at least for today."

Her eyes looked from me to Marco and back, "Fair enough. But please answer your phone when I call so there is no need for me to worry about you."

"I will take Jax with me to the city tomorrow and have her phone replaced. It was broken in the struggle with her attacker," Marco said.

Marco's reference to me in a familiar name wasn't lost on anyone in the room. Collin was the only one who responded to it. His sound of dissatisfaction matched the contempt in his glare. Who it was directed at I wasn't entirely sure.

"How did you find out where I lived anyway?" I asked Olivia as they headed for the door.

"Your Navigation device was one of the things that survived the accident." Olivia gestured to my bags they brought with them. "When Owen called us to get Trinnian's car he recommended we bring with us any belongings you may have at the manor. We had no idea what was going on until we got to his place and he explained in his brief vague terms what happened."

Olivia, Collin and I stepped out onto the porch while Marco remained on the couch. Collin continued on to Trinnian's Mercedes. I could only imagine what Owen said about me. Something told me I really didn't want to know.

"Owen had no idea where you were. He suggested that we should drop your things off at your house as opposed to trying to find someone that did not want to be found. However, I now understand why you were not answering your phone." Olivia paused on the bottom porch step. She turned to me and spoke, "I want you to know you will always be welcome in our home, regardless the outcome of the current situation."

"I guess it's safe to assume nobody has heard from Trinnian?" I asked.

"Nothing." She glanced back at the house before she continued, "It may not be any of my business but please use your gut instinct about the immortals you allow into your life. Just like in your human life not everybody has your best interest at heart."

"I promise," I said. Her comment seemed to imply more than the actual meaning of the words. I felt my eyes widen with the possible translations. "Olivia, nothing has happened between Marco and me. His number was the first one I came across in my panic," I quickly added in an attempt to defend my own honor.

"I did not intend to suggest such a thing," she said.

"Then is there something about him you think I should know?"

"I really do not know him well enough to pass judgment. Take my advice how you will. I was not trying to mask hidden meanings in the words. The face value of the statement was enough to serve my purpose," answered Olivia.

My paranoia did tend to get the better of me at times. I couldn't help feeling foolish for reading more into what she said than what she meant. Maybe part of it was subliminal guilt that emerged from the fact that I found Marco attractive?

Once again, I found myself uttering those same words to her that seemed to punctuate our interactions, "Thank you...again."

She smiled and strode off toward the passenger door of the car. Collin glared from within. His usual look of distaste carried a bit more malice behind it. I waved anyway and turned to the door. Marco stood in the doorway, watching them drive off into what remained of the night. And here I assumed Collin's hatred was directed at me. I was almost relieved that Marco had been the intended target this time.

"Are you ok?" asked Marco.

"Yeah."

"Well then, unless you plan for us to spend the day in the basement, we need to make our rooms sun proof," he said, gesturing me into the house.

His warm pleasant smile confirmed my suspicions. I was definitely attracted to Marco.

The sun proofing of the windows was done in such a manner as to not draw the attention of the neighbors in the light of day. After our project, we returned to the guest room to finish watching the movie. The credits started to roll when I got the impression Marco was watching me.

"Well, thanks for inviting me to finish the movie with you," I said. "I'm going to turn in."

I headed toward the door when I heard Marco get up off the bed.

"If you don't mind, I am going to take a quick shower."

"Sure, make yourself at home. Goodnight," I replied over my shoulder.

When I got to my room I turned to close the door. I caught a glimpse of Marco as he walked into the bathroom tugging off his black t-shirt. His back was criss-crossed with white scars. As he turned to close the door behind him I quickly pushed my door shut in hopes he didn't see me.

The shower turned off and I heard the shower curtain open. A few minutes later I felt someone sit on the edge of my bed. My first reaction was to pretend I was sleeping because my first thought was to admit I wasn't. Fingers lightly brushed across my cheek and pushed my hair back from my face. It became increasingly difficult to keep my breathing measured and to remain calm. I turned away onto my side, hoping to discourage any further touching.

To my relief I felt the bed move in a fashion that suggested my visitor stood up. I didn't hear footsteps retreating from the room as I would've expected. Instead, I heard the soft thud of material hit the floor and felt a body slip into bed behind me. The thin cotton of my night gown did little to disguise the fact that a naked man laid against me in my bed.

This was wrong. It wasn't that it felt wrong physically. It felt wrong mentally. Why was the body always so much harder to convince than the mind? I finally worked up the strength to protest and suggest Marco return to his room. Until I felt his gentle fingers move my hair aside and soft kisses cover my neck. My resolve tried to regain its foothold, even as the kisses turned to playful nips. A hand slid down my side to encircle my waist. It pulled us closer together, much to my surprise. I couldn't have imagined any space existed between us. When I felt his teeth graze the base of my neck, there was no question things had to stop. Once blood became involved I would no longer have the restraint required to stop myself from doing something I would regret.

"I'm sorry, I can't do this," I whispered.

"Well, then I guess I will have to apologize for assuming you were a whore then, won't I," said the man I had mistaken for Marco.

I was up and off the bed in a heartbeat. My reaction spurred on Owen's amusement, his laughter echoing off the walls of my room.

The room was silent when my eyes opened. Best of all, I was alone. With a sigh I sat up in bed, thankful it was only a dream. A knock interrupted my moment of relief.

"Yes?"

Marco poked his head into the room.

"I did not wake you did I?" he asked.

"No, I had just woken up."

"If you are feeling up to it, I would like to head to the city within the hour."

"That's fine. I need to take a quick shower." I didn't feel the need to explain why. "Do you think it's safe to take the bandage off?"

"Yes," Marco replied.

He entered the room and sat beside me on the bed. Gently, he started to remove the gauze. I tried to assist but he insisted he had it under control. He neatly unwound the bandage as I watched.

What if my dream would've turned out to not be a dream and it really had been Marco? Would I have been able to stop if I would've found myself staring into his soft brown eyes? I didn't notice he finished removing the gauze until his fingertips traced the light pink marks that were once gashes in my flesh. His feather light touch made my skin tingle and my breath shudder. It was too soon after my dream to not react to his touch. He heard the change in my breathing and looked at me. I found myself staring into his warm, sensuous eyes. I guess I was about to find out the answer to my question.

*   *   *   *   *

Owen ignored Petrus's calls for the past couple days. He was not sure he could carry on a civil conversation with him yet due to the headache he caused. Especially after being told by Margaret he was not allowed to be angry at Petrus for going to her. However, Owen was leaving town and figured he should call before departing. Not knowing how long he would be away or the reason Petrus tried to contact him in the first place. Reluctantly, he returned the call.

The conversation was a bit odd. Petrus insisted his reason for calling was about something he preferred not to discuss over the phone. He went on to request that Owen come to his place in person. Owen tried to explain to him that he was on a tight schedule and had to catch a plane in a few hours. Petrus promised it would only take a minute before he hung up. Owen grabbed his coat and headed out.

19

At some point, I quit breathing altogether. Part of me wanted to break away from Marco's unrelenting gaze. While the rest of me shamelessly hoped for so much more. It felt like playing a very intense version of that game where you try to make the other person look away first. Marco did. His hand retracted from my skin as if it suddenly shocked him. Just as quick, he was on his feet and looking at anything else but me.

"I should let you get ready."

No sooner were the words spoken, he left the room. It took me a second to start breathing again. Then another to get off the bed, grab my robe and head for the shower. The hall was mercifully empty as I made my way to the bathroom. Would it really have been that difficult to put more than one bath on the second floor? Stupid early twentieth century practical houses.

Somehow, we managed to avoid each other until I opened my bedroom door, ready to leave for the night. The door swung open to reveal Marco, who just so happened to be walking by headed for the stairs. The result of which played out almost like one of those ridiculous slapstick comedy routines, after you…no, after you…I insist, after you. I couldn't help laughing but neither could he. If nothing else, it served to return things back to normal. The awkward phase pushed aside for now, making our journey to the city much more comfortable.

The jet black BMW purred along the highway as we drove toward the city. Would I have expected Marco to drive anything else? Honestly, the car just seemed to fit him. Thus, people and their choice of vehicles naturally became the conversation starter. But eventually, the topic fell in my lap. He was interested in finding out about me. It reminded me of my first conversations with Trinnian. He too seemed to have a way with keeping the focus on me. Maybe it was a male vampire thing?

However, when Marco asked me about my career, that is when the conversation took a whole new turn. Before I knew it, I told him the whole story of my time with Trinnian from the beginning. At first it felt a bit awkward and then, toward the end, I almost felt physically lighter. Perhaps laying it all out like that was therapeutic. His questions stopped, I glanced over at him surprised by his sudden silence. He wore a grin that made me a bit insecure.

"What?" I asked.

"Remind me when we get to my apartment to hide all of the fireplace implements," he replied, laughing a rich honest laugh.

The amusement sparkling in his eyes somehow managed to make him that much more handsome, like he needed help. I had to admit, the incident with the poker was kind of funny now. The past couple of days did wonders for cleansing me of any lingering feelings of guilt I may have been harboring over that.

Before we headed to his bar, we replaced my cell phone. My new phone came fully loaded. Marco sold me on the fact that it would be to my benefit to have as much technology handy as possible, simply because you never know. His comment reminded me I hadn't checked my email since Sunday, before I left for Karl's funeral. It didn't seem possible that it was only Friday. The funeral felt like it had been light years away. Everything that happened to me occurred in a six day span.

Well, my motivation to quit my job was triggered by the feeling that I started to live for work and had no life. The days began to pass by with nothing in particular to discern one from the other. And now? Did I get what I wanted? Each day did seem to be full of action and excitement. So why did the phrase, 'be careful what you wish for', suddenly take on new meaning?

"Ready?" Marco asked.

I hadn't noticed we parked and the keys were no longer in the ignition. No telling how long we sat in that parking space, with me lost in my thoughts. I nodded. He came around the passenger side to assist me from the car. His hands sought out mine until he held them both.

"If you are not feeling up to this, I understand. You can go up to my apartment and relax while I go check on the bar," Marco said. His eyes filled with concern.

I shook my head, "No, really, I'll be fine." I threw in a tiny smile in an attempt to reassure him.

"I do not ever want you to feel like I am making you do something you do not want to." The unabated look in his eyes enforced his sincerity but his proximity was undermining my composure.

Did the Devil and an angel really sit on your shoulders in an effort to help you make decisions? Good advising from one side and bad from the other? I always thought that if this were true, the Devil definitely had an advantage. After all, wasn't he the ruler of Hell and an angel was simply a smaller symbol of God? Regardless, the Devil reminded me of the last time Marco and I got this close. It was like he insinuated that was really what Marco referred to. That truly being the case, I wasn't exactly sure how to respond.

My stare dropped from his seductive eyes to his sensual lips before I caught myself and returned my gaze to his. That must have been the signal because without a warning, he leaned in closer and his tender lips pressed to mine. I kissed him back willingly...or maybe, just maybe, the devil made me do it.

The parking garage occupied the basement of his building. We took a private elevator that dropped us off at a back entrance to his bar. I wasn't surprised to see the awkwardness back, if only on my end. As stupid as it sounded, I still felt a sliver of guilt each time I thought about Trinnian—which happened to conveniently occur each time I thought about Marco in a less than ladylike manner. With my hand in his, he led me into the bar. He escorted me to a stool right by the employee door we passed through. After making sure I settled in, he assured me he wouldn't be long before vanishing back the way we came.

In his absence, I caught myself thinking about our kiss in the garage. I pulled away and apologized first. Quick to comfort me, he blamed himself for doing exactly what he claimed he didn't want to do. I told him it wasn't his fault at all. It just felt like it happened too soon.

"Maybe one day, when you are ready, we will try that again," he said with a smile. "I would be a liar if I said I regretted doing it."

And just like that, the subject dropped.

The bar was pretty busy. Being the new kid in town, I didn't recognize any of the immortals. Which actually wasn't a bad thing since I felt pretty confident that Violet wasn't ready to reminisce about old times yet. Or that Owen wouldn't want to join me for a cocktail. Diana passed by with a tray full of empty glasses. She paused long enough to give me a smile and a wave. It was nice to know I didn't manage to piss everybody off.

With nobody to talk to I turned to my new phone. I had a message from Claire. Assuming I wouldn't be able to hear it very well and not concerned enough to ensure I would, I moved on. Emails were what I was after. I opened my account. There may as well have only been one message in my inbox because it was the only one I saw. It was from Trinnian, a few hours after he left me at Owen's. The blood in my veins felt like arctic slush. My hands shook so badly I needed to set the phone on the bar. The subject line simply read, 'I am sorry.'

"Everything ok?" Marco asked.

I was so blindsided by Trinnian's email I hadn't noticed his return.

"I'm not sure," I answered honestly. "There's an email here from Trinnian the night he left."

His expression showed signs of apprehension, "You have not read it?"

"No. Not yet." I glanced back down at the phone, unconsciously biting my lip.

"If there is one thing I have learned about you, it is the fact that you are much stronger than you give yourself credit for," he said. "Take your time, you will read it when you are ready."

He flashed me a reassuring grin before once again passing through the employee doors.

I exhaled and thought *screw it* as I opened the email. Ignoring the nauseous feeling in the pit of my stomach, I read the message.

Jacquelyn,

I am ashamed at my cowardice. I find myself unable to look you in the eye to even begin to try to justify my actions. However, you deserve an explanation. In doing so I do not expect or even hope for your forgiveness, my motives are not based on delusions of my own benefit. You have earned the right to know what is going on. My intent is to keep this brief and stick to the facts not wanting to monopolize your time any further.

Margaret was placed in my care by Owen about two hundred years ago. We were both sad and lonely souls that found comfort in the company of one another. The love that evolved between us was not strong enough for her to let go of the heartbreak of her past, unbeknownst to me. I came home one night to find that she tried to kill herself. It was not horrifying enough to witness her failed attempt at suicide, she actually begged me to finish the job. The anguish I felt was more than one person should ever have to suffer. The decision to end her life was not mine to make. Ultimately, the choice fell on the one that made her. Her fate rested in Owen's hands. A couple nights later Owen showed up to collect her. His rage was palpable as he vanished with her into the night. That was the last time I would ever see her. Or so I thought.

Over the years that have passed, I have learned how to endure the pain of heartbreak. I even supposed I forgave her betrayal at some point. The guilt that I woke with every night since has been relentless. It always felt like her death was my fault. I would have given my own life to be able to go back and make things right. Instead, I bore my burden of guilt in silence, eventually learning how to mask my suffering. As much as I resent Owen for keeping her existence from me, his actions have afforded me the opportunity to make amends. Not only with Margaret but with myself as well. I approach my situation with her in the same way I extend this explanation to you. There is no false hope that I will receive her forgiveness or even an invitation back into her life. I have been granted the chance most never get. The chance to try to make things right.

I never meant to hurt or betray you but I cannot ignore this opportunity to mend my broken soul.

Trinnian

The employee door opened and Marco settled onto the stool next to me. His presence managed to help me keep a hold of my chaotic jumble of emotions. I could tell he wondered whether or not I read the email. So I simply slid my phone across to him. I felt him look at me and I nodded without looking at him. Soon after, he finished reading and slid the phone back to me.

"Looks like they have everything under control, let's get out of here," said Marco.

We didn't speak as we made our way back to the elevator. The doors slid shut. I stared straight ahead, trying to determine what I felt. A little sad, angry, betrayed, everything I would've expected. The one feeling I didn't expect, was relief. No longer did I wait in limbo for a sign. Even more surprising was the fact that I understood why he left. Not that having the privilege of this information eased the sting of rejection. I couldn't honestly deny the fact that I wouldn't have done the same thing in his situation.

The hard lines of the elevator doors started to blur from tears glazing my eyes. I felt Marco's hand between my shoulder blades as he stepped in front of me and pulled me into the comfort of his embrace. His chin rested on my head while his hand stroked my hair. My arms encircled his waist and he kissed the top of my head. He pulled back and gently tilted my head up with his fingertips. A warm smile touched his lips.

"See, no more tears. I told you that you are stronger than you realize," he said, his fingers wiping away any remaining evidence of sadness.

"Not strong enough," I whispered, unable to resist the urge to kiss him.

Pulling me close, he returned my gesture with enthusiasm. The pleasure I felt in his kiss this time wasn't interrupted by thoughts of anything. Freedom from guilt made me even more aware of how badly I wanted him. His tongue teased mine playfully, sending shivers of excitement down my spine.

The elevator doors opened behind him and we spilled onto the floor of his foyer. He rolled over on top of me and pulled off his t-shirt, the sound of fabric tearing with his impatience. I took my cue from him peeling off my sweater. His finger tips traced along my jaw, down my neck, continuing on until they hooked around the front of my bra. He looked into my eyes. A sinister grin possessed his lips as his hand turned into a fist. With a devilish gleam in his eye he tore the lacy garment from my body and his hands smoothly explored my naked flesh. My fingers slid up his muscular arms to his shoulders. Before my hands could round his shoulders to his back, he grabbed my wrists and pinned me down against the floor.

A gasp escaped me with the sudden restraining movement. He lowered his lips to mine, kissing me softly. The change in him was unexpected, until I tasted the blood on his mouth. Arousal spread through my body like a flame to dry tinder. He pulled back. Taunting me, he bit his lower lip. Glistening crimson coated his lip, starting to form a droplet in the center. I struggled against his hold trying to reach it. His teasing smile tormented me before he ran his tongue across his lip, licking away any trace.

"Wicked, wicked man," I breathed.

He raised an eyebrow, leaning back in to kiss me…or so I assumed. At the last possible second, as I stretched toward him to receive his kiss hungrily, teeth latched onto the arch of my neck. And for the next hour or so, he proceeded to demonstrate what a truly wicked man he was.

The ringing of my phone wasn't going to stop. Every time it went to voicemail, a few seconds later, it would start ringing again. I tried to sit up but Marco held me tighter. We were still on the floor, a spent heap of flesh lying in front of the elevator amongst our cast-off clothing. He laughed at my attempt to free myself.

"Come on." I laughed back. "What if it's important?"

With a sigh, he released me. I dug my phone out of the front pocket of my discarded jeans. It was Olivia. I felt that nauseous sensation return to the pit of my stomach again. I answered anyway.

"Thank god!" Olivia said, sounding extremely irritated.

"Olivia, everything is fine. Just because I don't answer my phone, doesn't mean something's wrong!" I responded, a bit irritated as well.

"Really? I would not be so sure about that. Your friend Claire is here."

"What?" How in the world did she end up there? I looked at the clock on the wall, it read just after ten. "Tell her I left for the city earlier and will catch up with her there tomorrow. She can crash at my place tonight."

"Um, no...I think you need to come over here," Olivia said.

I felt the blood drain from my face, "Olivia, has she been hurt?"

"Not physically but she has seen too much to simply let her walk away."

"Olivia, please keep her safe until I get there," I pled, fear obvious in my voice. "I'm on my way."

She agreed and hung up. My heart sank. What the hell happened?

I flinched at Marco's touch. He turned me to face him.

"What is wrong?"

"I don't know but I have to get to Olivia's place as soon as possible." I started gathering my clothing with shaking hands. The words poured out of me in a hysterical babble. "My friend Claire is there, she's mortal. I don't know what she's doing. Why would she go there? She had no reason to be there."

CHAPTER NINETEEN

Marco grabbed me by my shoulders and pulled me to my feet. His action gained my attention, distracting me from my scattered thoughts.

"I am going with you," he said bluntly.

"No, Marco, it's not your responsibility to keep fixing my problems. I can do this." My tone wavered, betraying me.

"You cannot very well go get her without a car, now can you? Besides, I would never get to spend time with you if I did not help fix your problems."

He smiled in a way that made me understand I wouldn't win this argument. I surrendered.

We quickly dressed and headed for the parking garage. When we got to his car I remembered I had a voicemail from Claire. It actually turned out there were three voicemails...damn new phone.

The first came earlier that morning.

Jax, I'm gonna crash at your house tonight. My mom wants to take me to lunch tomorrow and I won't have to wake so early if I stay at your place. You know how I feel about the a.m. side of the clock. Talk to you later.

The second message was from early evening.

Jax...are you ok? I was prepping the coffee for the morning and when I moved the coffee maker there was fresh blood underneath where it had been sitting. Then I noticed the glass was broken next to the lock on the kitchen door. Maybe you got locked out and got cut breaking in? What's going on? Call me.

Third message was just a few hours old.

God dammit, Jax! I am officially worried. I called the emergency room to see if you went there to be treated. They had no record of you but suggested I call the police. I thought that was a bit extreme, knowing your rotten track record with cell phones. I found your navigator so I'm going to Trinnian's. Maybe you went back there or maybe he knows where you are. Please call me when you get this!

It all made sense now. All except for one little item, what exactly did she see?

20

The lobby was quiet when Owen arrived. Petrus had a new girl on duty, a human in her early twenties named Kayla. He was actually thankful to discover Lisette not working. She never took the news well whenever he left town. Any further headaches he could avoid at this point would be appreciated. This visit already contained more than its fill of complications and drama.

Kayla's attention flickered between Owen and the magazine she read. Her heavy dark framed glasses did not obscure the fact that she was very pretty. If anything, Petrus did have an eye for attractive women. She absently brushed her long, blonde streaked bangs from her dark eyes, looking up at him again as she turned the page. The natural brunette's shaggy hairstyle and heavy eyeliner gave her the rebellious look of a female rock star. Not to mention the black leather ensemble that seemed to be a requirement for Petrus's ladies. More often than not, they wore at least one leather item. Kayla's item for the night, a pair of skin tight pants that laced up the sides. Her long sleeved lace blouse did not even attempt to conceal the black silk bra she wore beneath.

Sitting impatiently on the couch in the waiting area, Owen looked at his watch. He already waited for nineteen minutes, long enough to be irritating. If Petrus made him wait much longer it would not end up being a pleasant meeting for either of them. He stood and walked over to the reception desk.

"Kayla, would you be so kind as to call him again?" Owen asked politely.

CHAPTER TWENTY

"Yes, Mr. Smith," she replied, picking up the phone and dialing. "He's not answering. He must be on his way."

"Thank you," he said, returning to the waiting area.

Instead of sitting, he paced back and forth, staring at the double doors Petrus would be coming through. He knew he was starting to make Kayla uncomfortable but he really did not care at that point. Much to her relief, Owen stopped pacing and planted his hands on his hips, looking at the doors as if he were trying to will them to open. Seconds later, Petrus stepped through.

"Owen, sorry to have kept you waiting," he said, crossing to the seating area, "but I had—"

"Can we just get on with this? I told you I am on a tight time schedule."

"Yes, of course, follow me."

Petrus turned on his heel, heading back through the doors toward the elevator. When they got in, Petrus hit the bottom button and the elevator hummed to life.

Owen glanced at his watch again, "What is this about?"

A sly grin slid across Petrus's face, "Patience old friend, patience."

The doors opened to a dimly lit hall. They made their way to an ancient rusty door at the end. It opened with a miserable groan to a small landing with a flight of stairs. They descended the stairs and entered another hallway. Owen looked at Petrus, who only shrugged in return before continuing on. At the end of the hall to the right was a newer door that must have been recently replaced, since the further they went the more rustic the surroundings became. Petrus opened it with Owen following close behind. Ahead of them, yet another flight of stairs, but these were so old they appeared to have been carved out of the bedrock.

"Oh come on!" Owen exclaimed. His fuse grew shorter by the second.

"Last one, I swear."

Owen rolled his eyes, shaking his head. Against his better judgment, continued on. They came to the bottom of the steps about twenty feet later. The spacious area they entered could have been hundreds of years old given the crude surface of the walls.

There were four heavy iron doors spaced out evenly in the surrounding walls. Petrus headed off to the far left door.

"In here," said Petrus.

Owen looked at him skeptically.

"Through this door and we are done?" Owen asked.

"Yes."

Before Petrus opened the door, Owen caught the scent of an immortal. One he knew, although he was unable to pin down the identity at first. The heavy door moaned painfully as Petrus forced it open.

There, chained to the wall, an emaciated vampire. His hands and neck bore thick metal cuffs secured by stout chains affixed to the coarse stone wall.

Even with the black hood over his head, Owen knew it was Silas. The once white T-shirt he wore was stained with dried blood and dirt. His arms were covered with cuts and bruises, the lack of blood hindering his healing process. When Petrus opened the door, Owen heard the distinct sound of chains moving, proof that Silas was alive and conscious. If he only had visual cues to rely on, he may not have been so convinced.

"No wonder he vanished into thin air, he has been underground," Owen mumbled to himself, stepping inside the cell.

"I stumbled upon him in an alley the other night after you came to see me. Figured you would appreciate my looking after him," Petrus said, following Owen inside.

Standing over Silas, Owen lifted the hood. The haggard man flinched, struggling against his restraints. His face bore the brunt of his beatings. One eye was swollen shut while the other blinked repeatedly, trying desperately to focus.

"Have you anything to say for yourself?" Owen asked Silas.

"Do I have any last words? Is that what you ask?" Silas inquired hoarsely. His throat was raw, a side effect of wailing in pain.

Owen crouched down to his level, "I am not going to kill you...if that is what you think."

"You can take him with you for a small finder's fee," Petrus offered.

180

The hood dropped, once again concealing Silas's face. Owen rose, turning to face Petrus. He stood there before Owen, his arms crossed in front of his chest, looking very proud of himself. It took all Owen's control not to lose his temper. Did he hear Petrus correctly? He was attempting to sell a vampire that had broken the terms of a judgment set against him? Petrus knew better. Law dictated there were only three immortals that were entitled to deal with Silas without consequence, his maker, his judge or Lattimer, the one immortal that outranked them all.

Of course there would always be those that tried to get around this for their own personal gain, as Petrus was trying to. The price that they paid when they were discovered hardly seemed worth the risk. In most cases, they served fifty years locked away in a cell, much like the one in which they stood. A few had even been executed, depending on anything else they may have been found guilty of at the time.

Owen's eyes narrowed as he approached Petrus, "Have you lost your mind? Do you think that because Lattimer is your maker that your actions will go unpunished?"

"Times are changing, Owen. When is the last time anyone was punished for such a thing?"

"Actually, the last time it happened...does the year 1863 ring a bell? How about the name Patrick Stockton? You do not think he was killed merely for being a liar and a cheat do you? He too tried to profit from holding a fugitive vampire hostage. I doubt you would lose your head as he did but I find it hard to believe you would by-pass the fifty years underground," Owen stated, heading for the door. "Deliver Silas to his maker tonight or I swear I will have you escorted along with him to Lattimer personally." He stepped out of the cell and paused, turning back to face Petrus. "Do not think for one second I will not be placing calls before dawn to make sure you have complied with my wishes," Owen said, leaving a rather sullen looking Petrus in his wake.

*   *   *   *   *

Olivia sat by the fire watching Collin pace. It had been a while since they enjoyed the fire pit, too bad it was not under better circumstances. She tilted her head back to soak in the cloudless, starry night. From the looks of it, tomorrow would be a perfect half moon.

As much as she tried to ignore it, Trinnian's absence felt like losing a limb. In an attempt to soften the ache of his loss, she turned her thoughts to more pleasant things. She wondered what he might be doing at that moment, if he noticed the same beautiful night sky. Sure, in all the years they knew each other they spent time apart. However, this would be one of the few times they spent apart that she had no idea where he was or if he planned on coming back.

She loved Trinnian but knew him too well. His loyalties would be the death of him. The promise he made to her lover almost six hundred years ago kept them from ever being more than just friends. That was his way. Everybody had something they believed in. Trinnian believed in the promises he made to the people he loved. Both spoken and unspoken.

Collin saved her from the unreciprocated love she carried for Trinnian. It was one of the things they had in common. He too carried with him an unspoken love that hid in the depths of his heart for one long passed. Olivia understood the grounds of her and Collin's companionship. She knew Collin loved her none the less as she loved him, in her own way. Theirs was a relationship with an understanding, if they could never have what they wanted, they had each other. And they were quite content with that.

Duty to his family was what forced Collin's hand. He had to turn his back on the woman he loved to step into his brother's role as husband and father. When his brother died unexpectedly, it was the honorable thing to do, according to his father. The love and respect he held for his father took away any choice in the matter. If his father wanted this of him, it would be done without question.

The decision in turn left Collin to watch from afar as his one true love Annabelle wed another. Their union tore a hole in his heart that would never mend. He went through the motions of living but was never truly alive. Each day that passed felt as hollow and pointless as the one before. His obligation forced him to share a home with a woman he despised and children that were not his. The passing of time did not bring with it acceptance for his fate. Eventually, he gave up speaking to his brother's wife entirely, if only to avoid her spiteful tongue. To the children, he remained the same Uncle Collin.

About a year later, Collin found out that Annabelle died from sickness. News of her death destroyed any ounce of hope he held on to. Depression dug its claws into him and he became an empty shell of the man he once was. Any excuse he could find not to be at home he would take.

Late one afternoon, he almost finished clearing a dead tree that fell over one of the roads leading into his property when he had an accident. Lost in his thoughts as he brought the axe down, it deflected off the log he intended to split and sunk into his leg below his knee. The damage was too severe to try making his way home, and nobody was within ear shot to hear his cries for help.

As night started to fall, Collin lay on the ground, ready for death when he became vaguely aware of a presence. His blood had caught the attention of an immortal, Trinnian stood by Collin listening to the final words of the dying man. He was rambling on about finally being free from his meaningless existence, delirious from blood loss. Trinnian had never encountered anything like it before. From his experience, people would beg until their last breath for a chance to live another day. Draining him did not seem right. Instead, Trinnian offered him a life far away from anything he had ever known. Collin accepted, no questions asked.

In Collin's mind, Trinnian saved him, spared him from another day trapped in his wretched life. The debt he owed Trinnian he felt he could never be able to repay. In return, he offered his loyalty as a friend and protection as a brother.

When Jacquelyn came into the picture, the change in Trinnian was like night and day. For Olivia, there came a sense of relief that he would no longer be alone. If she herself could not be the one to bring him happiness, there came a consolation in the fact that someone could. And when she got to know her, she really liked Jacquelyn. Collin, however, was cautious of her. Immortals have long memories. The time it took for Trinnian to get over the pain of Margaret, still fresh in his mind. To Collin, nobody could be good enough for Trinnian, and they would only end up hurting him. The incident with the fireplace poker enforced his belief and Olivia knew Jacquelyn would have to work twice as hard for Collin to warm up to her. That is, of course, assuming Trinnian would ever return.

Headlights coming down the road brought her back to the matter at hand. Petrus was delivering Silas to Collin. Olivia knew Collin felt he could not take back inflicting Silas upon the ones he loved but, to him, this was a step toward his own peace of mind. She tried to get a hold of Trinnian to let him know but, ever since the night he left, all calls went straight to voicemail.

The sleek, pearl gray Jaguar pulled around the back of the manor and parked just past the fire. Petrus got out, shook Collin's hand and gave Olivia a bear hug.

"I told him before I put him in the trunk I would use his long, flowing hair as a fuse to burn him alive if he dented the hood," Petrus laughed, running his hand over the smooth, unmarred surface.

"Thank you for bringing him to me," said Collin.

"Owen suggested it was the right thing to do," Petrus confessed.

He popped open the trunk to reveal Silas, still wearing the hood with his hands bound behind his back. Petrus pulled him out by his upper arm, his hulking size made the task seem effortless. Dropping Silas on the ground in front of the fire, he bent to remove the hood. Collin stopped him.

"Do not bother," Collin said, "I got it from here. You need to get back to the city."

"Thanks for understanding. I would not be so concerned but I have a new girl watching over things," Petrus explained.

He did not waste any time after they said goodbye. Petrus climbed back into his car and sped off.

"Watch him for a second," Collin said to Olivia and headed toward the outside entrance to the basement.

CHAPTER TWENTY

*   *   *   *   *

Claire used the car pulling away to mask her movement, sneaking closer concealed by the trees. She hid her car in the woods, not too far up the road just in case Jax was in trouble. Her actions were probably the result of too many crime shows. However, she wanted to be on the safe side. That was blood that she found at Jax's house after all.

She couldn't see Jax or her Volvo. No sign of Trinnian either, for that matter. What she did see was a person being pulled from the trunk of the car by an impossibly huge man. That person lay on the ground next to the fire, not moving. A woman stood over the body and another man walked off toward the house.

Claire hoped Jax wasn't here because something bad was happening. Even as she thought it, she couldn't bring herself to walk away.

The man emerged from the shadows surrounding the house with a shovel. Claire's hands covered her mouth in an effort to stop the sound of horror that wanted to escape. They were going to bury the body from the trunk. As the man with the shovel approached, the woman sat the body up and removed a hood it wore. Claire reached forward to the tree she hid behind to steady herself. It wasn't the body of a stranger. It was that guy Silas from the other night at Shane's pub. Jax said he knew Trinnian but she had been pretty tight lipped about anything else. She caught a subtle movement. Silas struggled against the rope that bound his hands behind his back. He was still alive. The man with the shovel spoke.

"You just could not leave well enough alone. You had to come back...and for what? Look at you, Silas!" he yelled, leaning down into Silas's face. Silas didn't flinch or turn away. He just stared back at the man without a word. "This is what your rebellion has earned you. The chance to be hog tied, awaiting your own death. Well congratulations."

The man took a step back and swung the spade. It connected with Silas's head, accompanied by a loud crack. His limp body flung to the ground from the impact. Claire's hands shot up to clamp over her mouth again. Tears ran down her face in terrified disbelief of what she was witnessing. The man approached Silas and stood over him with a foot on either side of his shoulders. He changed his grip on the handle and brought the shovel straight down on Silas's neck.

Screaming as the head rolled to the side, clearly detached from the body, Claire stumbled backward, falling into the underbrush. She scrambled to her feet, running as fast as her feet would carry her through the dark woods. The last thing she saw was the two murderers look in her direction. There was no doubt in her mind they were in pursuit.

21

We pulled into the familiar circular driveway. Marco parked in front of the dining hall, it was the exact same spot I parked in the first time I came to the Talbott Manor. A cynical voice inside my head wondered how much of that person still existed inside of me. I silently hoped at least enough remained for Claire to recognize. Maybe my thoughts were a tad bit melodramatic. Then again, some of the things I've said and done in the past week were almost like I watched someone else controlling my body. At the moment, I couldn't decide if that was a bad thing, especially when I looked into Marco's sultry eyes.

The doors to the manor opened as we approached. Olivia came out to greet us, followed by Collin. The smell of smoke hung in the air, laced with an unusual scent I couldn't quite identify. When we drove up I saw the glow of a fire coming from behind the house. I wasn't interested in their mid September campfire. My only concern was for Claire.

"Is she ok? Where is she?" I asked.

Concern emanated in my words. Marco shadowed me. His hand lightly touched my lower back as if to assure me of his presence, empowering and comforting me.

"She is fine, Jacquelyn," Olivia answered. Her eyes darted from me to Marco and back. "She is resting peacefully. It seems she worked herself up to the point that she fainted."

"May I ask what it was that she saw?"

"She saw me kill Silas," Collin said, stepping forward to stand next to Olivia. He looked from me to Marco just as Olivia

187

had. Except when his eyes returned to me I saw nothing but contempt. "You could have at least had the decency to wash him off of you before coming here," he sneered.

His glare shot to Marco before returning to me as if to emphasize specifically who he meant. I was absolutely mortified. Marco took a step toward Collin. I put my arm up to stop him while my other hand opened the email on my phone.

"What's your problem, Collin? Still haven't heard from your friend Trinnian?" I found the email, walked up to Collin and thrust my phone against his stomach. His hands clutched on to it out of reflex. "Well I have!" I locked him in my narrowed gaze before continuing past him up the steps to the house. "Now if you'll excuse me, I'm going to see Claire."

Her human scent was easy to pick up. I followed it into the living room where she lay unconscious on the couch. After I made sure she was unharmed, not that I didn't trust them, I gave a sigh of relief. Settling into the chair across from her I tried to figure out what I would tell her. How on earth would I explain what was going on? Though I've come to accept my fate, it all still sounded bizarre, even to me. Would she be afraid of me? Was this the end of our friendship? So many questions ran through my head, if she woke now I wouldn't even know what to say.

Olivia stepped into the room and motioned for me to follow her. She handed me back my phone as we walked outside. I could tell by her expression she had also read the email. It didn't bother me. They had as much right to know what was going on as I did, if not more. The fact that I was the only one he even bothered to contact was perplexing.

We reemerged into the night. Marco leaned casually against his jet black BMW. When he saw me, a smile spread across his handsome face. I didn't understand what it was about him that comforted me in his presence. As far as I knew it could simply be attributed to the fact that he was there for me at a time in my life when I had no one else. I may never know. What I did know at that particular moment, it was all I could do not to jump into the safety of his arms.

Collin was nowhere to be seen. I asked Olivia where he went. She simply replied he went to tend the fire. I didn't give it another thought. We sat on the front porch steps while she explained to me what happened.

When Olivia told me on the phone that Claire had seen too much, she wasn't exaggerating. Olivia finished her side of the story and I confirmed Claire's story from the voicemails she left for me. I couldn't help but feel responsible for what Claire went through. Her only motivation in coming here in the first place arose from her concern for me.

My mind kept replaying the same image over and over, Collin decapitating Silas with a shovel. I could see it in my mind as if I were there. No wonder Claire lost it. Even with the tolerance that came with being a vampire, I'm not sure I would enjoy an easy nights rest after seeing that.

It finally occurred to me what that scent was that hung in the air with the smoke. The burning remains of Silas. He was dead. The man responsible for my death would no longer roam free on this earth. Why didn't I feel something? Shouldn't there be some sense of relief? Satisfaction that justice had been served? Perhaps even an overwhelming urge to celebrate? I would think so but I felt nothing.

The air started to thicken with a tangle of emotions. It made no sense at first until the desperate need to escape came to the forefront. I had picked up on Claire's thoughts. Olivia and I looked at one another. She gestured for me to go inside.

"What am I going to say to her?" I asked.

"If that is your friend, why are you asking me?" Olivia replied with a grin.

I went inside, not sure of what to expect. Before I even passed into the hall I could see that Claire no longer lay on the couch. She was still in the living room. I could feel her ahead of me. With carefully measured steps, I entered the hallway.

"Claire, it's me, Jax," I said, trying to sound as calm and reassuring as possible. She didn't respond. "I'm coming in there. Everything's ok, it's just me. I'm alone."

Still, there came no response. I cautiously made my way to the end of the hall, hands up in front of me. It felt like the way to approach someone when you had the need to demonstrate you weren't a threat. The next step would take me into the room with her. I knew she was off to my right waiting for me. She held the fireplace poker braced over her head, ready to swing like a baseball bat. The irony found in her choice of self defense amused me. Fireplace tools must be the first weapon of choice for fighting vampires.

I figured I might as well let her get it out of her system. Braced for impact, I stepped into the living room. Sure enough, Claire took a swing at me. I grabbed the poker with both hands, turned and pinned her to the wall. She gaped at me with wide eyes, taken aback by my action. To her, it would have only appeared as a blur. The incredulous look on her face was priceless. I fought the urge to laugh. There was no time for jokes. She needed to understand the severity of the situation.

"Claire, if I let you go, do you promise to sit on the couch and talk to me?"

She stared at me for a moment before she nodded. I didn't pick up on any plans to try to attack me again, or run, so I let her go. Well, I kept a hold of the poker and stepped back to allow her to sit on the couch. After she settled in, I propped the poker against the wall but remained standing...just in case.

"Jax, I'm so sorry. I didn't mean to attack you." Her voice broke as she started to cry. "It's just that I'm so scared."

The tears ran down her cheeks as I stood there looking down at her. My heart ached for Claire, burdened by the knowledge that she suffered because of me. I sat next to her on the couch, putting my arm around her shoulders.

"I'm here now. Everything is going to be alright. You know I won't let anything happen to you," I said.

She wrapped her arms around me, resting her head on my collar bone and broke down completely. The sobs that wracked her body seemed to contradict what would be expected from such a tiny frame. I sat with her, allowing her to get it all out. It wasn't as difficult as I thought it would be to have her so close to me. Of course I found myself having to ignore the scent of her blood, although it didn't overpower me as I would've imagined. She finally calmed down and wiped away the last of her tears, pulling back from me.

"Jax, I saw that man kill Silas," she said, glancing toward the front door as if someone might hear her.

"I know, Olivia told me," I said. Claire looked at me as if she couldn't understand what I said. "Trust me, he deserved it."

"What?" she asked, sounding confused and appalled at the same time. She slid back away from me a little further. "What have they done to you?"

She eyed me as if waiting for the alien to pull off the mask resembling her friend. I wasn't sure how to answer her question. She already appeared so tormented. It seemed like the wrong time to spring the news that I was really a vampire.

"Nothing, Claire, they didn't do anything to me. Look…it's complicated." The words even sounded lame to me as soon as I spoke them.

"They did 'nothing' to the point where you now find killing people an acceptable practice? Jax, this isn't you. Something isn't right."

I sank into the cushions and let my head roll back against the couch, looking up at the ceiling. There seemed to be no way to explain this without sounding like I was crazy. Now I understood Trinnian's dilemma—and he had at least six hundred years of practice. I looked back at her, she sat patiently waiting.

"Silas killed me."

Claire's brow furrowed as she shook her head, "Is that some sort of metaphor?"

"No, not at all, actually," I answered. Sitting forward, I buried my face in my hands. This wasn't working. Then it hit me. I looked back at Claire with a smile. "We're going for a walk."

"Where to, if you don't mind me asking?" Her tone informed me she was running short on patience.

"I think all this will be easier for you to understand if I show you what's left of my SUV."

The look of bewilderment on her face was all I needed to let me know I regained her full attention.

Claire followed me outside. Thankfully Olivia joined Collin by the fire around back. I wasn't sure how she would react to seeing them again before everything had been explained to her.

Just like last time I came out, Marco was still leaning against his car. I felt Claire's grip on my forearm before it occurred to me that she hadn't met him. A grin of satisfaction touched my lips as I took in the same thing she saw. There was Marco, propped nonchalantly against his car. Bathed in the glow of the outdoor lighting, he could've been posing for a BMW advertisement. His European motorcycle jacket fit him like a glove. The worn black leather molded to his body, accentuating his physique as deliciously as the denim of his Levi's. When we left his place I worried so much about Claire, I failed to notice he put on a white t-shirt instead of the black one he wore earlier. My cheeks colored briefly from the memory of what happened to the other shirt. The blush didn't pass quick enough to be missed by Marco if the sly smile that flashed across his face was any indication.

"Claire, this is Marco." I stopped short of him intentionally, unsure I would be able to stand any closer without giving in to the need to touch him. There would be plenty of time for that sort of thing later. What mattered now was Claire. "Marco, I'm having a little trouble explaining things to her. I think if I show her my SUV, I might find it easier to get my point across." He agreed, knowing exactly what I had in mind since I told him the whole story earlier. "You're more than welcome to join us if you like."

There were a few different reasons for inviting Marco. The one that outweighed them all wasn't seeing the need to leave him behind with Collin. With all the chaos of the past few days, I really wanted to avoid any more.

We stepped into the woods headed for the quarry. Luckily, the sky was clear and the moon offered a sufficient amount of light. Marco still insisted on bringing a flashlight he had in his car for Claire's sake. He reminded me that even though we could see fine, she would probably feel more comfortable with a light source.

Marco fell back to give us a bit of privacy so I could relate my tale of the past week or so to Claire. I simply took a deep breath and told her the truth. She listened intently, taking it all in much easier than I originally would've given her credit for. I could tell she wasn't totally convinced. As long as she was past the point of hysterics and irrationality, that was fine with me. Not that those reactions aren't justified when you discover things like the fact that vampires do exist.

When I finished, she asked all the questions I imagine I would've asked. Thankfully, Marco stepped forward to help me with the ones I wasn't sure about. The majority of things we pick up through folklore about vampires weren't true, much to my relief. Garlic, crosses, bibles, holy water and silver don't bother us in the least. I knew the reflection myth to be false from my own experience. Of course we couldn't change into other forms like mists, bats or anything else. I assumed these were all things that Trinnian should've taught me. Go figure.

We entered the clearing to the quarry when she asked one more question I didn't have the answer to.

"I thought vampires could use some sort of mind control on their victims...talk them into doing things or erasing memories. So I guess that is a myth too since Olivia and Collin didn't do that instead of calling you, right?" she asked, looking from me to Marco.

I looked to Marco as well, "A myth, right?" Surely they would've avoided all of this if they could.

Marco shook his head, "No, we can charm humans just as easily as we can read their minds."

Claire suddenly looked really uncomfortable. Normally I would've found her discomfort rather funny. However, I was too distracted by the fact that Olivia allowed this to happen.

"Why would they have let things get to this point if they had it within their power to avoid this whole situation?" I asked Marco.

"Actually, I asked the same question when you went into the house to find Claire," he answered. "Collin did not think it was their responsibility to clean up your mess and he outright forbid

Olivia to do it. Apparently they did not agree on the subject because that is when Collin stalked off to tend to the fire."

I couldn't believe it. Collin really hated me that much that he would risk his own exposure to make my life difficult? Or perhaps he planned to kill Claire to shut her up if I didn't come for her? That would explain Olivia's desperation to get a hold of me. Claire started to get uncomfortable again. I needed to say something to put her at ease.

"Well, I was going to tell you anyway. I just didn't know where to begin," I explained with a smile. Hopefully that would get past Claire's radar because I wasn't even sure if it was a lie. "I suppose he just helped me get it over with."

Oh, but it was far from over with. I officially had it with Collin and his irrational hatred of me. Tonight it would end. Marco's hand rubbed my lower back, smiling down at me. He knew I was putting on a happy face. I returned his smile, thanking him in my own way for being there for me.

"We came to visit your Volvo?" Marco asked, like I needed reminded.

"Yes." I kicked off my shoes and started to unfasten my jeans.

"Jax, what the hell are you doing?" Claire asked, eyeing me suspiciously.

"Yes, Jax. Please, enlighten us," Marco said. He tried to suppress a grin, watching me slide my jeans down to my ankles.

I paused to explain before stepping out of my pants, "I'm going to go get a piece of my Volvo to show Claire."

Marco laughed, "Put your clothes back on and tell me what to get. You do not actually expect me to just stand here while you jump in there to do that?"

Happily I complied, yanking my jeans back up. He took off his jacket and t-shirt, handing them to me before reaching for his belt buckle.

"How did it get down there in the first place?" asked Claire. Her focus diverted to Marco's naked torso.

"A-hem," I cleared my throat to regain her attention, "I told you, Olivia and Collin brought it here to hide it."

Marco kicked off his Doc's, socks and stepped fully out of his jeans. He stood before us wearing only a pair of boxers. *God, I can't wait to get home,* was all I could think at that moment. I tried to be smooth and ogle him discreetly.

"What am I looking for?" he asked. His smirk let me know how smooth I wasn't.

"The rear bumper has a very distinct sticker on it."

"Jax, you don't have to prove anything to me. I believe you."

Even as she said it, I knew she wasn't being completely honest. I needed to make sure that she did believe me. I was running out of evidence. Only one more card remained up my sleeve but I hoped this might be good enough. Her tendency toward motion sickness didn't make the final option very enticing. Marco looked at me, awaiting my decision.

I nodded toward the water, "Thanks, Marco."

"Oh trust me," he said, walking backward to the edge with a devilish leer, "you will make it up to me later."

One more step and he disappeared, followed by a splash. Claire looked at me askance before she walked to the edge and used her flashlight to peer over. She knelt down in the dirt, the beam of her flashlight passed over the water. There was no sign of Marco. A couple minutes later she spoke.

"Jax, he has been down there for a while." She looked over at me sitting next to her with my feet dangling over the edge. Marco's clothing slung across my lap. I looked back at her and shrugged. The apprehension rolled off her in waves. "What if something is wrong, Jax!?" she asked. I could hear the anger seeping into her voice.

Panic got her to her feet. She started to take off her jacket.

"Oh for crying out loud, sit down," I sighed. Her prized leather jacket dropped heavily on the ground beside me.

"Hypothermia might have set in, he could be caught on something or hurt and you're just sitting there!" She stripped off her sweater and tossed it on top of her jacket, her skin looked like gooseflesh. "How can you just sit there?"

"Because I can see him, Claire," I said. The calm timbre of my voice immediately put her at ease. "Now put your clothes back on before you freeze to death."

She sat on the ground next to me, pouting while she pulled her sweater and jacket back on. Her flashlight skimmed across the surface of the water, making one last attempt to see him for herself.

A few seconds later Marco broke the surface of the water, holding the bumper over his head triumphantly.

"Sorry it took so long, I was debating on bringing up the whole thing. But I did not want to look like a show off," he said.

Unable to decide if he was joking, I shook my head and glanced over at Claire. Her eyes were fixed on the familiar symbol in the center of the bumper.

"You aren't lying about any of it, are you?" Claire asked.

I shook my head, looking her straight in the eye.

It had finally sunk in. First of all, she could always tell when I lied. Second of all, she knew how much I loved my SUV. Everything within her told her that I spoke the truth. Only time would tell how she chose to deal with it.

After he made his way up the steep quarry walls, Marco started to get dressed. I stood close beside him to hand him each piece of clothing as needed. When he bent down to pull his jeans on, I got a full on view of his back. The white scars that slashed his skin were slightly raised. I unconsciously reached my hand out to touch them as he stood up. He grabbed my outstretched hand and kissed it before letting go, reaching for his shirt. His expression became unreadable before breaking into his gorgeous smile.

He was pulling on his jacket when something on the other side of the quarry caught his attention. Stepping in front of me, he stared hard into the woods on the opposite side.

"What's wrong?" I asked, his protective gesture putting me on alert.

"An immortal is approaching from the direction of the city, fast," he answered. His probing stare fixed in the direction of the intruder. From the way my week had been going all I could do was brace myself for the worst.

196

22

Curiosity got the better of Claire, having placed me between herself and the approaching unknown. Her hands clasped onto my shoulders as she peeked around me. No doubt lingered in my mind whether or not she believed my story since, evidently, I became her human shield. Well, figuratively speaking anyway.

Marco hadn't moved a muscle since he told me what was happening. I figured he should be able to identify the approaching vampire by now. No sooner did I think it he relaxed.

"It is Augustine," he said, his tension completely gone by the time he turned to me.

"As in, *only* Augustine?" I asked, not ready to deal with Violet again so soon.

"Yes, he is alone." He took in my expression. "You did mention that you and Violet did not get along, if I recall correctly?"

"No, not really," I replied, although he obviously already knew the answer, judging from element of sarcasm present in his tone.

"You will be pleased to know that she would be more likely to go to your house than to come here. Whatever happened between the two of you cannot compare to the hatred that she and Olivia have for one another," he chuckled to himself before answering my questioning look. "Olivia and Augustine have a history. I will leave it at that."

Now there was a story I would love to hear. Perhaps one day.

He turned back in time to see Augustine step out of the trees opposite us. The speed in which Augustine rounded the quarry brought a gasp from Claire.

"You can do *that*?" she whispered in my ear, stepping forward to stand beside me. I nodded. "Sweet." Her awe struck comment barely audible.

"I have seen that look before, this is not a casual visit," Marco said in a hushed voice since Augustine was almost upon us.

As he approached, Augustine seethed with agitation. He started to speak before he reached Marco's side.

"Jacquelyn, you would have done us all a favor if you would have killed her!" Augustine fumed. Marco looked at me, raising an eyebrow in question. "I cannot take her incessant jealousy and false accusations another day! After you left us it took me three hours to convince her that we had not slept together. Then earlier tonight, we were walking through the city when I apparently looked at a woman with auburn hair. Violet made a snide remark about me being suddenly attracted to red heads. When I denied it, she said, 'So you did…make love to… her!' right before she slapped my face and took off."

I figured it was safe to assume Violet didn't use the term 'make love' by the uncomfortable glance offered to Claire and me before he said it.

"I told you she should have stayed at my place," said Marco. His hand casually stroked my upper arm, flashing a quick smile at me.

Augustine's lost expression was at odds with his decision not to comment on Marco's affectionate behavior. Instead, he turned his attention to Claire.

"Who is your lovely blonde friend, Marco?" Augustine asked, stepping toward Claire. "I find it hard to believe such an ugly man can attract two beautiful women at once." His Italian accent worked overtime, knowing it only added to his allure.

"Claire, this is my endearing yet narcissistic friend, Augustine," said Marco, ignoring his friend's playful jab.

Augustine took Claire's hand, pressing his lips to the back of it, "*Piacere mio.*"

CHAPTER TWENTY-TWO

"No, the pleasure is mine," Claire smiled.

Oh God help us. She got a chance to show off her arsenal of Italian for travelers. I knew her mini library of Berlitz pocket phrase books would come in handy one day.

"You speak Italian?" Augustine's hazel eyes lit up like a child's on Christmas morning, befitting of his boyish good looks.

"*Solo un po'.*" Did she just bat her eyelashes? My gag reflex was about to kick in. "I write for a travel magazine, it comes with the territory." She shrugged in an annoying coquettish manner.

I found myself half tempted to ask Marco if this was the result of being 'charmed' because if it was I wouldn't do it to my worst enemy. Instead I chose a less confrontational comment to make.

"I don't mean to break up this little meet and greet but due to the combustible nature of the majority of this party I think we need to start heading back." Claire still ended up giving me an irritated glare for interrupting her conversation. I pointed at the sky impatiently. "Not much nighttime left." The implication of my statement abruptly changed her demeanor.

Our group headed off toward the manor. Augustine asked Marco what he was doing there. Marco looked at me, I shrugged and nodded. He relayed the story of coming to my rescue in grim detail. Claire looked at me in shock and demanded to see my arm as she muttered to herself something about me holding out on her. I stopped and stretched the neck of my sweater down to show her my upper arm. The two thick pink lines that almost encircled it were slightly lighter than earlier but still noticeable. Claire ran her finger across the lingering evidence of the prior nights attack. Sadness clouded her eyes, apologizing that she couldn't have helped me. I put my arm around her shoulder hugging her to my side as we started walking again.

I became thankful for the gap created between us and the guys when I picked up on the thought running through Claire's mind. Her grief that came with the realization that our friendship was about to change forever was practically tangible. She glanced over at me to find that I had been watching her. Remembering that

I could read her mind reddened her cheeks. An awkward silence followed.

"You could probably join me if you want," I said. "Maybe Augustine would even do it for you." I elbowed her in a teasing manner, although not entirely joking.

Claire stared up at the stars before she responded. Her mood became serious. It didn't happen often. Perhaps for that reason alone, when it did, I always found myself listening a little harder and paying a little more attention than normal.

"I don't think I could handle being part of your new world," she responded, sorrow coating her words. "If you would've called me last night to help you, I'd have lost it. Honestly, I don't believe I'm strong enough. You've always been the tougher, more resilient one. This new existence isn't for the weak or faint of heart. I can't even imagine eternity, the very thought of which is pretty scary. The idea of sitting back and watching everybody I love die around me doesn't sound much like living. Not when you're constantly dying on the inside. There's a strange comfort that comes with having an end. One day, if and when I'm ready, I may want to have children. That wouldn't even be an option if I became a...if I became like you." Her inability to use the word vampire became as disheartening as her argument. I did my best to not let on that it bothered me, allowing her to continue. "Besides, you know how I love the sun. If I couldn't bake on the sand in the Bahamas every so often, I think I'd feel as if I'd been cheated. The life you now belong to isn't for me." Almost as an afterthought Claire added, "Most of all, I don't think I could kill another human being."

I looked down at the forest floor as we walked. There was still no feeling of remorse for the woman I'd killed. I began to acknowledge the fact that there wouldn't be either. The act had been justified in my mind. Given the chance, I had no doubt I would do it again.

"You'd be surprised what you're capable of," I said. Even to my ears, the words were void of emotion.

She searched my profile, not quite sure what to make of my comment. I could sense her fear but it wasn't of me. It was a fear that mirrored my own. If I changed this much in a week, what would I be like in a month? A year? A decade? I suddenly felt alone, unable to bring myself to look at Claire.

Swallowing hard against the lump forming in my throat, I caught myself staring at Marco's back. What would I do if I didn't have him? There would be nobody. Maybe Olivia...that would mean putting up with Collin.

The facts were undeniable, I would soon lose Claire. A tiny voice in my head told me this may even be the last time I see her. That's when I realized I'd been blocking out her thoughts, not wanting to know what she was thinking. We were almost to the manor when Claire spoke.

"I think I'm just going to leave now, if you don't mind walking me to the car." Her voice sounded hollow to me.

"Did you borrow Nickii's car?" I asked, trying to fill the uneasy silence that followed her words.

"No, she went out of town. I got a rental car," she answered.

"Why don't you have your mom follow you to the rental place to drop it off tomorrow, then she can take you back to my place after you two spend the day together. That way you can ride back to the city with us in the evening." As she thought it over, a sickening feeling crept into my stomach. The length of her pause prompted me to amend my statement. "You know what, don't answer now," I said, forcing a smile on my face. "Call me tomorrow and let me know then."

"Ok," she said.

Claire waited for me to jog ahead and tell Marco and Augustine to wait while I walked her to her car. Our silent trek to her vehicle was unsettling. When we said our goodbyes, I found myself at a complete loss, trying to decide if it would be our last one. When I broke down and peeked into her mind, she thought the exact same thing.

I felt helpless standing there, watching Claire drive away. The further she got the emptier I became. Marco's hands gently turned me by my shoulders. His expression was one of compassion and worry. He held me close. Everything in me wanted to cry. I couldn't bring myself to do it in front of him, again. He was more than likely finished being my personal damage control unit. Turning on the waterworks might be pushing it. Besides, I had to toughen up my exterior since I was about to face Collin.

Augustine quietly watched us curiously when we met back up with him. It would seem Marco didn't divulge the turn our relationship had taken. My consolation found in his discretion was immeasurable. The thought of another one of Trinnian's friends scoffing at me wasn't something I wanted to deal with at the moment.

With Claire gone, we resumed course back to the manor. I thought about what I planned to say to Collin. As much as I wanted to put an end to his blatant contempt of me, I wasn't looking forward to it. Olivia greeted us at the door. I asked her where Collin was, she told me I could find him around back by the fire. She embraced Augustine, inviting him and Marco inside while I went in search of Collin.

When I found Collin, he sat on a patio chair by the fire like Olivia said. Beside him was a vacant seat Olivia must have occupied before we arrived. I was primed and ready to give him a piece of my mind...until he spoke first.

"Jacquelyn, I owe you an apology," Collin said, looking up at me. He offered the seat next to him. I was taken aback but sat as requested. He continued while I settled in, "I have treated you unfairly and for that, I am sorry. However, you need to see things from my point of view to understand why I have behaved so badly. I am not the irrational, domineering man I may have appeared to be. In fact, you actually might still be alive if Trinnian actually listened to me."

He had my attention. I sat forward in my chair, curious to hear what he had to say. In light of the email from Trinnian, I guess he realized there was no reason left to sit in judgment of my every action. As I waited for him to continue, it occurred to me this was the first time since the night we met that his expression toward me held no sign of negativity. The warm glow of the fire seemed to soften his features even further. It was almost like talking to someone else.

"The night he met you is when it all started. You sparked a feeling in him that lay dormant for years. He changed that night. Olivia and I both noticed it, although I was the one that cautioned him to wait to see what would come of Silas's sudden appearance. Having firsthand knowledge of Silas and his unpredictable nature, I knew it would be to Trinnian's advantage not to be distracted. I tried to convince him at first that immediate action against Silas was not necessary, but his presence was still worth watching."

"However, as you know, Trinnian is one to think with his heart, leaving logic and reason to lie by the wayside. After Silas had shown up the night of the gallery opening, reinforcing my caution, he managed to contain himself. I did my best to convince him he did the right thing by staying away, to no avail. It was as if knowing you were out there was not good enough, he had to be with you. Olivia and I knew his feelings for you created a delicate situation that required the benefit of time to make sure you were the right one for him. He, on the other hand, could no longer wait, convinced he waited for you long enough. Trinnian simply refused to let Silas delay his happiness. That was the night of the funeral. And, well, we all know the outcome of that night."

Easing back in the chair, I allowed myself to absorb things from his point of view.

"So basically, here is the woman you were trying to encourage him to get to know gradually thrust into your lives permanently," I surmised. "I didn't even have a fair shake in your mind before I even opened my eyes. You were prepared for the worst and I only enforced it day one."

"Basically? Yes." He flashed a quick, slight smile. "You never had the misfortune of seeing him suffer the fresh, deep wounds of heartbreak. To stand by helplessly while someone you care about gets beaten down by the anguish of love lost...that is a living nightmare. Especially when it is one who already feels so intensely. Not to mention the same being that once saved you from suffering in almost the exact same place."

Having the luxury of knowing his side of the story made all of the evil glares and nasty comments make sense. I supposed I really couldn't blame him. His explanation brought to mind more than one occasion when acting in Claire's best interest may have made me look like a complete bitch. If I recalled correctly, I could've cared less what the people involved thought of me as long as Claire was alright. However, I didn't really want to think of her right now.

The embers in the bottom of the fire pit were a luminous orange. The dying flames weaved through the last fragments of flammable material. For a split second, I wondered if any of it was Silas. The absence of the unusual odor from earlier assured me nothing remained.

"Are we good now?" I asked.

"I think so."

I stood up, looking at the sky. Dawn approached which made being 'good' with Collin all the more reason to feel relieved.

"You don't mind if we crash here do you?"

Collin looked at the sky, "It is not like we have much of a choice." He smiled. It was a genuinely cordial smile that actually suited him.

I walked toward the house. The feeling of resolution was liberating. It wasn't that I needed to feel accepted by Collin as much as I didn't want to feel uncomfortable in his presence. Olivia was my friend and I hated the thought of avoiding her because of my unpleasant relationship with him. Speaking of relationships, I turned back as I almost made it to the back door.

"For the record, nothing happened between Marco and me before I received the email." I wasn't sure why I had the need to share that with him, I just had to.

"I knew, I just wanted to make sure," he said.

I smirked, shaking my head in light of his honesty and walked into the manor.

23

Olivia, Augustine and Marco were sitting in front of the fireplace when I entered the living room. Marco was settled back into a chair, staring into the fire, but he appeared to be miles away. The other two were talking about Augustine's plans as a newly free man.

When he saw me, Marco's demeanor changed. He regained the warmth in his eyes that emulated the kindhearted man I discovered him to be and was growing quite fond of. Any lingering distance that clouded his expression vanished.

I smiled to think that it was my presence that brought these qualities out in him. The relationship evolving between us was uncomplicated and relaxed. An extraordinary find, given the brief period of time we had known each other. I suppose it could be attributed to the fact that he may be hundreds of years old and simply accustomed to being able to predict human nature. After all, given the short time I'd been immortal, humanity still lingered. No matter how much I seemed to have changed already.

Olivia motioned for me to sit next to her on the couch.

"So…how did it go with Collin?" she asked.

"It went well, actually. He has come to realize that anything I did to make him dislike me was emphasized by his own negative predictions about my situation." I wondered if Olivia put him up to it. Not that it really mattered as long as he was sincere. "We even got permission to crash here tonight," I said to Marco. The news pleasantly surprised him.

205

"Thank God!" said Olivia. She sighed in relief, collapsing back into the couch. "It is difficult being caught in the middle of two people you care about."

"Now you know how I felt whenever you and Violet got into it," Augustine said to Olivia.

"*That* is hardly the same," Olivia protested.

"She has a point you know. Even at his worst, Collin never threw vases at me," I said to Augustine with a playful grin.

Olivia's eyes widened, "Jacquelyn! She threw a vase at you?"

"No. She was merely a witness to Violet throwing things at me," Augustine said, not joining in Olivia and Marco's shared laughter.

"I am sure there is something about Violet that we do not see that makes it all worthwhile," Marco said sarcastically.

"I used to think so," replied Augustine. "But whatever it was is long gone."

"You are fooling yourself. It was never there to begin with," Collin said, entering the room. He settled on the arm of the couch next to Olivia as he continued, "She has always been crazy. You remember when she got that gig in Vaudeville?"

Olivia did, apparently. With an agonizing groan, she buried her face in the couch cushion.

Augustine looked to the ceiling, shaking his head, "Please do not remind me."

Marco and I looked at one another at a loss. Unable to endure not knowing any longer, I turned to Collin and spoke up.

"What happened?" I asked.

Olivia's head popped up, "Augustine turned a neurotic French stripper into a vampire and now we all suffer!" she announced, throwing the offender a scathing look. "Always thinking with his crotch."

"To answer your question, Jacquelyn," Augustine said. His eyes narrowed as they cut to Olivia and back to me. "I was in Paris in the late eighteen hundreds when I fell in love with a beautiful burlesque dancer. She found out I was leaving for America and begged me to bring her along, professing her love for me. I was powerless to resist her innocent pleas—"

"That is not the story you told me," Marco said, cutting him off mid sentence.

Augustine's eyes begged him for silence that didn't come. Marco ignored him, turned to the three of us sitting on the couch to finish his recollection of the tale.

"He originally told me that he tried to break up with her a couple of days before heading to America. The night prior to his ship leaving, she was drunk and hysterical, insisting she would not let him leave. Before he knew what was going on, she came at him with a knife," Marco mused as if he could see it. "In her inebriated state, she stumbled and fell, impaling herself on the knife. He felt so bad he turned her."

Olivia and Collin exchanged a look of surprise before bursting into laughter. Augustine hung his head and sunk lower in his chair, having nothing to say in his own defense.

"Augustine, I apologize but I cannot have them thinking she had ever been sane," Marco told him, trying to justify his betrayal. "I would hate for them to waste sympathy or regret on her." He chuckled in response to Augustine's indignant grunt.

"Collin, we should really have Marco and Jacquelyn over more often." Olivia suggested in her amusement.

"What does that have to do with Vaudeville?" I asked.

Augustine's head popped up this time, his sly expression took in Olivia, "Violet landed a spot in a Vaudeville show in the city. It was a burlesque routine that included fire breathing. We came up here to the manor to visit one evening. Trinnian asked her to demonstrate the fire portion of her routine. I should mention that earlier in the evening Violet and Olivia got into it over...whatever senseless chance they found to bicker at one another that time."

"Oh please, you remember exactly what started it." Olivia told him, turning her attention to me. "Augustine and I used to be together a very, *very* long time ago. After Violet found out about our past together, she became extremely jealous and spiteful toward me. I was really getting fed up with it that night so I simply asked her if she was mad at me because Augustine still called out my name during sex. She was instantly furious with me. Later on I found out that a couple weeks prior my name *had* slipped while they were making love." Olivia smiled to herself, until her eyes met Augustine's. The grin slid off her face. She looked away trying her best not to laugh.

"*Anyway*, the story ends up with Violet setting Olivia's hair on fire during her routine. It took all Trinnian and I had to pull them apart." Augustine finished, taking advantage of his opportunity to laugh at Olivia's expense. His amusement tapered off quickly with a stony glare from Olivia.

Dawn showed its first signs, prompting the end of our gathering. We disbursed to our sleeping quarters for the day. Marco and I were to stay in the guest room. The same one I slept in last time I spent the night. I led the way as he followed me upstairs.

When I stepped into the hallway my attention became drawn to Trinnian's door at the end on the left, almost like having tunnel vision. I felt Marco's hand on my lower back as we drew closer to the end of the hall. The level of discomfort I felt approaching the door bothered me. Trinnian's essence lingered here, trying to invade my mind with memories I'd rather not revisit at the moment. I allowed myself one more glance before turning the opposite way into the guest room.

Everything remained as I remembered, except the bedding had been changed. Knowing I wouldn't have to spend the night ignoring Trinnian's scent was a relief. The thought of it alone conjured up a very explicit memory of us together on the bed.

Marco stepped in front of me, breaking me out of my thoughts. His fingers softly traced from my jaw to my chin, tilting up my face to look in my eyes.

"Are you going to be alright?" he asked with a note of sadness in his eyes.

"Yeah...I'm fine," I answered. "It's just a little weird being here."

I thought he meant to say something but he turned and headed for the bathroom. Not knowing what was on his mind bothered me. I grabbed his hand before he made it to the door, turning him to me.

"What?" I asked. "You were going to say something."

"I decided against it for a reason."

"Please, Marco, tell me."

He took a moment to study my face before he spoke.

"Would you go back to him?" The sadness that haunted his eyes now lurked in his voice. "If Trinnian came home tomorrow and wanted you back, would you go back to him?"

"No." I locked onto his eyes with mine. "Why would I want to do that?" I responded, savoring the warmth of his soft brown eyes. The answer came so automatically on its own. As if there wasn't a doubt in my mind.

His lips affectionately met mine and his strong arms embraced me while he steered us into the bathroom. Clothing was cast aside in total disregard, blindly making our way across the room. When we stumbled into the shower, Marco stopped kissing me long enough to whisper in my ear.

"I knew if I jumped into the quarry you would make it up to me later," he teased, nibbling on my earlobe. My body tingled, almost preventing my will to respond.

"Did I mention I'm sure I will need you to get something else out of the quarry tomorrow night too?" I said with a soft giggle before his mouth once again found mine.

Having depleted any remaining energy we had in the shower we collapsed on the bed. The entire night had been nothing short of exhausting, which had become the trend for me that week. I welcomed the mind numbing drowsiness, not wanting to lie awake worrying whether or not Claire would call tomorrow. Sleep found me quickly. My body gave in to it without a fight.

There was no end in sight to the desolate road I walked. Even with the benefit of my enhanced vision, it seemed to stretch on for eternity. Snow fell around me, coating the world in a façade of purity. The leafless trees that almost canopied the road stabbed cruelly into the winter sky. Their gnarled, dark branches were in stark contrast to the soft, white edges of the surrounding landscape blanketed by the snow.

With the approach of a new day, the sky started to pale. I didn't care about the impending daylight as I probably should. What I cared about was getting to the end of the road. Even if I couldn't see it, I knew what was there.

Somewhere in the distance ahead stood the massive limestone manor house I sought. It whispered to me through the trees, letting me know that within the comfort of its walls was the one place that I would never be alone. The bitter, frigid wind whipped around me, chasing away the whispers as if the gust that intruded believed I deserved to suffer in solitude.

Fear accompanied the urge to look over my shoulder. Surely Marco hadn't left me. He'd be there. Before I even looked I knew he wasn't. The absence of his reassuring touch was emphasized by my night gown flapping in the brisk wind. The fabric flailed behind me, unimpeded by his hand. My unassuming glance revealed the empty path behind me. Marco was nowhere to be seen.

The wind and the snow both subsided as I turned back to continue my journey. A crow suddenly cawed in front of me, flying straight for my head. I ducked in time for it to pass over me. Its abrupt ominous appearance sent a shiver down my spine. The lifeless trees that lined the road took on a foreboding presence. Panic started to build and my pulse quickened. I wanted to run but I couldn't. It felt as though something weighed me down.

The caw of another crow sliced through the eerie silence of the road. It came from somewhere off to the right ahead of me in the trees and answered by yet another off to the left.

Tears stung my eyes with the brightening of the sky, blurring my vision. I blinked them away in time to see two crows flying at me simultaneously. The only choice I had was to pitch myself forward into the snow. Terror consumed me. Pushing up to my knees I frantically scanned the tree tops for the black birds. The branches were bare and the road, once again, was silent.

I breathed a sigh of relief and sat back on my heels, brushing the snow from the front of the white cotton night gown.

Each swipe of my hand uncovered more and more blood that, at some point, ran down the front of me. My hands reached up to touch my mouth and chin. They came away covered in fresh blood. Whose blood was on my trembling hands? I looked up to see another crow swoop down toward me. In my haste to avoid the attack, I fell over on my side in time to see another crow gliding down to land just beyond where I had been sitting. Maybe they weren't interested in me after all. Perhaps there was something behind me I didn't notice. I turned to look behind me, not so sure I wanted to see what attracted their attention.

All I could see at first was a heap of iridescent black birds feeding on something in the middle of the road. Whatever they fed upon had been dragging behind me, leaving a trail of red as far as my eye could see. How could I not have noticed that before? There was a chain attached to my ankle that led to whatever it was that lie beneath the assemblage of at least two dozen crows. I jerked on the chain, much to the annoyance of the birds that started to caw loudly at me. The action parted the gathering enough to reveal their bounty.

It was a body. Even with the eyes pecked out and the skin sporadically torn away, I would recognize Claire's blonde curls anywhere. I screamed, frantically waving my hands to chase them off. Some flew away, others hopped back a few feet but they all squawked angrily at me. Scrambling toward my best friend's corpse, I was crying hysterically. I cursed the birds at the top of my lungs until my voice became raw. Her picked over body lay motionless before me. The chain that attached us was shackled to her delicate wrist, cutting brutally into her supple flesh. I couldn't have done this to her. How did we end up like this?

While I tried to make sense of what I saw, the crows were closing back in. One landed on her foot before I could chase it away, another set down next to her hip. I was quickly losing control of the situation. The birds, no longer intimidated by my presence, started to attack me. They swarmed, pecking and clawing at me mercilessly. I fought back, screaming for them to get off me when I felt two hands grabbing my arms.

My eyes opened mid scream. Marco held me down against the bed by my wrists. A gash across his cheek bled freely as did the claw marks on his bare chest. It took me a second to register my surroundings. We were in the bed of the guest room at the manor. Realizing I was safe, I relaxed. My panting breaths coming slower as Marco released me. There was no doubt in my mind I caused his injuries.

I apologized profusely. He hushed me and pulled me into his arms, refusing to listen to my pleas for forgiveness. His lacerations were already healing over and he insisted no harm was done. My restraint shattered. I could no longer suppress the tears that struggled to be released. Marco could throw his hands up in frustration and walk away if he chose. Maybe I wasn't as strong as he and Claire seemed to think. How could I be when faced with the truth in the form of a dream? My presence would end up being the death of Claire. If she did call, it would be my responsibility to break away from her.

24

The cell phone snapped shut. Owen leaned against the guestroom balcony, looking out over Lake Winnipeg, absently flipping the phone over in his hands. The crisp, clean air was a refreshing change from the stifling atmosphere of Manhattan but he hardly noticed.

Finally something had gone right. Silas was dead. Of course, the news could not just stop there. He received much more than he bargained for when he inquired about Jacquelyn. Owen cursed Petrus under his breath. If it was not for Petrus, he would not have had to call Collin in the first place. If it was not for Petrus, the whole Margaret fiasco would have never happened. If it was not for Petrus, Owen would not have been thinking about Lattimer. His threat to drag Petrus to Lattimer made him realize how long it had been since he came to Canada to see him. The trip already turned out to be more than he bargained for and Lattimer had nothing to do with it.

No point in putting it off any longer, he thought, striding through the room and into the hall. He made his way to the last door on the left before the hall opened into the grand marble staircase that descended into the foyer. The door led to a small landing with a spiral staircase leading down. This was Lattimer's two story library. He had more than one library in his massive estate, but this was his favorite. The immortal Owen sought occupied a leather wing back chair on the lower level.

"Well?"

Owen got halfway down the stairs when the question was posed to him. He shook his head, dreading the conversation about to happen. Lattimer picked a rotten week to go out of town, Owen thought, crossing to a vacant chair.

"Silas is dead," said Owen, casually settling into the chair next to Trinnian.

"You know that is not what I was referring to," Trinnian said impatiently.

Owen looked at his old friend for a second before speaking, "She is well."

"Owen, do not toy with me. I may have forgiven your silence about Margaret but that does not mean that I am terribly happy with you at the moment."

There would be no point in trying to hold out or hide anything and Owen knew it. He already told Trinnian about the fight he had with Jacquelyn the last night he saw her. Thus the reason Trinnian was not happy with him. Her whereabouts and activities since that night all came courtesy of the phone call to Collin.

"She is actually there," said Owen.

"At the manor? Why?" Trinnian asked. "I would think that was the last place she would want to be."

"It seems her human friend came looking for her and witnessed the execution of Silas."

"Claire? Is she ok?"

"I guess. Jacquelyn is talking to her now. They were headed off to the quarry when I was on the phone with Collin," Owen offered.

"So Jacquelyn is telling her the truth. Why did Olivia and Collin not charm Claire?" Trinnian asked. "I fail to see any reason why they would not take care of it themselves. Was it not enough that Jacquelyn had to suffer the blatant humiliation I inflicted upon her?"

"Collin did not think it was their responsibility to mend her life," Owen's matter-of-fact tone grabbed Trinnian's attention.

"You agree with this?" Trinnian considered Owen momentarily while waiting for an answer. "Everything is crumbling because of my irrational behavior." Trinnian mumbled, almost to himself, shaking his head.

"There is something else you should know," Owen said, ignoring his question.

Trinnian rubbed his forehead as if trying to soothe the onset of a headache, "Out with it, Owen, I am beyond your theatrics."

"Marco is with her."

Trinnian sat up straight, his attention returning to Owen.

"Marco de Navarra?" Owen nodded. "Why is he with Jacquelyn?" asked Trinnian. His furrowed brow confirmed the confusion in his tone.

Owen proceeded to fill in the blanks about his argument with Jacquelyn and divulge all he learned from his conversation with Collin. Everything from Jacquelyn staying at Augustine's the night she and Owen fought, to Collin and Olivia leaving her with Marco at her house the night she killed the intruder, to finally heading off toward the quarry with Marco and Claire. When he finished giving all the information he possessed, Owen sat back in the chair. Trinnian's expression was indecipherable.

"Does she know about Marco's past?" Trinnian asked.

"Why? What does it matter?" Owen's devil-may-care attitude finally set Trinnian off.

"Because, Owen," he said, his tone strained with frustration, "it is my fault she sought out the comfort of another man in the first place."

"She is no longer your responsibility—and a grown woman, I might add." Owen pointed out, unnecessarily. "Besides, last time I checked we are all murderers. Who is to say one of us is safer than the other?"

Trinnian stood, deep in thought, walking over to the shelves as if to examine a book.

"I should have never left that night."

"I assumed you were going to go to Germany."

"I was," Trinnian said, turning back to Owen. "By the time I got all my travel arrangements sorted the following night and arrived at the airport, I could not even bring myself to board the plane. While I sat there waiting for my flight, it occurred to me that Margaret was fine. Maybe my selfish invasion might ruin that. She was a very fragile soul at one time. I was not sure how much that changed. As much as I will always love her she did not want me in her life. For whose benefit was that really? I cannot say. I had to swallow my pride and let her live. I thought about coming home but I had done enough damage. Between walking out on Jacquelyn without a word and the email I sent her, there would be nothing for me to return to. Being alone in the manor would only emphasize that point."

"She only got the email earlier tonight."

Trinnian looked down at Owen before slowly sitting back in his chair. He shook his head and chuckled ironically.

"Well that explains a lot," he whispered. His was voice bitter, eyes cold.

"Why did you come to Lattimer's place?" Owen asked. "Simply to avoid going home?

"Partially, most of all I wanted answers. Even if I could not bring myself to speak to Margaret, I still had questions. I needed to know what happened after you left her with Lattimer. He would be the only one that would be able to tell me. I had this foolhardy idea that he could answer all the questions that I wanted to ask her."

"So you have yet to even speak to Margaret?"

Trinnian shook his head, "No, I decided there was no need."

Owen studied him momentarily before speaking, "It was all for nothing then?"

Trinnian met his accusing gaze, "I will know after I speak to Lattimer. Unfortunately, it is quite possible."

Owen stood abruptly, staring down at Trinnian. His fists clenched at his sides, resisting the urge to grab Trinnian by his throat took all his self control.

"Oh, I understand it all completely now," Owen growled. "You have finally gotten your revenge for me leaving Margaret with you in the first place. Do you really blame me? Do you honestly think I could have anticipated what would come to pass between the two of you?"

CHAPTER TWENTY-FOUR

The accusation caught Trinnian completely off guard. He shot to his feet.

"Have you completely lost your mind? How could you come to such a ridiculous conclusion? My motivation for ruining the relationship I had been waiting for well over a century was based on revenge?" Trinnian asked in total disbelief.

"I would have never believed you would toss the poor innocent newborn into the picture, that was why I never saw what you were doing," Owen said.

"I was in love with Jacquelyn!"

"Oh, I see, that is why it was so easy to abandon her."

How proud Owen was of himself to have seen through Trinnian's deception. His pride was soon lost as something snapped in Trinnian. The unsuspecting Owen never even had a chance to dodge Trinnian's fist, connecting with his jaw in a loud crack. Owen stumbled backward into the bookshelves, stunned as Trinnian landed another blow to his stomach, dropping him to the floor. His knee caught Owen's chin on the way down, knocking his head back into the hardwood of the sturdy bookcase. Owen fell forward. Trinnian stepped aside, prepared for the counter assault. Pushing himself up with his hands, Owen unsteadily sat back against the shelves. Blood from his mouth dripped off his chin onto his snow white shirt. His hand wiped the remaining drops away, the wound that spilled it already starting to heal.

Trinnian crouched down to speak to Owen. His words were acid spoken through clenched teeth, "You will not push another one of your disasters onto me. This was just the latest example of your infamous orchestrations gone wrong and I will not take the blame for it!"

The approach of an immortal prompted Trinnian to stand up. Joel, one of Lattimer's closest companions, appeared in the doorway next to them. He was responsible for the house and closely monitored all activity therein. His dark eyes took in the scene, looking from Trinnian to Owen and back.

"He tripped on the rug, Joel, he is fine," Trinnian told him.

The skeptical way Joel examined Owen, he was obviously not expecting the story to be supported. Slowly, Owen got to his feet.

"It was the strangest thing, the vindictive antique simply blindsided me," Owen said to Joel, pretending to flatten the edge of the oriental area rug with his toe. "But trust me, it will not happen again."

Owen's eyes cut to Trinnian before he retreated up the spiral staircase and headed toward his guestroom.

*   *   *   *   *

The world outside of Marco's BMW buzzed by, I observed its fleeting existence through the passenger window. Augustine sat behind me, carrying on a conversation with Marco while we sped along the highway in route to my house. I honestly didn't even know what they were talking about. My thoughts were consumed by what the night had in store for me. At first, there was a sense of relief in the fact that Claire hadn't called by the time I woke. That only lasted until I got out of the shower to discover the text message Claire left, agreeing to catch a ride with us to the city. I had a feeling I wasn't going to get off easy, that I would end up having to be the bad guy.

Claire met us at the door. I told them I wanted to pack a few things as we entered the house. Augustine gave Marco a hard time about his cleaning skills while I ascended the stairs to my room. I heard him tell Marco my house smelled like an abandoned blood bank. He wasn't too far off the mark. The odor of old blood definitely hung in the air. I could only imagine how much more I would discover next time I was home long enough to really clean the kitchen.

When Claire followed me upstairs, the level of my apprehension rose. Not wanting to have the conversation I needed to have with her until we had more privacy, I accepted her presence as motivation not to take any longer than I had to. I packed quickly, asking her about her time with her mom to avoid any other subjects. She went on to tell me about their day while I stuffed enough clothing and toiletries for a few days into a suitcase.

We were back on the road en route for the city in no time. I couldn't help listening to Claire and Augustine's conversation as we drove. Her flirting toned down a bit since last she saw him, although it was still in effect. They talked about her job, her family, what she did for fun, the usual getting to know you subjects. It surprised me to learn he and Marco knew Shane, the owner of our favorite pub. Marco explained it was good to know the competition, which made sense since I did know of at least one vampire that went there. Then again, I suppose Silas didn't count because, technically, he only went there because of me and no longer even existed.

Marco thought it would be best to drop Augustine off to oversee the bar until he got back from dropping Claire and me at her apartment. He explained that he didn't usually spend as much time away from it as he had in the past few days. Thus, he would feel better to have someone he trusted there. We pulled up in front of the nondescript apartment building. Claire appeared a bit confused. I told her I would explain later.

Augustine got out of the car, only to lean back in through the window to kiss Claire's hand, thanking her for the pleasure of her company. She beamed back at him. A flush of pink touched her cheeks. He suggested that next time he stopped by the pub, she should join him. She agreed, explaining to him which building she lived in. I looked at Marco and rolled my eyes. He simply shrugged and waited for Augustine to step back from the car before pulling into traffic.

The drive to Claire's was uncomfortably quiet. When we arrived at her apartment, Marco gave my hand a squeeze of encouragement and kissed me on the cheek. He knew what I was about to do, I explained it all to him when I woke from my nightmare. She didn't seem suspicious that I wanted to talk with her in private. I followed her through the entrance, looking back at Marco as he drove off. Knowing I would probably want the walk back to his place to clear my head I told him not to wait for me. Part of me wished I hadn't.

"I'm actually glad that you wanted to speak to me alone," Claire said as we entered her apartment. She hung her purse and jacket on the coat rack before wandering into the living room to plop down on the couch. "I hardly slept a wink when I got to your place with everything that you'd told me fresh in my mind."

Maybe I wasn't going to have to be the bad guy after all.

"I'm sure the bitter reality of it was a lot to swallow," I said. "You know it wasn't my choice. I didn't ask for this."

"Jax, I understand all that. I don't blame you for what you've become," Claire responded. "Therefore I can't bring myself to turn my back on you. I don't care what you are. You're still the best friend I've ever had on this god forsaken planet."

All I could do was stare at her dumbfounded. I thought I may have heard her incorrectly until she broke into a huge smile. She must have found the bottle of vodka I had in the freezer. Nobody of sound mind could be so nonchalant about the information she possessed about me.

"Claire, think about what you're saying," I pleaded. "The reason I wanted to talk to you tonight was to tell you that no matter how much you mean to me, it's not safe for us to spend time together anymore. Trust me, this is a decision I have not taken lightly and it kills me to have to make it. But you mean too much to me to put your life in danger."

"Why would I be in danger? It's not like any of you are the blood thirsty monsters exploited in bad horror flicks," she asserted. "You especially would never harm me...and besides, I kind of like Augustine."

"Ok, so what do you do the day he decides to turn you?" I asked, leaning forward in the chair across from her.

"Slow down! We haven't even gone on a date yet," she said defensively. "But I doubt he'd force me to do anything I didn't want to do."

"So you think it would be fair to let him fall for you then put a time limit on it?" I asked. "You do remember he is also a vampire and pretty much has no expiration date?"

"Why are you being so difficult about this, Jax?"

CHAPTER TWENTY-FOUR

"Why *aren't* you, Claire?" Anger seethed in my voice. She blinked to find me crouched in front of her. Her instinctive reflex made her jump at my sudden proximity. A predatory grin spread across my face, I heard her heart lurch with fear. The scent of her blood rushing through her veins made my body tremble with anticipation. I stood as I spoke, "At least there is something within you smart enough to be afraid."

I walked to the chair I had been sitting in and stood behind it, suddenly unsure of my ability to restrain myself. It wasn't until I indulged in her scent that I realized how hungry I was.

"You're just trying to scare me." The intimidation in her eyes was unable to support the confidence in her words.

I laughed. It was a cold, remote sound.

"If you only knew how hard it is to be near you right now..." My hungry eyes surveyed her from across the room. I saw a shudder pass through her body and tears fill her eyes. "I need to leave," I said abruptly.

The adrenaline triggered by her fright hung in the air like a fragrant temptation. I turned for the door, trying not to breathe in the aroma.

"Wait!" she cried. I turned to see the tears streaming down her face. "Please don't leave me, Jax." Her unrestrained sobs shook her body. "You're the only real friend I have." She stood, taking a step toward me.

"No, stay there," I demanded, making a subtle gesture for her to stop. My head swam in a disturbing mix of sorrow, anger and hunger. Tears began to sting my eyes. I had to look away from her. Claire's life would be in danger if she somehow convinced me to say. I had to go. "I love you, Claire," I whispered as I rushed out of the apartment.

Just two steps away from her door, I heard her collapse onto the couch, sobbing uncontrollably. My own tears spilled down my face. Finding the will to continue to walk away was one of the most difficult things I ever had to do. It was a close second only to turning my back on the one true friend I ever had.

I made it to the entrance of her building, leaned against the mailboxes inside the doorway and wiped away the tears in an

221

attempt to pull myself together. Every time I closed my eyes I could see the heartbreak on her face. I took a deep breath and stepped out into the night. The only thing I wanted was Marco.

25

Hidden in the shadows, Trinnian watched Claire's building, waiting for Jacquelyn to emerge. Her scent hung in the air when he arrived and he could easily sense her in Claire's apartment. To avoid detection, he put as much distance between himself and the building as possible while still being able to see the entrance clearly.

Prepared to wait all night if he had to, he knew Claire was his only hope. Jacquelyn had no reason to believe anything he could say to her, but she must know the truth about Marco. It had never been proven whether or not he killed his maker, Aloisia. However, nobody doubted he killed his wife and younger brother in his human life. Trinnian would not believe Jacquelyn knew of this and still chose to remain with him.

The door to the building opened to reveal Jacquelyn. Trinnian froze where he stood, watching her scan the street, only to relax when her scrutinizing gaze passed over him. Thankfully, she had not honed her skill as of yet. His considerable distance would not be taken as an immediate threat by any immortal strong enough to sense him. But close enough that, under normal circumstances, and given time, she would have recognized the presence of her sire.

The troubled expression she wore could not touch her beauty. The gravity of his regret hit him as if it never existed before that night. What had he done? How could he have been so foolish and inconsiderate?

From out of nowhere, a memory pressed to the foreground. The last time he saw her on those same steps was the night of the gallery opening. In that moment, he had been the recipient of her captivating smile that accompanied their playful banter. He could recall the blush of her cheeks when she slipped up, revealing more of her feelings than she planned and then, of course, his own misstep that ruined the moment. The memory faded, a dull ache made itself known.

She tugged the zipper higher on her suede jacket before descending the steps and heading off down the street. No doubt on her way to Marco's, he thought bitterly. He took no comfort in the fact that she looked so distraught. The ache grew with each step she took while he watched her fade away into the pedestrian flow. He wanted so badly to be able to chase her down and have her forgive him for his impetuously uncouth conduct. But, alas, he knew better. The wounds he inflicted ran too deep to excuse easily...if at all.

An immortal approached the street from the walkway along the side of Claire's building. Trinnian's attention had been so involved with Jacquelyn, he had not even been aware of the other presence. Violet came into view as a man moved toward the front entrance. She charmed him into letting her in. Her appearance threw Trinnian off. What was she doing there? Owen mentioned Jacquelyn and Violet got into a spat. What did that have to do with Claire? You barely had to know Violet to be aware of her self serving and vindictive nature. She was up to no good and that no good involved Claire.

Discretion was not always as easy as it sounded. Trinnian started toward the building using the quickest pace he could manage. Anything faster would risk drawing attention. Weaving through the foot traffic muttering apologies, his eyes never left her fourth floor window. A light that glowed within revealed a shadow passing by the curtains toward the front door. A young woman was entering the building as he crossed the street. She graciously allowed him inside. While the fog of charm with which he manipulated her lingered, he took the stairs two at a time unconcerned with his speed.

Trinnian arrived at Claire's apartment in time to hear a loud thud. The door was unlocked. He entered the apartment and caught a fleeting glimpse of Violet taking to the fire escape. She must have sensed him at the door. Claire had obviously been the source of the thud. Violet dropped her where she fed from her, if the twisted way she laid on the floor served as any clue.

Something about Claire's condition did not add up. The things he picked up from her mind were not making sense and she had not lost that much blood. He realized Violet didn't drop her, she threw Claire to the floor in a last ditch effort to kill her. Blood was spreading out from her fractured skull in the same lazy pace as it seeped from her throat.

Even if he could stop the bleeding, Trinnian knew she would have brain damage from the force of the blow. That was assuming she survived the head trauma to begin with. Only one solution could mend the lethal damage. Her death was not an option. Jacquelyn suffered enough because of him. He refused to allow her to suffer this.

*   *   *   *   *

The walk to Marco's was like wandering in a dream. The world passed by in slow motion while I moved along. My senses felt dull, like the space within me that Claire once occupied was an empty room. The fragile walls of which threatened to collapse without notice and crush what little remained of my heart. How much could one person suffer in a week and still continue on? I wasn't sure I really wanted the answer. More than likely, I exceeded the limit days ago.

Something tugged at the back of my brain, trying to get my attention. It was the presence of an immortal. I looked up to see Augustine approaching me. The urgency in his eyes stopped me in my tracks.

"Violet may be going after Claire."

He grabbed my arm, turning me around to head back the way I just came. His brisk stride set the pace as he led me through the pedestrians toward Claire's place.

"Did I miss something?" I asked. "She doesn't even know Claire."

"She was at Marco's building waiting for me when we pulled up. I opened the door and there she was in the hallway informing me that we needed to talk. I told her I had to get to the bar and had no time. She stormed out of the building and called me not long after Marco returned from dropping you off. I was headed up to my apartment when she called to say she was in my blonde girlfriend's building," he said. "She must have seen Claire in the car and heard her telling me where she lived."

My heart sunk. I knew how unreasonable Violet could be first hand when she became jealous of someone. Therefore, I could only imagine how brutal she could be to a human that found themselves the focus of one of her absurd jealous tantrums. I tried to break into a run, Augustine's steely grip kept me in check.

"Jacquelyn, I understand your rush but you must always use caution around mortals," he stated in a firm yet hushed tone. "You cannot charm a street full of witnesses."

I fully understood his argument, though it did little to suppress the caged animal that paced within. When we set foot on her block, my key ready in hand, it became increasingly difficult to watch my stride. A building away, Augustine's grip on my arm tightened. To my horror, he slowed down. I tried to pull away from him at the bottom of the steps leading to the door of her building when he spoke.

"You should wait here."

The words sent a terrifying chill through me. I stubbornly shook my head. Was he afraid that Violet would attack me? Or was it because Claire was dead?

"No, Augustine, I am going in."

My voice sounded so strong, my weak knees could've been a figment of my imagination. I broke free from his grasp, ran up the steps and unlocked the main entrance to the building. When we got to Claire's apartment, I hesitated at the door.

The scent of her blood permeated into the hall. I caught the presence of an immortal within. Pushing past me, Augustine entered the apartment.

Nothing could've prepared me for the scene that awaited us. All thoughts of Violet were thrust from my mind when the room before me came into view. I stepped past Augustine to make sure there was no mistaking what I thought I saw.

Claire was propped up on Trinnian's lap feeding from his forearm. Her blood covered the front of his light gray sweater and matted her hair to the side of her head. His dark eyes fixed on mine the moment I stepped through the door.

My hands clamped over my mouth in an effort to stop the rising scream from escaping. I shook my head in disbelief, fighting the desire to crumple to the floor. My hands fell limp to my sides.

"What have you done?" I whispered.

"I saved her life."

Trinnian's blank stare remained unchanged by his words. I felt Augustine's hands on my shoulders from behind, not sure if he attempted to comfort me or hold me back. With an annoyed grunt I shrugged him off and took a step forward.

"You saved her life?" I asked. The cynical edge to the question informed him of my opinion before I even continued. "Because she is no longer in fear of dying doesn't mean you saved her life!"

He pulled his arm away from Claire's mouth. She was too weak to object. Her eyes fluttered momentarily before her expression smoothed out peacefully. Somehow I knew that he completed the steps necessary to initiate her transformation. Trinnian carefully picked Claire up, placing her gently on a blanket spread out on the couch. Once he had her situated, he turned to face me.

"When I got here, I interrupted Violet feeding from her. She tried to kill her before escaping through the window. I did not have much of a choice. If she did survive her injuries, she would have surely been brain dead. What would you have preferred I do instead?" he asked, crossing his arms in front of him. "Let her die?"

"I know she would've preferred it," I growled. "Just because you have it in your power, doesn't mean you get to play God. Not everybody wants to live forever, especially when the price is so high."

I brushed past him to sit on the edge of the cushion next to Claire. The blood in her hair started to dry but I could still see where her scalp had been split and feel the fissure in her skull mending. Reaching in my pocket, I pulled out my cell phone. We were going to need Marco to help us get her out of here. There was no way we could've moved her discreetly on foot. If we could carry her down to Marco's car wrapped in the blanket, maybe she would draw less attention.

"I did what was in my power to save her because I could not bear the thought of you having to endure any further misery than you already have," Trinnian confessed.

I looked back at him, rising up off the couch. My eyes narrowed and my blood boiled.

"Don't you *dare* blame me for this," I snarled. Stepping toward him, I pointed at the door. "Get out!"

His expression grew cold, eyeing the cell phone in my hand. He glowered at me in disapproval.

"Maybe I should leave. We would not want you to feel awkward having me here when your new fuck buddy arrives," he scoffed.

My anger broke loose. I slapped him.

"GET OUT!"

His fingers absently touched his face at the point of contact. He looked from me to Augustine before indignantly retreating from the apartment, scarcely breaking stride to grab his coat on the way out. I stood trembling, staring into the empty hallway when I felt Augustine's hand on my wrist.

"I will call Marco," he said in a gentle tone.

Turning to see why he lifted my hand, my crushed phone sprinkled through my fingers to the floor like coarse pieces of glitter.

26

When Marco arrived, Augustine and I explained what happened, excluding Trinnian's rude comment about him, of course. His eyes studied me the majority of the time.

"I knew I should not have left you," Marco said when we finished.

"It really wouldn't have made a difference. What happened wouldn't have been prevented," I reassured him.

"Are you alright?" Marco asked me.

"Yes. I'm just upset. I knew something like this would happen to Claire because of me."

"Jacquelyn, it is not your fault. I should have taken Violet's presence more seriously when she confronted me at Marco's," Augustine said.

"We no longer have to be concerned with surprise visits from Violet. I have removed her code from the system. She has lost the ability to come and go as she pleases." Marco told Augustine. "You should have called me as soon as you knew of Violet's intentions."

"I'm actually glad he didn't. What we walked into was enough to deal with. Having you and Trinnian there together would've only made things that much more difficult," I said.

"I cannot say you are entirely wrong on that account," Marco said, offering me a quick smile. "I will bring the car around so we can take Claire to my place. She can transform peacefully in my guest room."

After making sure the coast was clear, Augustine carried Claire to the car wrapped up in the blanket Trinnian laid her on. We arrived at Marco's building taking the private elevator up to his apartment. I cleaned Claire up and dressed her in one of the nightgowns I packed in my suitcase earlier. It happened to be an emerald green silk nightgown she brought back from a trip to India for me.

When I got her settled into the bed, I sat by her side trying to allow her serene appearance to bring peace to my tattered soul. What if Augustine and I would've found her first? Could I have sat back and done nothing, allowing her to pass on as she claimed she'd have preferred? How selfish of me was it to secretly be thanking Trinnian for not letting her die? Marco returned from checking on the bar to find me sitting next to her.

"She will not wake until tomorrow, at the earliest. You have not fed today. Augustine can watch her if you like so we can hunt."

Knowing he was right, I agreed.

Saturday night made for a quick hunt, the weekend filled the streets with an ample supply of prey. After we both fed, I noticed that we were not far from Claire's apartment. I asked Marco if he wouldn't mind if we went by her place so I could pick up some clothing for her. Also, I wanted to clean up so she didn't come home to a pool of dried blood on her floor. She went through enough without having to walk in on the scene of her death. We changed direction, heading to her apartment.

When we got to Claire's place, I was fine, until I set foot inside. Emotion flooded my mind. The reality of what occurred here set in, along with the implications. Marco, my pillar of strength, reminded me of his presence with his gentle touch to my lower back. His very existence keeping me mentally grounded, like usual.

"I can have someone come do this for you."

"Claire wouldn't want anybody else in her apartment. This was her safe haven, her own private refuge from the world," I said. "It's already been violated enough for one day."

He turned me to face him, "What can I do?"

CHAPTER TWENTY-SIX

The concerned appearance he wore was becoming far too common place for my liking. Being in Claire's apartment with the task at hand would be difficult enough without him having to witness yet another emotional meltdown. Not that it was inevitable but it was probable.

"Why don't you go visit Shane at the pub?" I suggested before continuing in an attempt to obstruct the unavoidable protesting. "I just need a little time alone right now."

"Violet could come back, I do not feel comfortable leaving you alone."

"Do you sense her now?" He shook his head. "You'll be close enough to feel her presence from there," I assured him.

"I would feel better if you had a cell phone," he said eyeing the shattered pieces of my phone on the floor, noting the absence of a land line. "That way you could let me know when you are finished."

Walking over to Claire's purse, still hanging on the coat rack, I pulled out her cell phone and dialed his number. The phone rang in his jacket pocket.

"See, I'll be fine. This is just going to be easier for me to do by myself."

He saved the number and shoved the phone back in his pocket.

"I give up," Marco sighed. He approached me, taking my face in his hands looking me square in the eyes. "Call me if you need *anything*. I mean it, Jacquelyn. If anything happens to you that could have been avoided with a simple phone call…"

"I do seem rather helpless, don't I?"

"You are just having a very bad week," he smiled and kissed me before walking to the door. "If anything even seems slightly off, you call me."

Content with my nod, he slipped out into the hall. I immediately set to work cleaning up. The sooner I finished, the sooner I could be back to Marco's with Claire.

The hardwood floor cleaned up beautifully. However, her area rug was beyond help. I rolled it up and sat it by the door. Her building had an incinerator in the basement. I figured I would pack some things for her before I took the rug down. That way I could save myself a trip back upstairs and call Marco from the entry.

With her overnight bag finally packed, I gave the place one last glance before locking the door behind me and heading downstairs.

Damp, heavy air clung to me as soon as I entered the basement. I sat Claire's overnight bag and purse by the door, heading toward the incinerator with the rug bent over my shoulder. The sharp scent of mold and mildew hung in the air. My eyes played tricks on me the further in I walked. I caught movement in my peripheral vision. When I turned my head, I saw nothing. The irony of the creepy feeling wasn't lost on me. I was the monster that went bump in the night, I laughed to myself.

The incinerator was cold when I reached it. Thankfully, Claire showed me how to operate it once. I easily recalled her instructions and it came to life with little protest. When the flames reached full fury, I shoved the rug inside. It stuck out enough that the door wouldn't close, regardless how much I tried to force it further in. The thought of putting my hands inside wasn't very appealing. Apparently this was a common situation because, to the right of the incinerator, a three foot long metal rod was propped up against the wall. It reminded me of a fireplace poker, which in turn reminded me of attacking Trinnian. Oh, to be able to go back in time to that moment...

Creaking of hinges from somewhere behind me disrupted my overzealous jabbing at the carpet. I turned with my makeshift weapon in hand. Even though I saw and heard nothing, I felt the unmistakable presence of an immortal in the room with me. I walked slowly toward the door, gripping the rod like a baseball bat. My eyes scanned from one side of the room to the other with each step I took.

Off to my left, a door hung open that I hadn't noticed before. I could see stairs leading down to the perfect immortal hiding place. That would explain why Marco didn't pick up on their presence. They had been too far underground. Marco mentioned that bit of trivia to me during one of our conversations. My stomach knotted when I finally gave up on the hope that it was

232

only Trinnian and admitted what the back of my mind had been telling me. Violet was the immortal in the basement with me. No sooner did I accept it than she spoke.

"I hope you are proud of yourself," she said in her thick French accent.

The comment came from behind me. I spun to face her, swinging as I turned. She easily grabbed the end of the rod. I fought against her hold to break free my only means of defense.

"As I was saying..." She jerked the weapon from my hands and tossed it aside. It clanked its way across the concrete floor, coming to a rest amongst the clutter. Violet wore an arrogant smirk as she continued, "I hope you are proud of yourself. You have succeeded in coming between Augustine and me. Too bad you were not enough of a woman to do it yourself. You had to enlist the temptation of a human girl. I hope she didn't mean that much to you."

Her icy laugh sent chills down my spine. She took a step toward me. I stepped back, trying to buy some time, desperately looking for a weapon or a way out.

"I told you I never slept with him! What is wrong with you? Claire was my best friend. I would never have sacrificed her for any reason. Much less a piece of French gutter trash like you!" I spat.

I scarcely had time to flinch before I became airborne, crashing into a stack of discarded furniture against the wall. Pain from the impact shot through my body. My eyes opened, Violet stood before me with her head cocked to the side.

"Wow. That looked really painful. Did that hurt?" she asked. Her cynical commentary actually worked to my benefit. I became more angry than afraid. With my right hand obscured by a table top, I felt around blindly for a new weapon. The search came across the broken leg of a table. "That cut on your forehead may need...oh, no, it is almost healed," Violet said in a sickening sweet tone. A smile devised of mock compassion crossed her lips as she leaned in closer to examine the wound.

I pretended to recoil from her scrutiny, egging on the bully within her to come closer. When she got to the perfect spot, I swung with all my strength. The wood splintered from the force of the blow, knocking Violet off of me. She landed in the center of the room. Stunned, she lay on the floor clutching the side of her head. With no time to hesitate, I sprung from the smashed pile of furniture, pinning her to the ground. Twisting my hands in her hair, I slammed her head against the floor.

"Did that hurt? Because it looked really painful," I growled, smashing her head against the floor again. "Huh?"

Control left me completely. I smacked her head repeatedly against the concrete floor. The emotionally overwhelming events of the past week ran through my mind unimpeded while I viciously took it all out on her. All the pent up anger, pain and sorrow ripped free from the most primal depths of my being. What finally stopped my vengeful assault was when the hair I gripped so tightly separated from her mangled scalp. I sat back, scarcely able to look at her face. The sunken features resembled a deflated balloon. Locks of long dark hair dangled from my hands.

Pushing myself off her, I scrambled backward. The horror of what I had done sunk in. I stopped somewhere between her and the exit. Frantically, I tried clawing the strands of her hair from my trembling fingers before digging the cell phone out of my pocket. My hands shook so violently by the time I retrieved it, I could barely hit 'send'.

*   *   *   *   *

Trinnian walked into the pub, settling onto the stool next to Marco. An expectant grin touched Marco's profile before he spoke, his gaze never leaving the ice melting in his scotch.

"Well, well, well, if it isn't the illusive Trinnian Talbott in the flesh." He paused to take a sip of his drink. "To what do I owe the pleasure of your company?" Marco asked, turning to face his guest as he set his glass back down.

The smug look on Marco's face taunted Trinnian. Marco leaned against his forearms on the edge of the bar, his fingers laced together like this was simply a casual visit between friends. Trinnian knew beforehand the amount of self control that being in

Marco's presence would involve. He also knew that the man tested his resolve right at that moment. The bartender stopped in front of Trinnian placing a napkin on the bar before him.

"Shane," Marco addressed the man, "this is my old friend, Trinnian. Please, put his drink on my tab, whatever he wants."

Marco's exaggerated smile made Trinnian want to physically remove it from his face but he figured he would settle for verbally doing it.

"Good to meet you, Shane. Would you happen to have any wines from the Navarre region of Spain?" Trinnian asked.

From the corner of his eye, Trinnian could see Marco already started to lose his grip on his obnoxiously buoyant façade.

"No," Shane said, reaching for the wine list and handing it to Trinnian. "We carry plenty of others."

"I once heard quite a tragic tale about one of the oldest wine families of that area," he said, pretending to scan the list. "Adultery, murder, torture…how barbaric it must have been to live in the thirteenth century." Satisfied that Marco no longer wore his intolerable grin, Trinnian ordered. "I guess I will have what he's having," he said, nodding toward Marco's drink, handing the wine list back to Shane.

"Fair enough." Shane fixed the drink as requested and went off to tend to the patrons at the other end of the bar.

Marco's feigned pleasantries were over, "What do you want?"

"You are going to give Jacquelyn a history lesson," he answered, returning his attention to Marco. "She has every right to know about your penchant for killing your lovers, as I am sure you agree?"

"I paid for my sins a long, long time ago," Marco stated in a flat tone, meeting Trinnian's level stare.

"You think?" Trinnian inquired. "Did you pay for Aloisia as well?"

A lethal gleam flashed in Marco's eyes.

"Pretty determined to get her back I see." Marco's smirk returned. "I cannot say I blame you. She is quite a beauty. But she is so much more than that. Jax is smart, intense, honest,

BLOOD DESCENT

compassionate...oh, and of course, passionate." Marco's eyes took on a provoking quality. "Is it just my imagination or does she taste like Christmas?"

Rage got Trinnian to his feet, his face inches from Marco's, "*You* tell her or *I* will." Confident he got his point across, he turned for the door.

A cell phone rang, he heard Marco answer it.

"Calm down...I cannot understand you." Trinnian turned back to see Marco heading toward him. "Are you hurt? You are where? I am on my way."

Marco rushed by him without a backward glance. Trinnian followed. He knew the call came from Jacquelyn. He also knew that something very bad happened.

Trinnian followed Marco to the basement of Claire's building. Jacquelyn sat on the cement floor near the center of the room with her back to the door. Marco ran to kneel in front of Jacquelyn, placing himself between her and the body that lay only a few feet away from her. He gently placed his hands on her shoulders as he spoke.

"Are you hurt?" Marco asked, his eyes scanning her for injuries.

From the doorway, Trinnian could see Violet's lifeless body lying on the floor behind them.

"No," answered Jacquelyn. The word had a dead tone to it.

"What happened?"

"I came down to put the rug in the incinerator and she attacked me," she replied. "She accused me of forcing her and Augustine apart, using Claire to seal the deal."

"You did what you had to do to protect yourself." His hands cupped her face. "She was insane, Jacquelyn, it was going to happen sooner or later."

"I can't do this anymore, Marco," she said through fresh tears.

"What do you mean? You are fine," he insisted, trying to reassure her.

"I'm not cut out for the life of an immortal. I'm not strong enough."

236

CHAPTER TWENTY-SIX

Her shoulders shook with sobs as she broke down. Marco pulled her into his embrace, looking over her shoulder at Trinnian.

"But you are. I have seen your strength firsthand. It is one of the reasons I love you so much," he said, glaring at Trinnian.

"I love you too," she whispered, wrapping her arms around him in return.

Marco's victorious grin was all he could take, Trinnian had seen enough. In a blur he ascended the stairs and vanished into the night.

* * * * *

When I woke the next evening, Marco already left the bedroom. I could hear him talking to Augustine in the living room. Having to tell Augustine I killed Violet was one of the most difficult confessions I've ever had to make. Thankfully, his comments on the situation were about the same as Marco's. 'You were protecting yourself and someone was going to kill her sooner or later.' Even thought I could still see a trace of sadness in his eyes I couldn't say I felt much guilt, if any.

Marco and I spent a good deal of time cleaning up any evidence of foul play. Violet went into the incinerator along with the clothing I wore. I had been blissfully unaware of the amount of Violet that Marco discovered me saturated in until he suggested I strip down. After showering at Claire's and finding clothing that fit me, we made our way back home.

When I finally emerged for the night, Augustine got up off the couch, heading for the guest room. He stopped in front of me, placing a consoling hand on my arm.

"How are you feeling today?" he asked.

I found it odd that he should be so concerned about me. After all, I did kill his girlfriend.

"I'm good," I answered honestly. I did feel good. Anyone that wanted to hurt me no longer existed. Claire was safe, even if her new found life wasn't exactly the one she had in mind. My eyes sought out Marco. His adoring smile encouraged one from me in return. The best part of all, I had a beautiful man that loved me.

And after all I put him through he still wanted to be with me. My attention turned back to Augustine. "How are you?"

"Free," Augustine said with a smile. "I feel refreshingly liberated for the first time in about a hundred years. I was just on my way to check on Claire, if you will excuse me."

Augustine disappeared into the guest room, shutting the door quietly behind him. Marco patted the spot next to him on the couch.

"Come sit with me."

There was something in his manner I couldn't quite place. It lurked behind his charismatic smile. I complied, sitting on the couch next to him. He put his arm around me, pulling me close to his side and kissed my cheek. I turned to face him.

"Is everything ok?" I asked.

"Absolutely," he smiled. "I want you to know I meant what I told you last night. I love you, Jacquelyn."

I smiled to hear him say it again.

"I love you too, Marco."

"It has been a long time since I have felt this way about anybody," he said. His eyes took on a more somber expression, "That is why I need to tell you—"

"She is waking!" Augustine exclaimed, bursting through the guest room door. Just as abruptly, he vanished back inside.

I looked to Marco, unable to hide the mounting anxiety I felt.

"We can talk later," he said with a small reassuring smile. "Claire is going to need you."

The three of us stood around the bed. I tried to mirror their patience, but my fidgeting was a dead giveaway. Uncertainty weighed on me, churning heavily in my stomach. I was about to sit when Claire's eyes suddenly fluttered open. She stretched as if waking from a long sleep, slowly becoming aware of her unfamiliar surroundings. Propping herself up on her elbows, she took in each of our expressions individually. Her brow knit in confusion, until it all started to sink in. A look of realization crossed her face.

"God dammit, Jax!"

Epilogue

The sky opened up and the rain came down. It couldn't have waited until I made it to Marco's apartment, only a few blocks away. The newspaper I bought, with the intention of reading, now served a new purpose, a lame excuse for an umbrella. I tried not to be irritated by focusing on my relatively calm week. Then again, almost anything could be labeled as 'calm' compared to the previous week. Claire started adjusting to her new life reasonably well. I had Augustine to thank for that. The two of them were quickly becoming inseparable. She began to appreciate all the things she gained and dwelled less on the things she lost. I reminded her she could always get a spray tan, which she didn't find very funny. But it did seem to set her wheels turning. Me and my big mouth, did I set her up to be the world's first orange tinted vampire?

I didn't notice the limo parked in front of Marco's building until I heard the door shut. A burly immortal I'd never seen before approached, coming to a halt between me and the steps. His jet black hair meticulously parted and groomed, paired with his flawless black suit, gave him the appearance of a Wall Street broker. At least he was kind enough to include me in the shelter of his umbrella before speaking.

"Jacquelyn Livingston." His accent, which I couldn't quite place, made the words sound stiff. My name carried more of a statement than a question but, for the sake of argument, I assumed he was asking.

"Yes," I responded. My acknowledgement brought no change to his coal black eyes.

"My name is Nikos. Lattimer has requested your presence, if you will come with me?" he asked politely, gesturing to the back of the limo.

The name hit me like ice water. What could Lattimer, the oldest vampire in existence according to Marco, possibly want with me? I surveyed Nikos, thinking surely Lattimer could've sent a more welcoming driver for me to begin with. To say Nikos looked intimidating would be an understatement. His stony expression and brawny build made him look like a business man on steroids...who probably ate kittens for breakfast. His solemn appearance never changed, waiting patiently for my response.

"I need to go tell—"

"Marco will understand," he said, gently herding me toward the limo. He opened the door, helping me into the back seat. "Although you may want to wait until you speak with Lattimer to tell Marco anything," he added, shutting the door.

Something flashed in his eyes. My inability to interpret the look started to make me second guess my willingness to get in the limo.

Nikos climbed into the front seat and, before I could say a word, we pulled into traffic. A couple blocks later, I looked out my window to see Augustine and Claire returning from hunting. Augustine froze watching the limo pass. I doubted he could see me through the black tinted windows. However, his immortal abilities told him all he needed to know. Alarm invaded his placid features. He grabbed Claire's hand without a word and ran toward the apartment.

At that moment I understood the look in Nikos eyes. It was a warning.

Acknowledgements

ෂ෦෬෬෯෭෨෬

I would like to give a very special thanks to everyone in my life that supported me through this adventure.
First off, to my family for believing in me and encouraging me to the finish.
Now, the people that weren't obligated by blood relation, my test subjects, my muses and my readers. To be a bit more specific, Caleb Cornwell, Kristin Burns, Berni Stevens, Grayson Copeland, Debra Johnson, Lori Stevens, AJ Skinner, Mel Jokanovic, Lauren Coombs, Mazzadonna, Brittany Stevens, Hannah Rowe and Olivia Mistretta. You were all the driving force behind me...even if I did resort to bribary every so often.
Finally, I must thank Anna, Becky and Kassidy at the Signal Station in St. John's. If it wasn't for their hospitality, I may never have gotten through the final proof!

12598145R00157

Made in the USA
Lexington, KY
19 December 2011